# A Reclusive Heart

## by

## R.L. Mathewson

This is a work of fiction. All of the characters, organizations and events described in this novel are either products of the author's imagination or are used fictitiously.

Edited by Maura O'Beirne-Stanko and Lieve Van den Heuvel

e-book ISBN 978-0-9832125-8-4

ISBN-13: 978-1479338474

A Reclusive Heart: A Hollywood Heart Novel © R.L. Mathewson 2011. All rights reserved.

http://www.rlmathewson.com

**Other titles by R.L. Mathewson:**

Playing For Keeps: A Neighbor From Hell Novel #1
Perfection: A Neighbor From Hell Novel #2
Tall, Dark & Lonely: A Pyte/Sentinel Series Novel #1
Without Regret: A Pyte/Sentinel Novel #2
Tall, Dark & Heartless: A Pyte/Sentinel Novel #3
A Humble Heart: A Hollywood Heart Novel #1
Sudden Response: An EMS Novel #1

This book is dedicated to Lieve Van den Heuvel, who showed me what good chocolate really taste like.

As always a special thank you to Rhonda Valverde and all my forum buddies at http://www.vampireromancebooks.com

And of course to my children who will always be my inspiration and my little buddies.

I love you, Kayley and Shane....

even if you do frighten me from time to time.

## Chapter 1

"On behalf of Rerum Publishing House," Rick said, holding his glass of champagne up high. "I would like to congratulate our guests of honor on their five year anniversary!"

A loud round of applause broke out among the party guests as the happy couple smiled dreamily at each other. Nick glanced over at two of his closest friends and had to force a smile.

Rick, still grinning, held up his hand, motioning for the crowd to quiet down. "We are also here to celebrate a momentous occasion for Rerum Publishing House as well as for Dana Pierce. As of this month, all six books of her *Christian and Bailey* series have sold over a hundred million copies worldwide."

Nick watched as the luckiest bastard, as far as he was concerned, pulled a very surprised Dana into his arms and spun her slowly around while he gave her one those achingly sweet kisses that made all the women around them "aw" and coo. It just made him gag.

He loved his friends. He really did. They were great down to earth people with hearts of gold and had four of the greatest kids he'd ever met, but sometimes it was a little much for him to handle. Most of the time it didn't faze him, but other times like this when their love was practically a living thing reaching out to bitch slap everyone within a thirty foot radius, it was difficult.

It made every single woman around them get that hopeful look in her eyes just before they turned determined. Then right before his eyes, once level headed women turned into vultures, setting their sights on the single men around them in an assessing manner. Hell, five women were giving him that look right now, probably trying to determine what kind of husband and father he would make. Would he worship her? Be there for her? Be faithful? Take out the trash? The answer was pretty simple.

Hell no.

## A Reclusive Heart: A Hollywood Heart's novel

Marriage was not for him and every single woman out there should be thankful that someone like him stayed clear of the altar. Plain and simple, he was not the marrying type. Never had been and never would be. It wasn't that he didn't believe in marriage. He did, for the right people that is, and the right people most certainly did not include him.

Hell, he was a thirty-two year old man who'd never had a girlfriend, never wanted one. That was too much commitment and way too much drama for him. He didn't want to be responsible for someone else's happiness or be held accountable to remember shit like birthdays, anniversaries, Valentine's Day, or not to fuck her best friend when he was bored. No, that was just way too much to expect of him.

He was the guy that you went to for fun and always had been. As a kid he'd been responsible for giving more than half the girls in his class their first kiss. He loved women and they loved him. As long as they acknowledged that there would never be anything more than a good time and a good fuck or two, then all was good in his world.

For those who thought they could change him....

Well, they got what they deserved. He never lied or pretended to be something that he wasn't. He made damn sure of that. Any woman he took into his bed knew right off the bat that he was an asshole and that she better not get her hopes up where he was concerned. It just wasn't worth it.

He wasn't worth it.

"Congratulations to Edward and Dana Pierce!" Rick said, leading the room in another toast.

Even Nick held up his glass of scotch in their direction. Dana deserved this more than anyone. Seven years ago, she walked into their offices a broken down woman trying to keep it together for her two kids. Where most women would be bitter in her situation, Dana had thrived. She pulled her life together and shared her heart with the world. Then Edward stepped into her life and showed her what love really meant.

*Gag.*

Where the hell was this romantic shit coming from? He needed another drink and possibly a willing woman, or two. He glanced around at the marriage minded vultures and scratched the last part. He just needed a drink.

He made his way through the thick crowd of well wishers to the bar where he had to wait for twenty women to finish flirting with the bartenders and place their orders. Christ, couldn't Rick have hired a few female bartenders? If he had, he'd have a drink and a number by now.

"So, what do you think?" Rick asked, leaning against the bar.

Nick sighed, giving up hope of getting his drink anytime soon. "I think I should hire the staff for the next event."

Rick chuckled. "I think you're still banned from that job, buddy."

"That's bullshit. That party was memorable."

"Oh, yeah," Rick said, grinning. "Hiring strippers to function as staff was definitely one for the books."

Nick shrugged, unconcerned. "No one complained."

Rick threw him a disbelieving look. "Every single female guest complained. Many of them demanded your head on a platter."

Nick waved it off as he tried, once again, to get the attention of a bartender only to be ignored. Fuck. "The service that night was great."

### A Reclusive Heart: A Hollywood Heart's novel

"Yeah, it was. With each drink, the guests were offered a lap dance for half price and a few were offered a Happy Ending."

"See, now that's good service, nothing like the sausage fest you got going on here."

Rick looked at the long line of men being ignored and sighed heavily. "Guess I'm gonna have to do something."

"It's your party. Go nuts. I, on the other hand, am going home to my liquor cabinet and bed," Nick said, pushing away from the bar.

"Going home alone?" Rick asked, sounding surprised.

Nick gestured lazily to the crowd. "All these women are looking for Mr. Right."

Rick looked thoughtful for a moment. "You never know, it could be you."

Nick gave him a wink. "I have no plans to change my name from Mr. Wrong anytime soon."

* * * *

"Don't puke, don't puke, don't puke," Jamie said, pressing her forehead against the faux leather cover of her steering wheel.

She took a deep breath and exhaled slowly. This was no big deal, nothing whatsoever. This was just a job, a new job, the start of her new life. Nothing to worry about. It was just a brand new stage in her life because of-

Her stomach flipped over just thinking about her ex-almost boyfriend. Oh no, make that her new brother-in-law, and her ever loving sister Caitlyn. That fun little surprise was the reason why she was here. She needed this desperately. This was going to be the start of the new Jamie.

Not that she hated herself. She didn't. She just wasn't particularly in love with herself. She was too boring, too shy, and too plain. On top of that, she was pretty darn sure that she was the world's biggest pushover. Everyone knew she didn't have a backbone and had no qualms about taking advantage of that little fault.

No more. That was the old Jamie. The new Jamie was going to start saying no. She was going to take charge of her life. It was the main reason that she sold her internet publishing company and took this job. She wanted, no, needed to get out in the world and this was the perfect opportunity. This job would force her out of her shell and into the world.

"I'm good," she mumbled to herself, not really sounding all too confident, but it was a start. She pushed her glasses back up her nose and did her best not to vomit.

Taking one last fortifying breath, she grabbed her oversized purse, the one that really should be called a bag, and opened her door. After catching the small heel of her shoe on the floor mat and fighting her way to freedom, she opened her car door and stood up.

Satisfied that she hadn't vomited or passed out, she closed her door, hit the alarm and took a step forward only to come to a halt and stumble backwards into the car.

"What the...."

She turned around and frowned. Of course this would happen. She somehow managed to shut her bag in the car. Her cheeks burned as the sound of laughter reached her ears. She didn't need to look back to know that they were laughing at her.

Keeping her eyes and face averted so that no one would be able to identify her later and point and laugh at her, she disarmed the car alarm and removed her bag. This time when she closed the car door she made sure to remain a safe distance away.

## A Reclusive Heart: A Hollywood Heart's novel

Clutching the purse strap tightly in her hands, she headed for the front entrance of Rerum Publishing House, praying nothing else went wrong. She kept her breathing even as she walked up the sidewalk, into the lobby and to the elevator. She stepped inside, pressed the button for the fifth floor and exhaled slowly. Several people in the elevator threw her curious looks, but she ignored them.

She ran her sweaty palms down the front of her charcoal gray wool skirt and frowned as she inwardly groaned. Why hadn't she taken the time yesterday to try on her clothes? Oh, that's right, because Caitlyn and her little trio came into the store. She'd been forced to grab the first suit off the rack that looked like it would fit, pay up, and get the heck out of there before they spotted her.

It was either that or endure the fake looks of pity, rude comments, and Caitlyn's "little" stories about how Jamie never could keep any man's attention once they met Caitlyn. So yeah, she ran for it and apparently bought a suit at least four sizes too big.

The elevator dinged and people looked at her expectantly. It took a moment before she realized they were at the fifth floor. With an embarrassed flush and a murmured apology, she hefted her bag, er purse, and stepped out of the elevator and into a beehive.

"Excuse me," a woman in a much better suit than hers, said in a crisp tone as she rushed past Jamie.

Another murmured apology came from Jamie before she stepped back against the wall. She stayed there watching the chaos for several minutes before she broke out into a sweat.

Oh god, she couldn't do this.

She hurried the three feet back to the elevator and hit the call button, and then pressed it again and again. Where was it? She pushed her glasses back up her nose to get a better look at the elevator lights. It was on the ninth floor and she didn't have time to wait here.

Clutching her bag tightly to her body and averting her eyes to the floor, she turned and followed the Exit signs to the stairwell. Halfway there she spotted signs for the restrooms. After taking a quick glance up to confirm their location, she took another deep breath and scurried quickly through the swarm of people. She didn't release that breath until she was in the bathroom safely locked in the end stall.

After placing five paper barriers on the toilet, she carefully sat down, dropped her bag between her feet, and cradled her head in her hands. This had been such a huge mistake. She should have kept her company and resigned herself to being the strange woman with twenty cats that all the kids would point and laugh at in twenty years. The fact that she didn't like cats shouldn't factor into her decision.

Decision made, she just needed to come up with a plan to get herself out of here. She would just have to leave the bathroom and use the stairwell to leave the building. Then she'd go home and pack up her small apartment and find someplace where she could blend in and allowed cats. Maybe she'd use her new little fortune to buy a house and a new car. Wait, a house was too big for just for one person. Unless of course cats required their own rooms then she'd be all set. Then after she set up her house she'd start up another internet publishing company and everything would be peachy.

The only glitch in her plan as far as she could tell was that little issue of the signed contract stating that she was not allowed to start another internet publishing company and a few other factors that would keep her butt here working. She needed an antacid or something. She looked down at her oversized purse and frowned. She wasn't the antacid carrying type of woman. Although there was a good possibility that she had a half roll of spearmint Lifesavers or a few root beer barrels somewhere in her bag.

## A Reclusive Heart: A Hollywood Heart's novel

Deciding that a root beer barrel sounded great, she picked up her bag and nearly cried out in frustration as her bag tipped upside down, which normally wouldn't have been a problem except that somehow at some point her bag had opened. The soft whir of the air conditioning unit was momentarily drowned out by a loud gasp and the *clanking* sounds as everything in her purse hit the tiled floor.

"Why me?" she mumbled pathetically as she grabbed her purse and started to shove her personal belongings back inside. Things started to look up when she found a twenty dollar bill that she'd forgotten about and her favorite pen that she thought she lost a few months back. Well, maybe this wouldn't be so bad after all, she thought as she kneeled on the cool tile floor so she could reach several items that escaped the confines of the stall.

After a minute, it became obvious that her arms were just too short to reach the items that escaped the stall. Sighing heavily, she opened the stall door and crawled out, picking up items as she went. Two tampons and a quarter later, she was frowning at a pair of very large black leather shoes.

Her first thought was one of sympathy for whatever woman had feet that large. That feeling slowly disappeared as her eyes traveled up a pair of men's black slacks to a very masculine jacket, shirt and tie that in her opinion really looked good on the obviously fit torso. Slowly, ever so slowly, she looked all the way up and gulped when she saw beautiful, laughing, green eyes and perfectly combed, short, honey blond hair.

Why on earth did it have to be *him*? A month ago, when she came in for a meeting he had been the reason why she nearly choked on her own tongue. It was really unfair that someone so shallow should look so gorgeous. Really, it wasn't fair. No one person should be blessed this much. He had everything going for him in life and he knew it. It was a constant reminder to people like her that life really was unfair and was kind of sucky sometimes.

His eyes lit up with amusement as he held out a tampon to her. Not just any tampon, but a purple tampon with the words "Super Super Heavy" written in clear bold letters.

"I believe this is yours, Miss Harris," he said, sounding close to laughing.

Jamie grabbed the tampon and shoved it back into her bag as she quickly got to her feet all while avoiding his gaze. When he tried to help her up she took a step back.

"T-this isn't the women's room, is it?" she asked, knowing someone up there was having a heck of a time with her today.

"No, no it's not," that deep smooth voice that wreaked havoc on her heart, said.

She nodded. "Of course it's not," she muttered to herself. Really what else could she expect?

Still avoiding his eyes, she said, "Well, ah," she cleared her throat, "it's ah, very nice. Spacious, clean and all that."

He chuckled.

Darn it!

"I'll ah, I'll just go see what my desk looks like now. It was nice to see you again, Mr. Quinn."

"Oh, the pleasure was all mine," he said in an amused tone.

Another nod and she turned to leave only to have her escape halted.

"Miss Harris?"

She froze mere inches from freedom. "Yes?" she asked, her voice cracking.

"You have a little something on the back of your skirt."

## A Reclusive Heart: A Hollywood Heart's novel

Of course she did.

"Thank you," she said, trying to decide whether she should duck back into one of the stalls or risk further embarrassment by looking for the woman's room to remove whatever it was when Mr. Quinn took the decision out of her hands for her.

She heard the telltale sound of crinkling paper and gasped. Heat rushed up her neck to her face, leaving her to wonder if she could die from embarrassment.

"Got it," he said, chuckling.

"Thank you," she mumbled as she made her mad dash to the bathroom door, wondering what else could go wrong today.

## Chapter 2

Nick was still laughing twenty minutes later as he took his seat in the conference room. Who knew that hiring the little recluse would make his day? He certainly hadn't expected this little bonus. She'd certainly made his morning.

Ah, good times......

"What has you in such a good mood?" Beth or Janet or whatever the hell her name was asked as she took the chair next to his.

"Good coffee," he said, gesturing to his steamy cup of coffee. He wasn't about to further embarrass the poor recluse. He was an asshole yes, but a nice asshole. The poor thing was going to have a hard enough time here, he could just tell with that shy manner and frumpy clothes. There was no need to add to it. In fact, his plan was to stay away from the poor thing and sit back and watch. Maybe she'd provide him with another good laugh.

"So, Nick, I was wondering what you were doing tonight," Beth or Janet or was it Marcy? said.

"Washing my hair," he answered, hoping she'd take the hint and finally move on. For six months she'd been after him and not just for a good reason like hot sweaty sex. No, this one had relationship written all over her. She wanted to "change" him.

Yeah, good luck with that.

Even if he didn't date co-workers or clients he wouldn't touch this woman with a ten foot pole. She wore too much makeup, too much perfume, ugly ass clothes and was known to plan the perfect wedding ten minutes after some dumb bastard asked her out.

Before she could reply, Rick strolled in, looking pleased as punch with the little recluse following reluctantly after him. Hmm, Rick must have tackled her, because he was pretty sure the woman was going to make a run for it and never come back. Now she was here to keep him entertained.

## A Reclusive Heart: A Hollywood Heart's novel

Excellent.

"Have a seat," Rick said with a warm smile to the little recluse.

She smiled weakly as she took the chair across from him and looked shyly around, noticeably avoiding him. He took in her thick, too long strawberry blonde hair that was twisted into some horrible knot at the back of her head, her thick framed glasses and ugly baggy suit. Who dressed this woman? As if she sensed his gaze, a deep red blush crept up her neck. He didn't even bother to bite back a smile. This was just too good. He liked the idea of a woman leaving him alone *and* providing him with entertainment. It really didn't get any better than this.

Rick walked over to the chair at the head of the boardroom table and waited for everyone to sit down and settle in for the meeting.

"Good morning, everyone. I hope you all enjoyed yourselves last night."

There were several words of agreement before Rick continued. "Everybody did an excellent job. Edward and Dana sent their thanks this morning as well as an insane amount of pastries and muffins. So it would be much appreciated if at some point today all of you would stop by the break room and help us out with some of that food."

Several people nodded while most of the women murmured about diets and carbs. The only one that was silent was the little recluse who was eying the doorway like it was her new best friend. No doubt she'd make a mad dash for it if she thought she could make it unseen.

"I've got more good news. I know we're still all excited about Dana's book sales and for good reason. You've all worked really hard to help push her books and make them what they are today. I'm hoping we'll be able to do that with several of the new authors that we've recently acquired."

That caught several people's attention. A new author, a great author, could mean better pay, job security and a senior editor position. Nick wasn't too worried about the promotion since he was already a senior editor, but a great author under his wing could mean more pay and working with only the top authors like Dana Pierce. It meant more perks as well as months in Europe on book tours. He liked the perks. No, scratch that. He fucking loved the perks.

"Who did we sign?" Jeff, a junior editor asked with a calculating gleam in his eye.

Nick was curious about that. A few weeks ago he knew they were able to sign five of the forty-something clients that were signed with Miss Harris' internet company. Out of those five he knew the one he was going to grab. It was the one that he could easily see reaching Dana's status in five years. J.L. Lewis was going to be his client no matter what. She would be his Dana Pierce. He would take her from her already established e-book fame and set the world on fire. There were several others from her clientele that he wanted, but none of them had the potential that J. L. Lewis had. No, that author was his.

"I have a list here of who we've been able to sign and who we're waiting for. Miss Harris," Rick gestured to the blushing recluse, "was the owner of Harris Publishing House and has been able to convince many of them to take a chance with us and expand into print. Of those who haven't signed, we own their contracts for another book so we have plenty of time to prove that signing with us is in their best interest."

Several people glanced at Miss Harris with looks of surprise. The women sent her openly dismissive looks. Not a surprise. Miss Harris certainly didn't look like the type who could handle a telemarketer never mind an insanely successful business like Harris Publishing.

"Take one and pass the rest along. Here's the list of people we've signed, contracts we now hold and those holding out," Rick said as he handed a stack of paper to Jeff who greedily took his. Nick knew the second the younger man saw J.L's name. His entire face lit up.

## A Reclusive Heart: A Hollywood Heart's novel

Well, tough shit because J.L. was his.

"Rick," Jeff said, probably trying to grab J.L. before anyone else had a chance to see the list. "Who's getting who?"

Nick wasn't too worried. He knew how this would go down. The senior editors would meet. They'd take who they wanted and would leave the rest for the junior editors to fight over. He wasn't too worried about Rick trying to grab J.L. The man had his hands full with Dana's new book as well as the new book Dana and Edward just finished together. No, J.L. was as good as his.

"Well," Rick started. He cleared his throat and pasted a friendly grin on his face. "As part of the agreement between Rerum Publishing and Miss Harris as well as the clientele's request, Miss Harris will continue to oversee their work as our newest senior editor."

There was a long moment of stunned silence as every set of eyes in the room turned to the squirming woman. Nick felt all his good humor slowly disappear. This was.....this was.....

Bullshit!

J.L. was supposed to be his. He had plans. He already put out feelers for promotional events and the response he'd received was astronomical. This was not happening.

He shoved to his feet. "Rick, can I have a word with you?"

Rick sighed, but didn't look too surprised. The rest of the staff sent him grateful looks. Could they really be that stupid to think that he was upset on their behalf? That was just sad.

"That's fine. Meeting's adjourned," Rick said, grabbing his files and heading for the door. "Miss Harris?" Rick said to the nervous little recluse who looked like she was about to crawl beneath the table and hide.

"Yes?" she said nervously.

"Why don't you join us?"

If Rick thought bringing the woman into the meeting was going to keep him on his best behavior then Rick really didn't know him at all.

\* \* \* \*

This couldn't be good, Jamie thought as she walked into the large plush office. She followed Rick's gesture and sat on one of the leather chairs.

"Would you like something to drink?" Rick asked pleasantly.

"No, no thank you."

No, she wanted to get this over with and retreat to her new office and get to work and forget those hostile looks for a while. She knew from what Rick said that some people would be upset with this agreement, but she hadn't expected them to become angry like Mr. Quinn obviously was as he paced the office.

"Nick, why don't you have a seat?" Rick suggested as he sat down across from Jamie.

With a tight nod, Nick took the chair facing both of them. Jamie kept her gaze averted from the man, but knew he was looking, more like glaring at her.

"Look, Rick, this agreement isn't going to work out," he announced.

Rick leaned back in his chair, getting more comfortable. "Oh, why not?"

"Well, to be honest she doesn't have what it takes."

That surprised her. She'd been doing pretty darn well over the past five years. She started her company from scratch and made a name for not only herself, but for her clients as well.

"I would have to argue that," Rick said, earning her undying gratitude. "She took a bunch of unknown authors and signed them. Under her guidance, many of them have outsold printed authors in the same genre. I have no doubt that she'll be able to do the same here."

## A Reclusive Heart: A Hollywood Heart's novel

"E-books, Rick. She managed these people by phone and e-mail. She's never had to deal with promotional issues, venders or a thousand other issues a book in print brings up."

"She'll learn."

It was starting to disturb her that they were talking about her as if she wasn't in the room, but she kept her mouth shut. She hated confrontation, which could explain the whole ex-almost boyfriend/new brother-in-law thing.

"So, she's supposed to learn on the job? How is that fair to her clients, *our clients* now? They've signed with us expecting a certain level of professionalism and we're giving them a trainee? It's not going to fly. What about J.L. Lewis?" At the mention of that name Jamie cringed. Rick sent her an amused look before giving Nick back his attention.

"J.L. could very well be the next Dana Pierce." That made her puff up a bit. She knew J.L. was decent, popular even, but as good as Dana Pierce? That was unexpected.

"If we leave J.L. with a trainee she'll never go anywhere and we'll have missed a golden opportunity. Come on, Rick. Don't do this. It's not fair to any of the authors or the company."

"What makes you think she can't do this?" Rick asked and she had to admit that she wondered the same thing.

"Besides a lack of experience in promoting and handling a book tour, not to mention conventions? Well, I would have to say she's too shy, quiet, can't make eye contact, she dresses like a bag lady with jury duty. She needs a haircut and some make-up wouldn't exactly hurt. Her glasses belong on Erkel. She doesn't have the killer instinct to get the job done. For Christ's sake, Rick, she's just sitting there meekly while I'm tearing her apart and you think she can handle someone like J.L. Lewis? She'll wreck her career in record time."

Miss Harris gave him a shocked and hurt look. Damn if he didn't feel like he just kicked a puppy, but she needed to hear the truth.

"That was uncalled for, Nick," Rick said, trying to hand Miss Harris a box of tissues. She shook her head, averting her gaze.

"It was dead on and you know it, Rick. If you want to train her, go for it, but don't leave J.L. in her incapable hands."

Rick sighed. "I wasn't going to, but you didn't exactly give me a chance to discuss it with you."

"You weren't?" he asked, sounding surprised.

"No. Some things are going to be changing around here. For you at least."

Jamie bit her lip to stop herself from protesting. This guy was a...he was....a jerk! Did she really trust him to handle J.L.'s career? No, but she didn't have a choice anymore.

"What do you mean?" Mr. Quinn demanded.

"What I mean is you will be training Miss Harris. You will help her get the look she needs as well as the skills."

"Rick, that's not-"

"In return, you will also get to sign J.L. Lewis as your client. As well as oversee the rest of her clients."

"Seriously?"

"Seriously."

"That's great! I already made some contacts. I think if we get her face out there and get her to do a few interviews before we start the book tour for her new book that we'll be able to count on huge sales for the printed book as well as the e-book."

## A Reclusive Heart: A Hollywood Heart's novel

Jamie cringed further into herself. Interviews? Book sales? Could J.L. do this?

"Before you get too carried away, Nick, you should probably know something," Rick said.

Jamie couldn't help but glance at the man from the corner of her eye to see his reaction. She didn't want to, but she found herself helpless to do anything else.

"If you have a problem with Miss Harris then you're not going to be too happy with J.L.," Rick said carefully.

"And why is that?"

"Because I'm J.L. Lewis," Jamie answered softly.

## Chapter 3

This was definitely one of those "oh, shit" moments. He just insulted the woman he was dying to sign. Granted, he thought he was insulting the hermit standing between him and the author he wanted to sign.

Ah hell, there was nowhere to go but forward with this one.

"You're J.L. Lewis?" he asked in what he knew was his most charming tone. Apparently the little hermit didn't know that because she only nodded.

A thought occurred to him. "Rick, how exactly is she supposed to represent other clients if she is busy writing and promoting her own work?"

"She won't be. Her job here is strictly editing. She's easily one of the best editors I've ever come across. Her clients trust her and we can work with that. They know their books will be handled by others and they're fine with that as long as Jamie gives their books a final look over before they go to print."

"So, her job here is just to give the final editorial approval before a book goes to print?" Nick asked.

Rick nodded. "That and to write and promote her books. You're right about her potential. I really think she'll reach Dana's level with the right help."

He'd heard of pampering authors before, but this was ridiculous. They created a job for her to keep her happy? It was ludicrous to pay her as an editor when she really was a proof reader.

"These authors need someone to work with. A proofreader isn't what they need. Who's going to promote their work or organize book signings?" he asked.

She frowned. "I'm not a proof reader."

"No, you're not," Rick agreed, to keep her happy? Nick wasn't sure.

### A Reclusive Heart: A Hollywood Heart's novel

Rick turned his attention on him. "I've decided to let you have first pick. The rest of the clients I want you to assign away. What I suggest is that Miss Harris gets the manuscripts right before they're ready to go to print."

Nick frowned. "So, you're making us proofreaders?"

"Only on these clients. It's what they want. She's known for having a sharp eye and good taste. She never takes out too much and she has a hell of a knack for detail. Other than that I want you to handle her. I need you to get her ready and start promoting her books. I want her to go on tour with a few lectures, book signings and interviews. I want it at the same level we give Dana, but unlike Dana we don't have to hold back because of the kids. I trust you know what to do."

He caught the panicked expression on Miss Harris' face, but ignored it. He had more important things to focus on right now like not doing a touchdown dance. It would probably come off as unprofessional. He'd save it for his office.

Shit.

There was so much to do. He needed to call the printers, get a decent picture on her book, set up interviews, book signings, book tours and a convention or two wouldn't hurt. His eyes drifted towards the little recluse. First, they had to give her a makeover, nothing major. Just her hair, her eyes, makeup and good god those clothes had to go. If they could make her look more nerdish or even plainish that would be preferable over hermit.

He couldn't help his shit eating grin that seemed to make the little hermit more nervous. He knew just the women to handle this little overhaul.

* * * *

This was depressing, Jamie thought as they drove through a plush neighborhood. Seems things hadn't changed. She was still the world's biggest pushover or doormat. Really, labels didn't matter at the moment because her life just plain sucked.

How pathetic does someone have to be to just sit there and take it politely while someone trashed everything about her? Pretty darn pathetic. Instead of putting her foot down and demanding a different agent to handle her career, she was in a car with a big jerk who wouldn't stop smiling smugly even though he was having a conversation with someone on his cell phone. He'd been on that thing since they left Rick's office, setting up this or that.

She really wished she knew where they were going. Call her crazy, but it would have been nice to have been told, correction, asked to go wherever it was they were going. She was pretty sure he hadn't said one single word to her since they left Rick's office. As soon as the door closed behind them he attached a hands free piece to his ear and began his marathon of calls. It wasn't until she sat down at her new desk and logged onto her computer to start editing Margo O'Malley's latest book that she realized he'd followed her. Without a word, he picked up her bag and handed it to her, gesturing for her to follow him.

Well, it was just one more person to add to her list that knew she didn't have a backbone. This was just super, she thought dryly as they pulled into a long driveway of a huge white one story house.

Finally Mr. Quinn ended his call and got out. Obviously he expected her to follow after him like a puppy. Deciding against sitting in the car, mostly because it would look like she was pouting, she followed him to the front door.

"Um, where exactly are we?" she asked.

He looked over his shoulder at her and ran his gaze over her, making her feel like a bug under a microscope. Finally, he looked at her face and sighed as if it pained him to speak with her. "We're here because you need a complete overhaul and I don't have the time to do it. So, I'm going to ask a friend of mine to do it for me."

Fire scorched her cheeks as embarrassment once again won over frustration. She knew she wasn't exactly a prize, but would it kill the man to sugarcoat it for her? Perhaps a few white lies here and there?

## A Reclusive Heart: A Hollywood Heart's novel

"Oh," was her only response.

The front door opened to reveal a man with more muscles than any one human needed. He looked Nick over and nodded his acknowledgement before turning his gaze to her and frowned.

A bodyguard? What kind of friend that would help with her appearance needed a bodyguard? Then it hit her. He was bringing her to one of his many lady friends. A model perhaps? She'd heard about him. Heck, she saw the man operate a month ago when she attended that meeting. He seemed to hit on every waitress at the restaurant. It was kind of insulting to say the least.

"Who exactly are we meeting with?" she whispered, feeling suddenly nervous under the bodyguard's glare.

"Dana Pierce," Nick said casually as if he were ordering a burger.

Her brows shot up and her heart practically leapt out of her chest. He brought her to the home of Dana Pierce! Was he insane? The woman was a world famous author and actress and did she mention the woman had been in Maxim magazine a total of five times? Nope. She couldn't and wouldn't do this. Next to Dana Pierce she would look like dog food.

She turned to leave only to have the back of her coat grabbed. In seconds she was being dragged inside a house that had a surprisingly down to earth feeling to it.

"Hey! Let me go!" she hissed.

"I don't have time for this, Miss Harris," Nick said unapologetically.

"Uncle Nick!" several small boys yelled excitedly.

He released her, causing her to stumble. With the help of the bodyguard, she avoided going head first into the front door.

"Thank you," she mumbled.

"You're welcome, ma'am."

Jamie brushed her coat down and turned around to see two little shirtless boys around four years old happily latch onto Nick's legs. An older boy, also shirtless, who looked to be around eight or nine, hugged Nick, careful of his smaller brothers. There was no doubt that they were brothers. She would have known that instantly even without knowing that Edward and Dana Pierce had three sons and one daughter. They looked exactly alike and exactly like Edward. That was kind of interesting considering the oldest one was not Edward Pierce's biological son. It was kind of eerie.

As discretely as she could, she did a quick glance over the oldest boy. She remembered the incident that occurred five years ago with this little boy. Everyone heard about it. It was hard to turn on the television or pick up a paper or magazine for a month after it happened without seeing a reminder. A babysitter from a well known and trusted agency had a little alcohol and drug party with a guy in this very house and left the two young children alone. As a result the little boy suffered severe burns when he tried to cook food for himself and his sister.

After that incident a new law was enacted called the Cole Child First Act. It required all California agencies that dealt with the care of a child, handicapped or elderly person to do a federal background search on employees instead of a simple state background check. Monthly drug tests were now mandatory and the laws were tougher. From what she read she was pretty sure the woman who caused Cole's injury was still doing time along with her boyfriend.

At least it looked like the boy didn't have any scars. She shifted her gaze away quickly. No need for people to think that she was some sick-o or something. Though, she was sure that she wasn't the only one who threw the kid curious looks.

"Where's your mom, Cole?" Nick asked.

Cole stepped back and gestured towards the kitchen.

### A Reclusive Heart: A Hollywood Heart's novel

"Alright, guys. I have to go talk to your mom, but I'll see you early tomorrow afternoon at your game. Okay?" he said as he bent forward so he could look Cole in the eye.

Cole beamed. "Can we feed the ducks afterwards like last time?"

"We sure can, buddy," Nick said with a fond smile for the boy. He kissed Cole on the cheek and the two little ones on the top of the head before he gestured for her to follow him.

She was starting to feel kind of awkward being in someone else's house without an introduction. That feeling of awkwardness was nothing like what she experienced when they walked into the kitchen.

They walked in on Edward and Dana Pierce during a hot and heavy make out session! To make matters worse they didn't stop. Dana pierce cupped her husband's face as she practically devoured his mouth while he cupped her backside, holding her tightly against him.

Well, at least she could easily say those magazines that Caitlyn read were wrong. Edward and Dana Pierce did not seem to be on the verge of an ugly divorce. In fact, it looked like they were on the verge of tearing each other's clothes off.

She turned around, not sure who she should be more embarrassed for, her or them. Nick on the other hand didn't seem to be too worried. Out of the corner of her eye she saw him lean back against the wall and cross his arms over his chest. He looked almost bored.

"If I could interrupt you for a moment?" Nick said, grabbing her arm when embarrassment demanded that she make a run for it. He pulled her back and in one swift move had her turned around so she could face the couple they just walked in on. Did this make her a peeping tom?

Instead of looking angry at the interruption they looked amused. Edward pressed a sweet kiss to Dana's mouth and nose before stepping back.

"You know," Edward drawled as he leaned against the counter, "most people would have just walked out and given us a few minutes. Maybe knocked on the door or something."

"Sorry," Jamie muttered automatically, still not quite meeting their eyes.

"Who's this?" Dana Pierce asked in friendly tone? Jamie wasn't sure mostly because her ears were still burning from embarrassment.

"Oh," Nick said as if she was an afterthought. "This is the favor I need your help with."

"Does this favor have a name or are we all supposed to follow your rude example? Honestly Nick, sometimes I wonder why I love you so much," Dana said, stepping forward.

"Hey!" Edward snapped.

Nick grinned hugely.

She rolled her eyes playfully at her husband. "Don't give me that look, you know I have a soft spot for Nick."

"That's funny, because I have a hard-" Nick began only to be cut off by Dana slapping a hand over his mouth.

Dana smiled warmly as she looked at Jamie. "I'm sorry that my very rude friend here is being, well....himself. I'm Dana and this is my husband Edward. We're very pleased to meet you......," she prompted smoothly.

"Jamie Harris," she managed to answer.

"It's very nice to meet you, Jamie. Would you care for something to drink?"

"No, thank you," she said, feeling really nervous and wishing Nick would release her so she could make a run for the car or the border, whichever was more convenient.

## A Reclusive Heart: A Hollywood Heart's novel

Dana nodded, turning her attention back to Nick. "I'm going to remove my hand now. Behave yourself," she warned sternly, but the smile she gave him kind of defeated the tone.

"Now tell me what this favor is that you need," Dana said, walking back to her husband to lean into him. Edward's arm automatically came around her waist to hold her.

Jamie had to look away again, feeling like she was intruding on another private moment. It was obvious that this couple was madly in love. Something she would never experience.

Wow, that was a really depressing thought.

"I need you to take Miss Harris out for a complete makeover."

Dana frowned as she looked back at Jamie. No doubt she too thought it was a hopeless task.

"Not that I could ever say no to you-"

"You better be able to say no to him," Edward practically growled, making Dana smile.

"-but do you mind telling me why she needs a makeover and what it's for so I know where to focus?"

Nick sighed. "She's an editor, well really an author Rerum has signed and I'm her editor. I need to get her ready for some PR, but I don't have much time."

Dana frowned, looking thoughtful. "Have I read anything you wrote?"

Nick chuckled. "Most likely, but she writes under a penname."

"Oh, what name?" Edward asked, kissing the top of Dana's head.

"J.L. Lewis," Nick announced to her horror.

Why must the man do things like this? Did he enjoy humiliating her? First with the tampon and the toilet shield, then he put her down in Rick's office for a good half an hour. Now he was determined to have a good laugh at her expense. Like Dana Pierce really knew who she was. Puhlease. That was so ridicu-

"The J.L. Lewis of the Immortals on Earth series and Vampires of the Heart series?" Dana Pierce asked with a deadly serious expression.

Wow, Jamie thought, Dana Pierce heard about her books. That was pretty cool. Maybe she had some advice or something about her books. Of course she probably only heard about her series from Rick. Jamie really doubted someone like Dana Pierce actually read her work.

"That's her," Nick said casually.

Dana's jaw dropped.

Jamie became worried.

"Honey? Are you okay?" Edward asked.

Not bothering to answer, Dana rushed towards her scaring the crap out of her. Dana took Jamie's hands into hers as she gushed, "I am such a huge fan of yours! Oh my god, you have to sign something!"

## Chapter 4

"You know, you don't have to do this," Jamie mumbled.

The two women who'd practically dragged her here, slowly turned around, looking horrified. "I *love* makeovers!" Amy Benet, Edward Pierce's baby sister, gushed.

Dana chuckled. "She's just hoping we let her out of this." She gave Jamie a warm smile. "Don't worry. This will be fun."

Jamie wasn't so sure of that as she glanced past the two women towards the open floor of the upscale beauty parlor.

"Besides Rerum Publishing is paying for this so I say enjoy it," Dana said with a firm nod.

Amy quickly agreed, making her fight back a smile. These two women were nothing like she expected. Never in a million years had she expected that Dana Pierce would drag through her house to her private office so that Jamie could autograph a piece of paper for her. Nor did she expect Dana to call her sister-in-law and brag rather excitedly that J.L. Lewis was in her house. That of course made the other woman screech and demand that no one move until she got there.

Now they were embarking on what could only be described as a day of torture. The other two women argued with Nick for over an hour about what needed to be done. When Nick explained what he wanted done she frowned along with the other two women. Even Edward Pierce looked a little confused. The way he explained it she could have sworn he expected her to turn out nerdish.

Thankfully, the other two women shot him down. When he argued, Dana enlisted the help of her three boys and little girl to chase a laughing Nick out of the house with water guns. The new game plan now was hair, makeup, laser eye surgery if it turned out she was a candidate and then clothes.

Jamie didn't have much hope, but didn't say anything. She knew she wasn't pretty. Caitlyn was the pretty sister. Everyone always said so. Jamie was the smart one, the responsible one. It was the role she was born into and she accepted it without complaint. Never once had she even considered, well not really at least, having a makeover. What was the point? There wasn't enough makeup in the world to turn this ugly duckling into a swan. No point in wasting her money.

She didn't want to waste Rerum Publishing's money either, but the two women were so excited and happy to do this with her that she couldn't bring herself to tell them that it was pointless. She just hoped when this was all over that they weren't too disappointed.

* * * *

Nick glanced at his watch as he stepped out of the car.

"Shit," he muttered as he headed for the front door. It was a quarter to nine and he was more than two hours late in picking Jamie up. Dana was going to be pissed, but there was no helping it. He just spent the last eleven hours on the phone, computer and overseeing five assistants all so he could make J.L. Lewis' introduction to the world perfectly smooth.

This was the big chance he'd been waiting for and he wasn't about to let anyone mess it up, not even J.L. Lewis herself, especially not J.L. This was his big break. This was his "Dana Pierce." When he was done, everyone was going to know who J.L. was and it would all be thanks to him.

Before he got the chance to knock on the door, it was pulled open. A disheveled looking Dana stood in the doorway with a silk pink robe wrapped around her body. Her lips were puffy and glistened from a recent kiss and her hair was mussed.

He couldn't help but smile. "Did I interrupt something?" he asked innocently.

## A Reclusive Heart: A Hollywood Heart's novel

Dana blew out an exasperated breath, sending a strand of hair out of her face. "You're late."

"Aw, were you waiting for me? Does Edward need some help?"

"I seemed to manage just fine on my own," Edward said, walking into the large living room, wearing nothing but a pair of unbuttoned jeans and a shit eating grin.

Nick frowned as a thought occurred to him. As hot and heavy as Edward and Dana were for each other, they would never ignore a guest to play mattress leap frog.

"Where's Miss Harris?" he asked.

Edward wrapped an arm around his wife and pulled her back into his body. "The girls dropped her off at her car a couple of hours ago."

"Damn it! Why didn't someone tell me? I need to see her tonight and see how things turned out so I know how we should proceed with press releases."

Dana shrugged. "We did call you, but she wanted to go home and I don't blame her. She was really upset."

"Upset?" Crap. The makeover hadn't helped one bit and the little recluse was heartbroken. No doubt she thought a snip here and there and a little blush was going to perform miracles. He could have told her not to expect much, but wouldn't that have just been cruel?

"She had a big shock tonight, Nick. Just leave her alone and let her get used to it, okay?" Dana, always sweet, kind and considerate, said. If only he could listen to her, but he couldn't. He had a job to do and that meant going over to Miss Harris' apartment and seeing how much damage control he had to do. If it was really bad he'd have the photographer do some touch ups after the photo shoot tomorrow.

Normally he'd invite himself in and make a nuisance of himself to mess with his friends, but tonight he had work to do. After thanking them for all their help, even though it probably hadn't done much, then again he hadn't expected much, he made his way over to Miss Harris' apartment.

He wasn't entirely surprised to discover the little recluse lived in an average city neighborhood. There wasn't much to set this place apart. It looked to have a convenient store, a package store, and a small bakery that promised half off coffee rolls every Thursday with the purchase of a large coffee.

Even her building was average, a three level brick building with a basic security door and buzzer. There was absolutely nothing special about it. He walked up the two front steps and looked over the apartment listings. Not surprising that the little recluse lived on the third floor. It was out of the way and the perfect floor for a little hermit.

He pressed the button marked "J. Harris," and waited. When no response came he hit the buzzer again.

"Hello?" Miss Harris' voice sounded from the raspy speakers.

"Miss Harris, it's Nick Quinn. You were supposed to wait for me so that we could go over your schedule for the next four weeks."

"Oh, I'm sorry. I just-"

He cut her off. "It's no problem, Miss Harris. We can go over it now if you'd buzz me in."

"It's kinda of late," she responded quickly.

"It won't take that long. I promise. At the very least, I need to go over tomorrow's schedule."

"Can't we go over it tomorrow morning?" she asked, sounding hopeful.

He had to smile. Poor thing must be so humiliated. Well, it was best to get it over with and see what he had to work with.

## A Reclusive Heart: A Hollywood Heart's novel

"I'm afraid not. We're not meeting at the office, Miss Harris. I really need to speak with you."

"You're speaking to me now," she pointed out.

Nick closed his eyes and prayed for patience. The first day wasn't over and she was already causing him problems. He had no doubt that he could get the little recluse under his thumb. He'd use his charm, false flattery and if that failed, which it never had, he'd just use the little fact that she was a pushover to his advantage.

"I prefer to speak with you in person, Miss Harris, instead of discussing Rerum Publishing business in public for the entire neighborhood to hear."

"I'm, uh, tired. So, um, this will have to wait until tomorrow. So, um, goodnight," she said. A small clicking sound followed, letting him know she turned off her intercom.

Why that little......

Did she really think she'd get rid of him so easily? She really had a lot to learn if she thought she could dismiss him.

He picked another buzzer at random.

"Hello?"

"Pizza delivery," Nick said.

"I didn't order any pizza," the guy said.

"Are you sure? It's all paid for."

"Oh, wait. Um, yeah, I think my wife did," the guy said obviously lying. A few seconds later he was buzzed in.

He walked through the paste white foyer to the stairs and took them two at a time. A few minutes later he was knocking on the little recluse's door. No answer. There was nothing but silence.

"I know you're there, Miss Harris. I can wait here all night if that's what it takes," he said in a bored tone as he leaned against the doorframe.

Her answer was a small gasp. He had to laugh. Yeah, his little recluse was going to do what he said when he said it. Then it was smooth sailing from here on out.

"Miss Harris, please open up so we can talk."

"No."

"Miss Harris, I can stay here all night. Why don't you save us both some time and open up now? The sooner we get this over with, the sooner you can go to bed," he promised in a reassuring tone, but he really couldn't help but wonder how bad the makeover was.

Did she look like Frankenstein or a drag queen?

"No."

"Miss Harris," he said warningly. He was getting pretty aggravated now.

"You can stay out there as long as you want. I for one am going to bed. Goodnight," she said.

She wouldn't......

She did!

The light beneath the door disappeared. A minute later he heard a door shut. No doubt it was her bedroom door so she wouldn't have to hear him.

"Son of a bitch!" He rapped on the door for a moment.

Nothing.

He waited another five minutes, feeling like an idiot. No woman ever made him wait. It was unheard of. The fact that this little recluse had pissed him off like nothing else.

## A Reclusive Heart: A Hollywood Heart's novel

"This isn't over! I'll be back!" he said to absolutely no one. Scowling at the door one last time before he left. This was far from over.

## Chapter 5

"This is Jamie Harris," Jamie said in a hoarse voice, hoping that she wasn't overdoing it.

"Hello, Miss Harris, how can I help you?" one of the office assistants asked cheerfully.

"Could you please tell Rick that I'm going to be working from home today? I'm afraid I caught something yesterday."

"Miss Harris, could you hold please?" she said before she placed Jamie on hold without waiting for an answer.

Jamie opened her mouth to say she couldn't hold, but didn't get the chance. She suddenly felt like a kid playing hooky from school. Maybe she should just hang up and shut her phone off. As long as she edited a few books today they should be happy, right?

She paced her small bedroom, mentally berating herself for not just hanging up. It was easy. All she had to do was press the "End" button and then turn off the ringer. Then she could spend the rest of the day wrapping her mind around everything and make sense out of the little surprise she had yesterday.

Of course it all could have been a fluke yesterday brought on by a very vivid imagination. It was most likely a side effect of an overactive imagination, the two glasses of champagne she drank at the spa and the wishful thinking of the other woman affecting her eyesight. Not to mention the laser eye surgery. That probably altered her sight, making her see things that really weren't there.

No doubt about it. Her mind played a trick on her, a mean trick, but a trick nonetheless. She'd been with two women she didn't want to disappoint and she saw what she knew they wanted to see, but it wasn't true. That woman wasn't her.

She wasn't.........

## A Reclusive Heart: A Hollywood Heart's novel

She wasn't beautiful, wasn't cute, wasn't that woman that stared back at her at the spa through the mirror. She just wasn't. Jamie was the sensible, boring, quiet one. She was just background, wallpaper and nothing more. She didn't draw attention unless it was to point and laugh at her. Caitlyn was the natural beauty. She was the daughter her parents adored. The one her mother babied and pampered even though Caitlyn was the oldest. She was the one her mother brought to the beauty parlor when they were little, because she was a natural beauty, not Jamie.

Jamie paused midstride as she caught a glimpse of the surprising beauty in the mirror. She was beautiful. Her hair was shorter, ending just below the shoulder blades with a hint of soft curls. It flowed like silk with every movement. Jamie pushed back a strand of her hair behind her ear and was somewhat startled as the beauty before her did the same.

It was so wrong. The woman before her was too beautiful. It couldn't be. It definitely couldn't be that simple. A day at a spa and a shopping trip and she looked like this? Impossible. If it was really that simple why hadn't her mother done it for her years ago? Her mother loved to go to the spa, so wouldn't she have brought Jamie along with Caitlyn if something like this was even possible?

Caitlyn was the favorite, everyone knew that, but wouldn't her mother have been happy with two beautiful daughters? Shouldn't she have tried for Jamie's sake? A small sob escaped her before she could bite it back.

Why had her mother been so sure, so adamant that there was nothing to her? Exactly when had Jamie been designated ugly, useless and nothing more than Caitlyn's plain little sister? Why?

With a shaky hand she pushed her hair back and smiled nervously as the golden silky hair slid perfectly back into place. She traced her newly thinned arched brows. With her glasses now permanently gone, she could see her features better. They were softer than she thought they would be. Her skin was definitely softer and healthier looking thanks to the torture she endured yesterday.

She'd never done much for herself in the way of beauty. What was the point? she thought. All those years and all those put downs from her family kept her in her place. She never ventured past the basics of self-care, never even considered that there might be more for her. Why would she?

All those years......

She'd been such a fool.

Was this the real her? she wondered as her eyes moved down the little pink tank top Dana picked out for her yesterday. She'd never worn anything that fit her so well before. Normally, she picked clothes that were plain and way too big. Anything that helped her blend in and not attract attention made her happy.

Now she couldn't help but smile. As a child she'd always been stick thin. It wasn't until college that she finally began to fill in. Not that anyone would notice thanks to her wardrobe. She never thought her body was anything special. Plenty of women had breasts, hips and a nice figure, but the difference was that those women had a pretty face to go along with the package and now so did she.

She smiled as she looked down at the cute pink flannel pajama pants that hung low around her hips. They were a little bit baggy but in a complementary way. They looked really good. It really surprised her how good she felt and how feminine these clothes made her feel.

For the first time in her life she'd enjoyed shopping. When they entered the store, out of habit she wondered over to the discount area, not because she was broke, but because that's where the plain clothes were. Dana and Amy shared an amused look as they dragged her away.

Under their guidance and direction she bought everything from shoes to simple lingerie. Her bedroom and half her small living room were now filled with shopping bags. An excited smile tugged at her lips at the thought of going through everything and playing dress up.

## A Reclusive Heart: A Hollywood Heart's novel

She felt like such a girl today! It was exciting and scary and she couldn't wait to get started!

"Miss Harris, please hold while I transfer your call to Mr. Quinn," Jennifer suddenly announced, breaking through the Christmas morning-like euphoria Jamie had going on.

"Ah, that's not really necessary!" Jamie hurried to say, but it was already too late. As the last word flew out of her mouth she heard the audible click of the phone being switched to a different line.

"Good morning, Miss Harris," Nick said smoothly. "I hear you're not feeling well this morning."

"I...ah, that is...I'm......," she rambled on nervously.

"You're planning on working at home today I gather."

"Yes," she answered quickly. Then she remembered that she was supposed to be sick and cleared her throat and tried to make her throat sound all scratchy-like, "Yes."

"You don't sound too good."

Relieved that he was buying it, she relaxed a little. "Yeah, I think I just need a day or two to recover. I should be fine in a few days, but in the meantime I'll just have to work here." She added a little sigh at the end to make it sound like she wasn't entirely happy with the idea of skipping the office for a few days.

"I see," he said.

"So, I'll see you in a few days?" It came out more of a question than she planned. She really needed to work on being firm. No wonder people walked all over her, she thought, disgusted with herself. Well, she'd fix that later today with a trip to the book store. She was going to buy every self-help book there was on being more affirmative.

"Hmm, perhaps I should stop by and see how you are. I could bring you something to eat and perhaps some tea for that sore throat of yours and we could go over a few things," he offered.

He wanted to come here? Oh no, no, no, no, that couldn't happen. Today was her fun day. Today she was going relax and be girly. She couldn't do that with *him* here! Plus, she didn't want him to burst her bubble.

Right now she felt pretty and womanly. If he looked at her and still saw the same old Jamie it would break her. She liked this new Jamie. She wanted, no, *needed* to be this Jamie.

"T-that's okay. I don't want you to get sick."

"Oh, but I don't mind. Why don't I swing by?"

"Er......"

"I can be there in ten minutes. I can see how you are and we can get some work done," he said.

"Well, I-"

She was cut off by the beautiful sound of someone knocking at her door. Thank god for annoying neighbors. No doubt Mrs. Brigs wanted to tell her to turn down the television that wasn't on or it was Mr. Ames accusing her of stealing his mail, again. Heck, even the landlord informing her of a rent hike would be more than welcome at this moment.

"I have to go. Someone's at the door. So, I'll just see you at the office in a few days. Bye," she said quickly, not giving him a chance to respond, knowing he would just find some way to come by.

She tossed her phone onto the couch as she made her way to the front door. At least she bought herself two more days before she had to listen to Nick Quinn tear into her again, she thought as she opened the door.

## A Reclusive Heart: A Hollywood Heart's novel

A small whimper escaped her as she came face to chest with Nick Quinn. Oh, this was so not good.

\* \* \* \*

Nick didn't even bother looking at the little recluse as he swiftly backed her up. He had more important things to do like get inside her apartment so he could assess the damage and see what needed to be done in order to make this work for him.

Once he backed her into her apartment far enough he shifted her away, she may have stumbled, he wasn't really sure or cared at the moment. He turned, shutting and locking the door. Satisfied that he had her where he wanted her, he placed the new laptop on the table by the door and let out a relieved sigh.

Admittedly, last night he'd been a little pissed that the little recluse wouldn't let him inside so he could do some damage control, but he went home and regrouped. He went through the itinerary he'd worked his ass off yesterday to set up and added a few things, deciding that he could in fact be generous and allow the little recluse a few hours to console herself after her failed makeover, but that time was over.

He turned around to get his first glimpse of the made over little hermit and frowned. Where the hell had she gone now? He swore under his breath as he scanned the small organized living room and didn't find her.

"Miss Harris?" he called out. He stepped past the couch and a half dozen shopping bags and quickly scanned the adjoining kitchen. Nope. No little recluse there.

He wasn't too surprised when she didn't answer. No doubt she thought he'd eventually get bored and go away. Not a chance in hell of that happening, he thought as he looked at his watch. They needed to go over a few things, pack, get to a photo shoot, pray for a miracle, go to Cole's game and then catch a flight to Boston. This was his chance to make his mark and he wasn't about to fuck it up.

"I'm not going anywhere, Miss Harris. The sooner you get out here the sooner we can get to work," he announced as he put his hands on his hips in an effort to keep himself from tearing the little apartment to shreds to find her.

Shaking his head in disgust, he walked back to the door and grabbed the laptop. He was pretty sure Rick never had to go through this much bullshit for Dana. The reason for that was pretty simple, Dana had been motivated to get out there and ignore her doubts and fears.

She'd been trapped in a loveless marriage with a worthless piece of shit that cared more for his computer and girlfriend than he had for his family. Writing had been Dana's only means of escape. She'd worked her ass off day and night to perfect her craft and it had paid off not only for her, but for Rerum Publishing and definitely for Rick.

Nick wanted what Rick had. He wanted to be a leader in the industry and most importantly he wanted to leave his mark on the world and Miss Harris was the key. If he couldn't get her to cooperate and get in line with his plans he would be good and fucked. There was no doubt in his mind that she'd be switched to another editor if he couldn't pull this off quickly. His bosses were practically drooling at the idea of having another author of Dana Pierce's caliber and they wouldn't tolerate mistakes.

With that in mind he knew that he had to entice the little recluse into doing what he wanted. He sat down and removed the new laptop from the bag. As it powered up, he looked around the small room. Beyond the basics like furniture, a small television and a computer there really wasn't anything special about this room.

The only wall decoration was a framed diploma. Other than that there were no pictures of friends or family. No knick knacks or keepsakes to be found. Now that he really took the time to look around the only area of the room that looked lived in was the computer area. While the rest of the room was spotless and bare, her desk was not. It was piled high with papers, probably manuscripts, books, candy bar wrappers, a jar of hard candies and a very old mouse pad.

## A Reclusive Heart: A Hollywood Heart's novel

Realization hit and he knew how he was going to get what he wanted. This little recluse was truly that, a recluse. She was a young woman with no life or experience outside of her books or computer.

That's why she'd sold her successful internet company and taken a job when she didn't need one. This little recluse wanted to experience life, to make changes and take chances. All he had to do was offer her those opportunities and he'd own her ass.

He placed the computer on her bare coffee table and opened up the document he'd been working on only an hour ago.

"Miss Harris," he said, trying to sound casual, "I'd like to apologize for upsetting you. I realize that this is all a bit sudden and overwhelming for you. I believe Rick made a mistake in assigning me to you." He ignored the snort of agreement that came from somewhere in the vicinity of the tan door, probably the bathroom, and continued.

"I think this is all too much for you, too soon. I'm going to call Rick and have you switched to one of the junior editors. He'll make sure to keep things simple. You probably won't even have to leave the office." He paused to let his words sink in. No doubt she was feeling relieved at the reprieve.

"If you don't mind, I need to make a lot of calls. I have to cancel flights, hotel rooms, conferences, book signings, and conventions." He sighed heavily for effect. "I guess I can wait for most of these calls until I get to the office since they'll take hours. I had you booked all over the country. The one in Hawaii will be kind of tough to get out of." He paused for a few seconds to allow that to sink in.

"It's really a damn shame because I think you would have really enjoyed yourself. I know touring can be a lot of work, but it's also a lot of fun," he said as he opened his e-mail to make sure that all his travel confirmations were set. "But they're also a lot of fun, new experiences, trying new things, meeting new people. I think this could have been really good for you, but I'm not going to push you into something that you're clearly not ready for."

Nick waited, watching the bathroom door like a hawk. He bit back a groan of frustration, knowing he had to remain cool and calm if this was going to work. His eyes darted back to her desk and he couldn't help but grin when he spotted the scratch ticket.

"You wouldn't happen to know the area code for Vegas, would you? I booked you there next month and I need to let them know-"

"Vegas?"

"Yeah, I..." his words trailed off as he turned his head and found the little recluse standing in the bathroom doorway, fidgeting nervously with her fingers. She stood straight, but avoided looking at him.

There were few things in life that left him speechless and this was one of them. The drab, frumpy little recluse that he'd left with his friends was gone. In her place was a very pretty and adorable woman. She wasn't the most beautiful woman he'd ever seen, she wasn't Dana Pierce level pretty, but she was definitely hot.

He ran his eyes from her newly cut silky hair over beautiful caramel eyes, cute little nose, the bottom lip that was fuller than the top, small oval chin, slender neck, surprisingly full breasts accentuated by a baby pink top, a slender waist, nicely shaped hips and short, yet nicely shaped legs.

## A Reclusive Heart: A Hollywood Heart's novel

One very important question came to mind, why in the hell had she been covering all that up? That thought was immediately followed by the realization that this new look would definitely work in his favor. Before all he had was her work to push the name. Now he had a beautiful face to back the work. This would be easier than he thought.

"Where else would I be going?" her quiet voice tore him from his thoughts. He gave himself a mental shake and focused on the problem at hand, convincing her to take a chance with him.

He moved to the end of the couch, gesturing to the computer on the table. "The whole itinerary is right there if you'd like to take a look," he said casually as if he wasn't nervous as hell.

She looked close to bolting again, but curiosity clearly won out. She sat down on the couch, careful to keep her distance from him and scrolled down the list. He knew she liked what she saw by the way she was trying to bite back a smile.

"And there would be time for me to do other things?" she asked hesitantly.

Oh, he had her. J.L. Lewis was his.

"Absolutely."

## Chapter 6

"What are you doing?"

Jamie quickly shifted the new laptop on her tray so that the monitor was now facing the airplane window.

"Nothing," she said quickly.

Nick frowned down at her. Even sitting down he towered over her, intimidating her. She inwardly sighed, wondering when she was going to catch a break. Thankfully, and much to her delighted surprise, first class seats really were spacious. All throughout her photo shoot and meetings this morning she feared being squished between Nick and some unknown, probably smelly person, during the six hour flight, but luckily the airline bumped them up to first class at the last minute. It probably had something to do with Nick flirting with the ticket woman.

She wondered if he would use that lovely little talent for the rest of their flights during their tour. It would save her nerves. Not that she couldn't handle sitting in coach. She could. The few times she'd flown were in the coach section and she'd survived.

No, her concern was being squished in by Nick. He intimidated her and made her feel uncomfortable. The man was far too bossy for his own good and with her being the world's biggest pushover that wasn't exactly going to help. Space was her friend. As long as she had that she could breathe and think clearly. Well, sort of....

"If you're not working then I need the computer," Nick said, sounding grumpy. He hadn't been happy when he discovered that she didn't own a laptop. When she quietly suggested they bring her desktop with them he glared at her. Just glared. For about a minute she held back her apology for not owning a laptop. She knew it was stupid, but she couldn't help it. Finally she couldn't hold it back any longer and apologized and promised to buy one.

## A Reclusive Heart: A Hollywood Heart's novel

He didn't speak, but his eyes narrowed on her and she would swear to her dying day that they looked calculating. It made her take a nervous step back. After another moment of making her squirm, which she really didn't appreciate, he told her they would share his new laptop until he could find one that met his specifications for her.

She really didn't understand why they couldn't just pop into a Best Buy and pick one up and told him that. He just shook his head and told her he'd handle it. That was fine with her. She really didn't care and was more than happy to play around with this one. It was pretty cool. For the first ten minutes she played around with it. Then she felt kind of guilty about that so she started editing John Bishop's latest novel only to stop doing that ten minutes in because she wanted to see if it was her turn in an online Scrabble game. It was. Since then she'd been kicking some cyber butt if she did say so herself.

"Well, if you're done, do you mind if I got some work done?" he asked calmly enough so she passed the computer over, but not before she quickly closed the Scrabble window and erased the web browser's history. No need to poke the tiger, she thought.

Deciding this was probably the best time to use the bathroom, she stood up. "Excuse me," she said as she flattened herself against the back of the seat in front of her, there was more room in first class, but she liked to get as much space between herself and the man watching her with an amused expression as she could.

"Where are you going?" he asked, looking back at the screen.

"Bathroom."

He nodded as if she'd asked for permission. She almost snorted. She might be a pushover, but she wasn't that pathetic. She quickly made her way to the first class lavatory and sighed as she spotted the "Occupied" sign. Deciding that it was better to wait here instead of in her seat, she leaned back against the wall and prepared for the long haul.

"Excuse me, is this the line for the bathroom?" a deeply masculine voice said, drawing Jamie's attention.

She looked over to answer the man and found herself speechless and probably blushing. He simply smiled at what was probably her impression of a dying goldfish while she tried not to drool. This man was GQ level handsome, not as handsome as Nick or Edward Pierce, but close enough to fray her weary nerves.

He held out his hand, expectantly. "Since it looks like we're going to be line neighbors I thought I should introduce myself. I'm Sean."

Was this man flirting? Oh, he definitely was, judging by the glint in his eyes. Jamie barely stopped herself from looking behind her to search for the beautiful woman that obviously had his attention. It took her a few seconds to realize that he was flirting with *her*.

She forced herself to take a calming breath as she shook his hand. This was so new and unexpected. Men did not flirt with her. They simply didn't.

"Jamie," she said quickly when she realized she was only holding his hand and staring. Oh, she so sucked at this! He probably thought she was the biggest freak on earth. Any second now he'd give her a polite smile and step back. Obviously he couldn't walk away completely. There were no other bathrooms available. The poor man was stuck in line with her. Even she felt bad for him. Why couldn't-

"Is that your husband?" he asked, still holding her hand she'd like to point out, as he nodded towards Nick who was now scowling at his computer.

She laughed. She really couldn't help it. The very idea of Nick Quinn being interested in her never mind married to her was truly laughable.

"You have a very pretty laugh," Sean said, giving her a boyish grin.

Jamie took her hand back and pushed an errant strand of hair back behind her ear. "Thank you."

## A Reclusive Heart: A Hollywood Heart's novel

"So, I take it he's not your husband," he concluded, sounding pleased.

She was about to tell him that Nick was her editor, but didn't mostly because she still wasn't comfortable letting people know who she was. So instead she said, "We work together."

"Ah, I see," Sean said, leaning in closely, but not too close to make her feel uncomfortable. "Is this your first time going to Boston?" he murmured in a rather sexy tone.

Jamie couldn't help but smile. "Yes, I've been meaning to go for years, but never had a chance," she said, thinking she also never had anyone to go with or any reason to go. She had friends, but no one she really wanted to take an adventure with. Her eyes darted to Nick. She didn't really want to do this with him, but he was giving her a good reason to try new things. Also, having him around made her feel a little safer and a little more confident to take a chance.

"There are a lot of new experiences to be had," Sean said as if he could read her mind. "In fact," he said leaning closer, "those experiences can start right now, if you want. There's nothing stopping you from doing whatever you want."

She was just about to open her mouth and ask what sort of new experiences could be had on an airplane when the bathroom door opened. Jamie was barely aware of the middle age man smiling sheepishly as he stepped past them. Her mind was suddenly racing with ideas.

"Excuse me," she said absently as she stepped around Sean. "It was nice to meet you. Um, it's all yours," she said, gesturing awkwardly to the bathroom.

He simply shrugged. "I didn't really have to use it. I just wanted an excuse to meet you."

"Thank you," she murmured shyly as she practically raced back to her seat, eager to start working on a list while crazy ideas raced through her head. Could she really do this? she wondered.

There was only one way to find out, she thought as she quickly, but carefully, moved past Nick to get back to her seat. She sat down, looked at Nick, fidgeted and fidgeted some more as he typed. Finally he let out an annoyed sigh.

"What is it?" he asked irritably.

"You wouldn't happen to have a piece of paper and a pen handy, would you?" she asked quietly. She really did not like the idea of putting this down on paper, mostly because it was private, but there was also her little tendency to lose things.

He sighed long and loud. "Do you need to work?"

She opened her mouth to tell him no, but then reconsidered it. "Yes, yes I have to work," she lied.

"Fine," he said, saving his work before passing over the laptop. "There's a folder on the desktop with your name on it. I'd appreciate it if you kept everything you worked on in there."

That would definitely make this easier, she thought as she shifted in her seat so he couldn't see the screen. She opened a new word document and quickly titled it, "Things to Try List."

\* \* \* \*

Nick barely stopped himself from rolling his eyes as the little recluse shifted in her seat so he couldn't see what she was working on. As long as she worked, he really didn't care and judging by her focused expression and fingers tapping away at a rather impressive pace she was no doubt working on her next book.

A new book would be the perfect finishing touch to this little tour. Granted, it would probably start a whole new tour, preferably a European tour, but he would deal with it. He thought about asking her what her new book was about, but decided that he'd ask in a couple of weeks. Right now he didn't need to add plans to market a new book into his already hectic schedule.

## A Reclusive Heart: A Hollywood Heart's novel

In a few weeks when everything settled down and his little recluse was firmly under his thumb he'd start working on her new book with her. He knew getting her to do things his way was going to take some time, not much considering how easily she folded under a simple glare, but it was still something that needed to be done and quickly.

There was too much to do and not very much time to do it in to let the little recluse have much of a say if any. He needed to be able to make last minute decisions that would benefit them both and he didn't have time to hold her hand through every issue. It would just make it a lot easier, for him, if she left everything to him. All she needed to do was work, edit if it made her feel important, and show up and smile when and where he told her to, which he thought with a content sigh, wasn't going to be an issue.

Four hours later he knew he had her exactly where he wanted her. From here on out there weren't going to be any problems. She accepted his word as law, which she should. In fact, if all women listened to him as well as his little recluse did, his world would be perfect.

He watched as she looked around the hotel foyer nervously. When her eyes landed on the Gold Ballroom's bulletin board announcing the romance writer's convention the following day with a special appearance by J.L. Lewis he had to bite back a smile. The blush and look of surprise on her face was actually kind of cute, but it also let him know one very important thing.

Jamie was easily intimidated.

This was going to be so fucking easy. All he had to do was give her a little nudge every now and then, sprout bullshit in her ear and he'd have her doing everything he wanted.

* * * *

"Where the hell are you?" Nick bit out harshly.

"Out," Jamie said, nibbling her bottom lip as she looked around.

"Where?"

Good question.

She looked down at the complimentary map she'd picked up in the hotel lobby before she started this little adventure and frowned. Why did they have to make everything so tiny? Because the map was the size of a brochure, she thought with a sigh.

"Well?"

"I'm out."

"You're out?" he asked tightly.

"You said you wouldn't need me until tomorrow morning so I decided to walk around and grab a bite to eat," she said, turning the map slightly to the side and frowned. Was that little brown spot the symbol for a restroom or an ATM? Not that it mattered since all she wanted to do was go to the Museum of Science.

Visiting a museum probably didn't seem like a big deal and it wasn't. But she decided to break into the whole "Try new things" agenda slowly. Besides she was only killing time until tonight. Tonight she was going to go to her very first nightclub and she was pretty excited about it.

She'd never been to one. Not even when she was in college. The closest she'd ever come was a sixth grade dance that Tommy Perkins invited her to as a dare. She'd learned that fact after he grudgingly danced one slow dance with her and his friends started laughing their butts off at him. It had been a memorable moment indeed.

But that was in the past and had no bearing on her life now. Although she was really nervous, she was also pretty excited. She'd always wanted to try something like this, but could never find the courage. Now that she was on this trip she was going to force herself to try new things. By the time this was over, she hoped that the old Jamie was good and buried and that she liked the new Jamie.

### A Reclusive Heart: A Hollywood Heart's novel

A loud sigh broke into her thoughts. "Fine. Just head back to the hotel now so that we can go over some things and I hope you ate because it's probably going to be a long night."

Her shoulders slumped as she opened her mouth to tell him that she'd be there soon, but something stopped her. She didn't know what it was, but it gave her a moment's pause. Yes, this was supposed to be a working trip, but he'd said that she wasn't needed until morning so she'd made plans. He really couldn't expect her to drop everything at a moment's notice to accommodate him, could he?

If she went to him now then he'd know that he could push her around and she was done with that. That Jamie was long gone. The new Jamie wouldn't be jumping for anyone. She'd wasted too many years of her life hiding in the background and letting her life slip by her. She was done.

When she was supposed to work, she'd work her buns off. She'd write, edit and do the hundred or so things that he expected from her that just thinking about gave her heart failure, but when it was her time, she was going to enjoy her life for once and no one was going to stop her, least of all the overbearing bossy jerk.

"I can't. I have plans," she said as her eyes landed on a sign for Duck Tours and widened. That sounded like fun, she decided as she headed towards the sign.

"Well, break them. I need you to work."

"Sorry. Can't," she said distractedly as her eyes landed on a large boat/car. Now that looked like fun.

"*Jamie*," he said tightly in warning, but she was barely listening as she handed the friendly cashier the money for a ticket.

"Gotta go!" she said excitedly as she stepped into the small line to get into the boat.

"Don't you dare hang up. I need to-"

She hung up as a cute guy in his early twenties helped her onboard. As she sat down, all thoughts of her overbearing boss disappeared until she was only left with excitement.

She had a feeling she was going to love the new Jamie.

## Chapter 7

He was going to strangle Jamie.

When she'd hung up on him hours ago he thought it was a mistake. He quickly learned the error of his ways when the next ten calls went straight to voicemail. When she didn't show up within the next hour like he fully expected her to he'd become a little irritated with her and decided to catch her when she came back to the hotel.

Either he was losing his hearing or she was the quietest woman in the world, because she somehow managed to sneak into her room, the room next to his, shower, change and sneak out without him knowing. Well, that wasn't entirely true. When he stepped out of the shower he heard her door click shut.

At that point he'd been willing to forgive her for ignoring his summons and pulled on a pair of sweatpants quickly before he stepped out into the hall to knock on her door only to catch a glimpse of her as she stepped onto the elevator all decked out in a black cocktail dress and further pissing him off.

After he got dressed, bribed the bellhop to tell him where Jamie was headed he hunted her down at a nightclub of all places. He scanned the long line, hoping he'd find her, but he hadn't. Somehow Jamie had gotten into the club and he'd been forced to get into the line and wait a damn hour as he kept an eye out for Jamie.

Now he had her in his sights and it was taking everything he had not to go over there and strangle the nervous little recluse. For the past half hour he bided his time as he watched her, hoping his damn temper would go down. It hadn't. So he watched as she sat at the crowded bar, sipping her drink as she cast wary glances towards the dance floor. Every now and then someone would bang into her as they signaled for the bartender and he knew even twenty feet away that she apologized each and every time.

Whenever a man approached her, the little recluse would blush bright red, mumble something, fidget in her seat and send the guy away. Then she'd watch him walk away, frowning. Why the hell was she here if she wasn't interested in a guy or the very least, dancing? Since he spotted her she hadn't left the stool.

Well, that was fine with him since it would make getting his hands around her neck a hell of a lot easier. He didn't know why she was here, didn't care and he sure as hell didn't care that she looked sad. The only thing that mattered to him at the moment was that she fucked with his night. With that in mind he made his way through the crowd.

A minute later he glared at the asshole standing next to her until he moved away and he could take his place. She didn't realize that he was there. She was too busy watching the dance floor to notice anything going on around her.

When a whole minute went by and she didn't notice him, he signaled for the bartender, a hot blonde with an inviting smile. One look at him had her ignoring the customers vying for her attention.

"What can I get for you?" she asked as she looked him up and down. As she dragged her eyes up his chest to meet his eyes she licked her lips. She'd been obvious about her perusal of him, he had not. In under ten seconds flat he knew if she was fuck worthy, she was.

Maybe he'd pick her up as a treat to himself for all the bullshit his little recluse had caused him tonight, but then he remembered the shitload of work that waited for him back at the hotel. Oh well, it wasn't like he wouldn't find a willing woman or two during the tour. When everything calmed down and he got his little recluse in line then he'd allow himself to indulge, but not before then.

"Scotch on the rocks," he said, noting the way his little recluse froze up at the sound of his voice. He kept an eye on her in case she decided to make a run for it as he picked up her drink and took a sip and nearly winced. Who the hell came to a bar to drink soda? Apparently his little recluse did, which was fine with him since it meant that she'd be able to work for a few hours with a clear head.

## A Reclusive Heart: A Hollywood Heart's novel

"Another Coke for the lady," he said, gesturing to Jamie and not really caring about the ice cold glare the bartender threw at her.

He leaned against the bar and waited for Jamie to turn around. When she only continued to sit there rigid as a board he sighed heavily as he grabbed the seat, ignoring that beautiful ass of hers, and turned her around. When her eyes widened and she noticeably swallowed, he felt somewhat appeased. The moment he had her under his thumb he'd feel a whole hell of a lot better.

"W-what are you doing here?" she asked, trying to shift back on her stool and away from him.

"I came to help you," he said absently while he watched the bartender move onto another customer. Well, it looked like he wasn't getting his drink tonight.

"Help me?" she asked, frowning, not adorably, he decided. He didn't find a damn thing adorable or sexy about her. Not at all. He especially didn't like the way her dress pulled up mid-thigh, giving him a glimpse of beautiful light golden legs that probably had other men groaning. He was not one of them and didn't care if she looked good, really good, he decided absently a second later as he ran his eyes over her legs one more time.

"Mmmhmm," he said, forcing his eyes up and over a sinfully tight short black cocktail dress covered body. Much better than that frumpy suit she wore the other day, he decided. "You obviously got lost on your way from your room to my room so I came to help you," he explained tightly, mentally daring her to argue.

He wasn't having it. Not tonight. He had too much to do and not enough time to do it in. If this tour was going to work then he needed to have her onboard and doing whatever he told her to do with minimal bullshit.

"Okay, I'm ready to go," she said meekly as she stood and headed for the door with her shoulders slumped and her eyes on the floor.

What the hell?

Not that he was complaining. He wasn't, but he just hadn't expected it to be this easy. Hopefully this would be the last little act of rebellion that he'd have to deal with from her. At least it damn well better be, he decided as he followed after her.

* * * *

"Oh my god, I love you, J.L. Lewis!" a woman screamed, startling her.

As discretely as she could she leaned to the side to see who was screaming, only to groan. A large woman wearing a homemade t-shirt with her penname plastered on it was jumping up and down excitedly with five other women sporting the same shirt.

Maybe it was time for a break? she thought, shooting a hopeful glance towards Nick only to see him shake his head firmly, once. That's all it took for her to paste the weak smile back on her face and turn around in her chair to greet her next fan.

Only an hour into this and she wasn't sure that she could do it any longer. This was too much for her. She wasn't used to this much attention and every time a new person stepped up for her autograph she had to fight back a surge of panic that threatened to drop her to her knees. This wasn't her. If last night had taught her anything it was that she couldn't handle things like this.

Why the hell had she sold her business and taken this job? Because she was an idiot and thought that if she forced herself into a situation then her survival skills would kick in and she'd be able to acclimate. It was a really stupid plan, she decided as she signed her name, barely able to register what the person in front of her was saying. When she walked away smiling, Jamie felt her shoulders slump in relief only to tense right back up when the next person stepped up.

## A Reclusive Heart: A Hollywood Heart's novel

This was a bad idea. She couldn't do this. She didn't care if they sued her and demanded that she give all the money back. She just couldn't do this. This wasn't her life and she didn't want it to be, not anymore, and definitely not after last night. She needed to go home to her small lonely apartment and resign herself to the fact that she was meant to be alone forever.

"Excuse me," she said, her voice shaking as she stood up and knocked her chair over. She felt her face burn as every head turned in her direction with looks of amusement and confusion.

Why the heck hadn't she snuck out of her room this morning and made a run for it? She wanted to, planned to, but just as she grabbed her bag, Nick banged on her door and demanded that she get her buns going so they could prepare for this morning, but nothing, not the three hour lecture or the pointers that he gave her had prepared her for this. She hoped that she'd be able to deal once she sat down at the small table covered with stacks of her books, but she'd been wrong, so wrong.

The moment she stepped into the large ballroom she felt the same discomfort she'd felt last night when she'd stepped into the club. All day yesterday and up until last night she'd felt excited and even giddy at the prospect of trying new things. That all ended the moment she stepped into the club.

Within seconds she realized that she didn't belong, but wouldn't allow herself to leave. As she made her way to the bar she prayed that no one would notice her, but they sure banged into her. Once she found a seat, she sat down and refused to leave. After thirty minutes she somehow managed to grab the bartender's attention and got a drink, because by that point she'd needed sugar, badly.

All of her excitement and plans ended the moment she saw the dance floor. She'd been intrigued even as she felt her newfound self-esteem deflate. She didn't know how to dance and was too scared to give it a try and she wanted to, so badly, but couldn't bring herself to take a risk. She was weak and as pathetic as Caitlyn said and this whole experience proved it.

"Are you okay?" the older woman standing in front of her asked with grandmotherly concern that should have eased some of her panic, but it didn't. She needed to get out of here now.

"Excuse me," she said, swallowing as she took a step back. "I-I just need a drink of water."

"Here you are, J.L.," Nick said smoothly as he handed her an ice cold bottle of water. He picked up her chair, put an arm around her shoulders and helped her back into her seat.

She looked up at him, sending him a pleading look, but he ignored it. He flashed a smile at the woman in front of them that had the other woman blushing.

"I hope you'll forgive me. I should have brought her a bottle of water an hour ago," he said charmingly to the woman, but the way he maneuvered her back into her seat both impressed and irritated her. "I'm very sorry, J.L.," he said with an innocent smile as he jammed his foot behind her chair to stop her from escaping again.

"Thank you," she said, forcing a smile as she made a show of opening her water and taking a sip.

"He's so sweet. You're so lucky to have someone like him helping you," the woman gushed and Jamie was tempted to tell the woman that she was more than welcome to take him when he gave her a nudge.

"Thank you," she said, already guessing the reasoning behind the nudge to her side. "I don't know what I'd do without him," she said with that forced smile even as her brain screamed for her to do something else.

*Run.*

"I'll be right here if you need me," Nick said, taking two steps back to lean against the wall. To anyone else it probably sounded sweet and considerate, but she knew damn well that it was a threat.

## A Reclusive Heart: A Hollywood Heart's novel

If she tried to move so much as an inch out of her chair he'd be all over her. The message was clear, if she moved he'd drag her right back and probably staple her butt to the chair. Knowing it was useless to argue, she pasted that smile back on her face and forced herself to get through the rest of the signing.

For the next eight hours she put up with him shoving water at her as an excuse to remind her to keep her butt in the chair, forced to take pictures with fans even though the whole thing made her feel uncomfortable, and four denials for a bathroom break. When she told him that she was hungry and asked for a break, he handed her a stale package of crackers he'd bought out of the vending machine in the hall.

By the end of the whole thing she was mad, exhausted, humiliated and more than done with Nick Quinn. She might be stuck doing this because of her contract, which he reminded her of thirteen times throughout the day, but that didn't mean she was going to be stuck with him.

"Where are you going?" he demanded as she walked past his room and headed for her own.

"We need to discuss our strategy for the interviews tomorrow," he said, gesturing towards his room, but she ignored him and kept going.

She grabbed her room card, jammed it into the slot on her door's electronic lock and kept jamming it until Nick took it out of her hand with a bored sigh.

"What the hell are you doing, Miss Harris?" he asked as he opened her door and handed her back the keycard.

"First, I'm going to order the biggest steak this hotel has since you starved me," she said, sending him a narrowed glare. "Then I'm going to call Rick and ask him to replace your psycho butt!" she snapped as she went to slam the door shut in his face.

He stopped the door with his foot and hand and shoved it open. Knowing it was pointless to try and shove him out of her room since he easily outweighed her by a hundred pounds, she walked over to her bag, *er* purse, and dug through it.

"You signed a contract, Miss Harris," he reminded her tightly. "You have a contractual duty to finish this tour. You can call Rick up and complain all you want, but it won't change a damn thing."

"I already know that," she bit out distractedly as she dumped her purse over and of course more than half of her belongings tumbled off the bed and onto the floor. "I made a promise and I intend to keep it," she said, frowning when she didn't spot her phone among the contents on the bed. With a small groan, she dropped to her knees and began searching through the mess on the floor. She shoved aside a paperback, checkbook, tampons, half a roll of Lifesavers and still no cell phone. She blew a loose strand of hair out of her face as she looked around the beige rug. Where the heck was her phone?

"Then I see no reason why you need to call Rick," he said.

She had to snort at that. "Of course you don't."

"If you're upset about the amount of work that we have ahead there's nothing that I can do about that. Those are the obligations we have and if we want your launch to be a success we have to do it," he explained slowly as if he were talking to a child, further irritating her.

"I have no problem with the work," she admitted as she peered under the bed and sighed. It wasn't there either.

"Then what's your problem?" he demanded.

"You," she snapped, not even bothering to look up at him.

"You need me, Miss Harris," he explained, sounding pissed. "I'll guide you through this process, get you into the best venues and make sure you're a success."

## A Reclusive Heart: A Hollywood Heart's novel

"Anyone from your company could do that," she pointed out, wondering where her phone had run off to.

For a moment he didn't say anything and she was glad. It gave her a chance to focus all of her attention on finding her phone and figuring out what the heck she was going to say to Rick. She didn't want to get him in trouble despite how much he irritated her, but she didn't see any way around it. If she didn't say something he'd walk all over her and that's the last thing she needed right now, especially after last night.

"Finally," she mumbled when she spotted the sleek black phone peeking out from the corner of the light tan couch. She reached out to grab it only to gasp when a large tan hand swiped it up. She turned her glare up at him.

"You need me," he said as he put her phone in his pocket, probably thinking that she wouldn't make a grab for it.

He was right, darn it!

"No, I don't," she argued tightly as she came to her feet, holding her hand out expectantly.

"Really?" he asked with a cocky arch of his brow that she didn't like, not one bit.

"Really!" she snapped back.

"Then how do you expect to get through your *list* without my help?" he asked, and judging by his smug grin she didn't have to ask what list he was referring to. "Face it, Miss Harris. You need me."

## Chapter 8

This was going to be too easy, he thought as his little recluse looked up at him through wide eyes as her mouth worked soundlessly. After her little rebellion last night he should have realized the odd little list he'd come across late last night would be the key to getting her under his control, but he'd still been angry that she hadn't jumped when he told her to. That was fine because now it seemed that he could offer her what she desperately needed.

Him.

The only reason she agreed to come along on this tour was to try new things and apparently she desperately wanted to get out there and expand on that little goal, but there was only one problem with that. She was shy, painfully so. That was the reason she didn't leave her barstool last night and the reason why she damn near bolted every time someone said hello to her today. If the only way to get her to stay and start behaving was to go through each item on her list with her then that's what he would do.

If it meant that she would listen to him then he'd do all the things on her list that had him rolling his eyes last night. Half the things on her list he'd done before and actually enjoyed so that wouldn't bother him. Of course, the only way to have time to do anything on her list was to get their work done. She'd realize that and work her cute little ass off and do what he told her to do. Then he'd help her get through her list, but only if she did everything that he wanted first.

"I-I don't need you to do that list," she mumbled pathetically even as a bright red blush crept up her cheeks, painting her a liar.

"So you'll be able to do all of those things on your list?" he asked before adding, "by yourself?"

## A Reclusive Heart: A Hollywood Heart's novel

She worried her bottom lip as she shifted nervously in front of him, but she didn't say anything because they both knew the truth. Without him, she wouldn't have the balls to do anything on her list. There was a reason why she was a little recluse after all. She was too damn afraid to get out there and grab life by the balls. Without him she'd only be able to write about life instead of living it.

He shook his head as he walked over to the hotel phone. "Face it, Miss Harris, you need me more than I need you."

"No, I don't," she said weakly, probably some half ass attempt to stand up for herself, but he barely paid attention as he picked up the phone and ordered room service.

When he was done he sat down on the small love seat and relaxed as he watched the little recluse struggle to come up with a decent argument. When a minute passed and she still hadn't been able to say anything more than a mumble he decided to take pity on her.

"Why don't the two of us come to an understanding on the matter?" he suggested casually. "During this tour I will go with you and do anything that you would like to try. In return, you will show up to book signings, interviews, conventions and anything that I need you to do on time and say more than two words to your fans. You will also make yourself available when I need you."

She licked her lips nervously and he knew he had her by that little calculating expression on her face. She wanted this, badly. Not that he could blame her, he thought with a tiny ounce of pity. One look at that list and it was more than obvious that the woman hadn't truly lived. It was actually pathetic to think that last night had been her first visit to a nightclub or a bar for that matter since that was also on her list.

He should probably feel bad for her and if he didn't need her so damn badly he probably would. But the truth of the matter was this made his life easy. She would do exactly what he wanted and in return he'd help her with her little list. The only downside that he could see of course was that he would have to give up what little spare time he would have during this tour to see to this ridiculous list of hers.

Then again if it worked to keep her in line and smiling on cue then he would suck it up and deal with it. Besides, her list was pretty simple and wouldn't take long to go through. They'd finish it in two weeks, three tops, and then he'd have her undivided attention for the next several months. Actually, this could actually help him out in the long run as well. She'd learn to listen to him and trust his judgment and he could plan future events with J.L. Lewis without fear that she'd cause him any problems.

"You're willing to go with me and do whatever's on my list?" she asked slowly as if she didn't trust him.

Smart girl.

But as long as she did what she was asked he would fulfill his side of the bargain. It was a simple enough agreement.

"Yes, but you have to do what I ask if you want me to go with you," he clarified. Work came first and he needed to make sure that she understood that.

She nodded slowly. "That sounds fair."

"But I'm warning you, Miss Harris, the moment you stop doing as you're asked, you're on your own with that little list of yours."

Another nod.

"Okay then," he said, getting to his feet and gesturing towards the door. "Let's get some work done."

* * * *

## A Reclusive Heart: A Hollywood Heart's novel

"I don't remember this being on your list," Nick said accusingly as he glared down at her.

It took everything Jamie had not to cower beneath that glare, but somehow she managed it. Actually, she was quite proud of herself for that little move, but that didn't exactly help with the man scowling down at her.

She cleared her throat nervously. "Yes, it was," she lied.

His eyes practically narrowed to slits. "I don't remember seeing going with you to a chocolate convention on the list."

"Well, it was a really long list. You probably just missed it," she lamely explained as the man standing in front of her stepped back and bumped into her, almost knocking her down. "Sorry," she mumbled pathetically before she could stop herself. Her cheeks burned with embarrassment as Nick's glare intensified for some reason.

"It was a very short list," Nick said as he put his hands on her shoulders and gently moved her out of the way as the man in front went to bang into her again. He moved her closer to his side and she was pretty sure she'd rather be rammed into by the rather rotund man in front of her than to be this close to Nick. The man was too damn intimidating and being this close to him was making it kind of difficult to lie to him, but she was willing to give it a shot.

"It was long, very, very long," she said, nibbling her bottom lip as she averted her eyes.

"It was one page, double spaced," he bit out.

"Um, no it wasn't." But it was. At least it had been until last night when he finally dismissed her for the night. After he shoved the laptop in her hands with the expectation that she was going to work for a few more hours even though it had been well past eleven at night by that point, she revised the list......a little.

She'd meant to work for at least an hour just to appease the big bully, but when she logged onto the computer and started to work all she could think about was her list and all the new possibilities that went along with their new agreement. Even though she fully planned on doing the things on her list, things that she'd been sure she could handle on her own she was now going to venture out and do *everything* that she'd always wanted to do but was always too chicken to even try.

For three and a half hours she'd added things that she'd only dreamed of doing until she passed out at her hotel room desk. She was pretty sure she'd covered everything, but if she hadn't she knew she could always add it later, well she hoped at least. Judging by the disgruntled look Nick was sending her, she realized that she may have to find a way to sneak a few things onto the list, because right now she had a sneaking suspicion that he wasn't going to be happy when he found out that the list went from one page to ten or twenty or so.

Then again, this chocolate convention hadn't been on the list at all, but she'd overheard one of her fans talking about it earlier and mentally added it to the list. Nick had assumed that she'd want to try to go to the nightclub again tonight and had been shocked when she told him what she really wanted to do. She'd hit a nightclub again soon, especially if she had him by her side, but tonight she was all about the chocolate.

Seriously, what kind of woman would be able to pass up a convention center filled with chocolate from all over the world? Okay, granted she'd almost passed it up, but only because she always felt like an oddball whenever she went to any event by herself, but then she remembered that she didn't have to. While she was on this tour she had her own personal tag along buddy, a buddy that would help her do all those things that she'd always dreamed about doing, but didn't have the guts to try.

"Exactly how many items are on the list now, Miss Harris?" he demanded as they moved forward in the line to enter the convention.

## A Reclusive Heart: A Hollywood Heart's novel

She nearly rolled her eyes at the "Miss, Harris". She knew they weren't friends and knew this agreement had nothing to do with friendship and everything to do with getting what they both wanted, but if he continued to call her Miss Harris other people would question why a handsome man was spending time with her. They'd probably assume she paid him and she really didn't think she could deal with anymore unwanted attention.

"The name is Jamie and I have no idea how many items are on the list," she whispered, ignoring her burning cheeks.

He sighed heavily as he grabbed her arm and practically dragged her along the moving line. "I suppose it would make things easier if we were on a first name basis," he grudgingly agreed as they paid for their tickets. She considered paying for his ticket since he was doing her a favor, but then remembered that he wouldn't allow her to order a hot fudge sundae last night after dinner because he considered it an interruption. So she didn't feel bad when he had to dish out twenty bucks to get in.

Once the man in front of her headed to the right and she could see what waited for her, she gasped. It was just so darn beautiful. There were booths filled with chocolate and everywhere she looked she saw signs for free samples. She'd probably have a stomach ache later but she didn't care. It would be worth it.

"Okay, so go grab a few pieces of chocolate and let's get out of here," Nick said, gesturing for her to move her buns.

"Are you insane?" she asked, surprising herself, but really he had to be. They were in a convention center that featured two levels of chocolate and if he really thought that any woman in her right mind would be able to choose just a few pieces of chocolate out of thousands and be satisfied then he was crazy. It was either that or he was on drugs.

He rubbed his hands over his face before dropping them to his sides, looking annoyed. "You're going to hit every vender, aren't you?"

She nodded solemnly as she headed to the first one in front of her. "At least twice," she admitted as she accepted a chocolate dripped strawberry and nearly moaned in ecstasy as the tasty combination hit her tongue.

"This is hell," she thought she heard him mumble, but decided to ignore him as she moved on to a vender that hade creamy white chocolate.

\* \* \* \*

"Well, I hope you learned your lesson," he said as he slapped a hot face cloth on the whimpering woman's forehead and sat down at the small hotel room's desk.

"It was......worth it," she said, turning over on the bed to move into the fetal position and hold her stomach.

"Sure it was," he agreed dryly as he logged onto his computer to check the next day's itinerary. "You can hardly move without saying 'oh, god', but I'm sure the fifty pounds of chocolate you consumed that will probably be making a reappearance real soon was well worth it," he said dryly.

"It really was," she agreed, groaning.

He sent her a glare before returning his attention to his computer as he tried not to think about the four hours of his life that he'd never get back. He really couldn't understand how anyone could get worked up over chocolate like that, but apparently his little recluse had. She'd dragged him from vender to vender to vender until he considered strangling her cute little neck. Finally when he didn't think he could take another minute of someone shoving chocolate in his face she grabbed her stomach and muttered five of the sweetest words he'd ever heard, "I don't feel so good."

## A Reclusive Heart: A Hollywood Heart's novel

Thankful that the hell was finally over, he practically dragged her out of the convention, ignoring her sad little attempts to break free and go indulge in more free samples, threw her in a taxi, and hauled her ass back to the hotel where he fully planned on getting at least three hours of work out of her. He held up his end of the bargain and he fully expected her to do the same.

Speaking of the agreement......

He opened her folder, clicked on her "To do" list and nearly swore when he saw the insane number of pages she'd added. After sending her one last glare that she ignored because she was squeezing her eyes shut while mumbling, "Ow, ow, owie," he returned his focus on the list that would no doubt make his life a living hell. He swore that if she had another convention on the damn list that he was going to spank her ass.

What the hell.........

He hadn't seen this coming, but hey if this was what she wanted he could do it. At least she'd made the list interesting, he thought as he went through each item as he tried to figure out which ones they could manage to do while on this tour and the ones that were impossible. By the time he was done going through it he had a newfound respect for the little recluse. He'd never thought the woman whimpering on his bed would be interested in some of the more interesting things, but he couldn't deny that the list pleased him.

This definitely just got a lot more interesting.

## Chapter 9

"Faster!" Jamie practically squealed in his ear.

He couldn't help but chuckle as he squeezed the throttle of the rented bike and sped down the deserted highway. Jamie's arms tightened around him even as the sound of her laughter reached his ears over the loud roar of the bike's engine.

This was her first time on a bike and he could already tell that the woman had fallen instantly in love. He'd chosen this item off her list because it was one of his favorite things to do. Whenever he felt stressed or just needed a break from it all he jumped on one of his bikes and hit the road. Granted, he didn't do it as much as he would love to these days, but it was still one of the few things that made him relax, sex was the other.

Since he hadn't had sex in a while and it didn't look like he was going to be able to indulge in his favorite pastime, at least not while he was on this tour, then this was the next best thing. Thankfully, the little recluse seemed to love it as much as him so he'd be able to do it a few more times while they were on this tour. That would definitely help since Rick contacted him that morning and told him that Rerum Publishing House wanted to extend the already long tour.

They'd only been on tour for two weeks, but it seemed that every city they visited had a huge surge in J.L. Lewis sales that more than made up for the cost of this promotional tour. It seemed that J.L. Lewis was well on her way to setting new sales records for Rerum Publishing House and Nick couldn't be happier. He knew this woman was the key to his success and so far she'd proved him right.

A week ago several of her books managed to make it to number one on all the important book lists and even some that weren't. It seemed as though everyone had J.L. Lewis fever and he knew that it was only going to get better. There was already talk from networks about making several of her books into television series and a few major boys in Hollywood were hinting at a movie deal. That would mean more exposure and even higher sales and Nick couldn't wait.

## A Reclusive Heart: A Hollywood Heart's novel

It wasn't necessarily his job to influence the little recluse on what she should do, but he'd talk her into doing whatever deal benefitted him. The more exposure she had the better he would make out in the deal. Hell, he was already toying with a European tour after this. For most authors he'd force himself to step back even though everything in him screamed to move his ass, but this was Jamie he was talking about here.

She had no life or real friends to rush back to so he knew it wouldn't take much to convince her to keep going. Tours normally could become tiresome and stressful for authors, but he knew that Jamie actually enjoyed traveling, sleeping in different hotels and trying new things. Even when she was exhausted and they had to travel late at night she still had a smile on her face.

He'd be able to keep her happy. As long as they had the list he owned her happiness. They'd been doing this for two weeks and he knew she was addicted to that damn list. She loved trying new things and with him there she seemed relaxed and able to go through with her little list. The two times he had to put off the list she'd tried to do things on her own only to end up stressed and intimidated. That of course pleased him because it meant that he hadn't outlived his usefulness. She needed him for this list and he needed her for this tour and possibly a European tour immediately afterwards. It really depended on what Rick could come up with.

"Do you want to head back to the hotel?" he asked when he noticed the setting sun.

"No!" she said, sounding close to pouting, which actually pleased him.

He loved riding and wasn't ready to call it a night either. This was one of his favorite things in the world to do. Normally he didn't involve women in this activity because they bitched a lot, but surprisingly he didn't mind bringing his little recluse with him. She loved this and couldn't seem to be able to get enough. The only other woman that he'd enjoyed this with was Dana Pierce, except in her case she'd been on her own bike while trying to kick his ass racing.

They hadn't ridden together in five years and he missed it. He missed spending the time with his friend, but she was married now and had a busy life. He understood that she had other things holding her attention these days, but he still missed that time with her. They still spent time together, but it wasn't the same.

Before Dana he'd never spent time with a woman just to spend time with her. She made it easy to be with her and relax, somewhat. He'd never really been able to let his guard down with her and just enjoy her company, but it had been close. Oddly enough, he was able to do that with Jamie. It probably had something to do with the fact that they both knew what they wanted from this agreement. There were no secret agendas and he didn't have to work his ass off to flirt with her to get something out of her. He had the list and knew exactly what she needed.

For the first time since Dana, sex didn't matter with a woman. Well, that wasn't completely true. Much to his horror he was attracted to the little recluse. It was hard not to be. She was a cute little sexy thing with an infectious laugh and a genuine smile that pleased him. She never pretended around him and didn't play some of the drama bullshit games that other women played. She was real, wholesome, and it didn't hurt that he could now tell that she had a killer body. That was just a bonus.

Nothing would ever come of his attraction to her. She was his client and technically his employee. Besides, he had a two fuck limit and she wouldn't understand. Jamie had relationship written all over her and wouldn't understand that with him there would only ever be two nights. Sleeping with her, no correction, fucking her, because he never slept with a woman, would make continuing this tour impossible and it sure as hell would make a European tour out of the question.

## A Reclusive Heart: A Hollywood Heart's novel

Sex would screw this agreement up real quick and when she realized that she couldn't have him she'd be on the phone with Rick, demanding that he send someone else to take over Nick's job. There was no way in hell he was risking losing J.L. Lewis for sex. If his attraction for her became a problem he'd find a willing woman to slate his lust and forget about it since one woman was just as good as another.

\* \* \* \*

Note to self, sitting on the back of a motorcycle for seven hours is really bad for the butt, Jamie noted as she walked stiff legged to her hotel room's bathroom, but with a smile. That had been a lot of fun, a lot more fun than she ever thought possible. She already decided that when this tour was finished she was going to buy a bike and get her license. She briefly thought about asking Nick to go with her to pick it out, but then remembered that the agreement would be over and she'd be on her own. That thought scared her, but not enough to back down. This was something she wanted to do and thanks to Nick, she knew how much fun it could be and wasn't going to allow herself get scared off.

Thanks to Nick she was trying new things and finding new interests. Having him accompanying her made her feel relaxed and safe. With him around she didn't stand out. Well, she kind of did, but that was only because she was with an incredibly handsome man. She'd take that rather than stand out because she was the lone loser shifting nervously while trying to appear not to be alone any day of the week.

Having people look at her with open pity wasn't exactly her idea of fun. She hated the looks people sent her when she went out to eat by herself, to a movie, the mall. Then again, she had stood out thanks to the way she dressed. When she dressed in plain oversized clothing she'd hoped to blend into the background, but now she realized that actually made her stand out more. With her hair shortened and her new clothes she actually blended in a lot better, but she still wasn't comfortable doing most of the things on her list on her own.

She was deathly afraid that she'd embarrass herself or screw something up. It made it a lot easier to try new things with Nick. She'd never met anyone more comfortable in his own skin and she never had to worry about being too nervous to try something when he was around. It also didn't hurt that he'd done a lot of things that she wanted to try so it was just a matter of him showing her how to do something. With Nick around it was like having her own personal tutor on life, a tutor that was also a slave driver.

From the moment she woke up until the moment he declared that she had free time, he worked her to the bone. If they weren't going over possible interview questions, the proper way to give an interview, what not to say, working on her books, or editing someone else's book, they were traveling. It was a grueling schedule and if she didn't have the List to look forward to she'd probably be begging for him to slow down.

But there was no way she was going to give up the List. Thanks to Nick she was trying new things and loving it. She was starting to feel more comfortable and eager to try new things.......other things that he wouldn't be able to help her with. There was another aspect of her life that she' always ignored, well, not so much as ignored as never finding anyone interested. Now that she was discovering a whole new Jamie she decided it was time to give the other part of her life that she'd sorely neglected over the years a try.

She was going to have a sex life.

A really good sex life, she decided. She'd do all the things she'd only imagined and she'd do them with whomever she wanted. The old her was gone and so were her prudish or rather virginal ways. She was twenty-five years old and ready to pop her cherry. She was too old to be a virgin and definitely too old never to have been kissed. Okay, so she had been kissed in eight grade by Gerald Logan, but that shouldn't count because he'd kissed her on the cheek and only because someone dared him to do it.

## A Reclusive Heart: A Hollywood Heart's novel

Now she was more confident and eager to give it a try. There were so many things in that genre that she wanted to attempt, but was too nervous to try, but now all that was behind her. She was the new Jamie. Granted, this new Jamie required a little bit of help, but that was neither here nor there. If she wanted to have sex then she was going to have it, lots of it. She did sort of, kind of wish she could ask Nick for a few suggestions, but she didn't want him to know about this or think that she was asking him to step up and take one for the team.

The very last thing she wanted was for a guy to have sex or touch her because of an obligation. She wanted a man to want her, need her even if it was just for a night. Nick would probably think that she expected him to handle her needs as if they were a part of the list and she didn't. She knew the man would never touch her and didn't want her, which was fine because she wasn't delusional.

Nick flirted with absolutely every woman. He sweet talked them, charmed them and made them all want him, except for her of course. With her he didn't bother flirting with her or sweet talking her into doing something. No, for her he used intimidation and the List. As long as even part of her was still a pushover and that List existed then he wouldn't need to waste energy trying to sweet talk her. Besides, her heart didn't need the confusion.

It was bad enough that she'd developed a bit of a crush on the man. She didn't need him to confuse her by flirting with her and making her think that he was interested when her mind knew that he wasn't. She appreciate that they had boundaries. It made this a heck of a lot easier. He was her boss and List buddy and that was all.

She took a quick shower before dressing in a pair of soft green flannel pajama pants and a pink baby t-shirt and rushed to the desk in her room only to remember that Nick had the computer. Worrying her bottom lip, she tried to decide if this was something that could wait until tomorrow. After a minute she realized that it couldn't. If she didn't make this new list then she'd be up all night tossing and turning as the possibilities raced through her head.

Decision made, she grabbed her key card and walked out of her room and across the small hallway to Nick's door. She knocked on the door and was about to knock on it again ten seconds later when he still hadn't opened the door when it was suddenly opened and she found herself stumbling forward. As her face plastered against warm damp skin it occurred to her that Nick might not be dressed.

Taking a fortifying breath, she stepped back, averting her eyes of course as her cheeks burned and mumbled, "Can I use the computer?"

Nick sighed heavily as he walked over to his desk and picked up the laptop bag. When he turned around, she allowed her eyes exactly ten seconds to look over one of the best bodies that she'd ever seen before quickly looking away. The man was large and ripped and that really didn't help with the blushing.

"Make sure you get some sleep. We're catching a train at eight," he said as he handed her the bag.

"I'll be ready," she promised, taking the bag as she let her eyes quickly shoot to his bare chest and boxer clad body one last time before looking away and rushing back to her room.

Seeing a man in nothing but his underwear should be no big deal at her age, but sadly it was. It just went to prove to her that she desperately needed sex. Having sex would make her feel normal and less shy around men, she decided as she sat on the bed, crossing her legs as the computer powered up. She opened her file and was just about to add to her list when she realized just how stupid that was.

She created a new file and named it, "Grammatical Errors," figuring that Nick wouldn't bother looking at that file. After creating a new word document and typing the title, "Sex List," she stared blankly at the screen for several minutes.

Where should she start? she wondered. After a few minutes she figured that she should start with the basics. There really was no need to rush into sex. There were plenty of stopping points along the way to help ease her into this.

## A Reclusive Heart: A Hollywood Heart's novel

*Sex List*:

Buy condoms

Learn to flirt (Probably best to learn by watching Nick)

Buy books about sex and positions

Watch a porn (nothing weird and take notes)

Kiss a man. (Best bet to find a man to kiss is at a bar or club)

Buy sexy lingerie, nothing flannel

Have sex, lots and lots of sex.

Visit a sex store and get the basics (Make sure to ask the clerk what the basics are.)

Learn how to give oral sex (men seem to like that for some reason)

Have sex in a car.

Have sex in a pool or ocean.

Have sex in an elevator or stairwell.

After tour ends use newfound sex knowledge to please boyfriend.

Probably should find a boyfriend.

That list seemed reasonable, she decided as she saved the file and got ready for bed. Tomorrow she'd start working on her new list.

By herself.

## Chapter 10

"We're running behind," Nick said when his little recluse practically ran out of the elevators towards him.

"I know. I'm sorry," she said even as she dropped her suitcase and large duffle bag by his feet. "I'll be right back," she said, rushing off towards the hotel's small convenience store and leaving him standing there like an idiot.

The only thing that saved her from a good throttling was the fact that she was in the store and back out in under sixty seconds with a small brown paper bag clutched tightly to her chest. Deciding that he had a pretty good idea of what it was and in no way wanting to invite her to discuss her womanly problems with him, he said nothing as she shoved the bag in her duffle bag and stood up, not quite meeting his eyes.

"I'm ready," she said, blushing a darker red than he'd ever seen on her.

Deciding to take pity on the poor thing, he gestured for her to walk ahead of him while he threw his laptop bag over his shoulder and grabbed his bag. He wasn't exactly surprised when she didn't say a single word during the taxi ride to the train station. Poor thing was easily embarrassed, he thought with pity as they picked up their tickets and then waited for the train. Still she didn't utter a single word.

After about thirty minutes his sympathy was coming to an end. Being embarrassed was one thing, being mortified to this level was unhealthy and not normal. He considered explaining to her that she didn't need to be embarrassed about that sort of thing around him since he'd been raised by a half dozen strippers who were really hookers who danced every now and then, but decided against it. His past was nobody's business.

## A Reclusive Heart: A Hollywood Heart's novel

When the train finally arrived and they were ushered onto the train he damn near sighed with relief. He'd pull his computer out and get some work done while his little recluse got over this and she really needed to get the hell over it. They were going to be working together for several more months to come and really didn't need to this bullshit every month.

"I'm sorry, sir. The seats have been overbooked. I'm afraid we only have one seat available. One of you is going to have to stand," the conductor said with a what-are-you-going-to-do shrug.

If they hadn't already checked their bags they'd be getting the hell off the train and hauling ass to the airport, but they couldn't. The airport in South Carolina was a good two hours away from their hotel while the train station was only ten minutes away. They'd lose too much time switching now and would miss the book signing.

With a sigh, he gestured for Jamie to take the seat while he went and found a spot to stand near the bathroom. She looked like she was going to argue when he sent her a glare that told her to sit her cute little ass down before he spanked it. After a slight hesitation she nodded and sat down in the aisle seat.

He was just resigning himself to cramped legs and boredom when he spotted a middle aged man sporting the door to door salesman look pause in front of her. While Jamie was looking out the window the man was looking at her, looking rather pleased as he quickly slipped his wedding ring off his finger and into his pants. Nick watched as the man ran his fingers through his hair and straightened his tie before approaching Jamie and gesturing to the seat next to her with his train ticket.

Oversold train his ass. He was going to have a word with Beth or whatever the hell her name was in transportation, he told himself as he watched the asshole strike up a conversation with the little recluse. She really was a naive little thing, he decided as he watched the asshole charm her. When she smiled and let out a small laugh that seemed to please the man and piss him the hell off he decided to intervene.

Clearly she was in over her head and he was helping her. It had nothing to do with the fact that she'd given away one of the smile and laughs so easily to the asshole when he had to work his ass off to earn one. It didn't. She was his responsibility and therefore it was his job to make sure that no one but him took advantage of her. With that in mind he walked over to her.

"Up," he said, gesturing for her to stand. When she only stared up at him, looking adorably confused, he grabbed her hand and gave it a quick tug. Once she was on her feet he moved in and sat down, throwing the asshole a smug grin as he gave Jamie's hand another little tug that had her falling on his lap. He ignored her surprised gasp as he righted her on his lap and got comfortable.

"What are you doing?" she whispered as another beautiful blush crept up her neck. It made him wonder if she blushed during sex. Before the thought left his mind he was shifting her again and trying not to notice how warm and soft her ass was. Hell, he really needed to get laid.

"Getting comfortable in our seat. Why?" he asked as he closed his eyes and settled in for the ride.

She shifted again, but didn't say anything and neither did the guy next to him. He really didn't expect to fall asleep so when he was suddenly jolted awake when the train came to a stop he was surprised. He was even more surprised to find his little recluse fast asleep in his arms. She was curled up quite nicely in his arms with her head resting on his shoulder.

"Lucky bastard," the guy next to him muttered as he stood up and squeezed past him.

Ignoring him and how good Jamie felt in his arms, he gently shook her awake. When she mumbled something and tried to turn over in his arms he gave her another shake that thankfully did the trick. She slowly opened her eyes, looked at him sleepily for a moment before she blinked. He watched in fascination as her eyes widened almost comically a split second before she bolted from his lap.

## A Reclusive Heart: A Hollywood Heart's novel

As much as he hated to admit this, she'd felt damn good in his arms and he didn't like that one goddamn bit. He was a man who liked his space and didn't need a damn thing from anyone. Sex didn't count. That was just a way to work out stress and get off. He sure as hell didn't hold any of the women after he had sex with them.

If a woman entertained him in bed he'd consider her for a second bout of sex, but nothing more than that. Then again, if she'd been too needy, brought any drama to the bed or displeased him in any way he was out the door before she was done screaming his name. He liked his sex bullshit free and without all that relationship crap.

Some women got a little pissed and irritated about his view on sex, but he didn't care. If they even hinted at any drama he lost interest and moved on to the next woman. He liked to deal with women who knew the score before he fucked them. There was no future with him and he made damn sure that they all knew it.

\* \* \* \*

"What do you want to do after this?" Nick asked as he looked over some papers the bookstore manager gave him.

"Um," she said, clearing her throat and trying not to appear nervous, "I was thinking about looking around the mall for a laptop."

He frowned at that, but didn't bother looking up from the paperwork. "I told you I'd find one for you."

She stopped herself from pointing out that he'd promised to do that a few weeks ago, but she knew with their busy schedule and her List that he hadn't had much time to look around. Well, tonight she planned on rectifying that. Not only did she need her own computer to work, but she also needed it to-

"What's with the sudden rush?" he asked, still reading.

To watch porn, she almost blurted out but somehow held it back. Tonight for the first time ever she was going to watch porn. She'd never seen it before, always avoided it, but tonight she was going to watch one and take notes. Admittedly she was curious.

It wasn't as though she was completely oblivious to the act. She read romance novels and saw love scenes in movies so she felt that she had a pretty good knowledge base of the act, but she'd never actually seen the real act, but tonight she would. She'd pay attention, learn what men liked and what she could expect when it came time to have sex. She might be a virgin, but that didn't mean she wanted the first guy she slept with to know that. That was her business.

Granted, she'd didn't necessarily need to shell out a lot of money to watch a porn, but she didn't want to use Nick's computer in case it left evidence behind and she sure as heck didn't want to have to order one of those movies she'd seen advertised in some of the hotels and have anyone find out that she was doing this. She also didn't understand why anyone would pay thirty bucks to watch a movie.

"I'll take you after this," he said, not sounding particularly happy about it, but then again he had been spending all of his time with her. She imagined a man like him wasn't used to going without sex and probably needed a night off so he could do that. Then another thought occurred to her, one that made her curious, could men get cranky if they went without sex? If so, was it like PMS? Could she expect mood swings and sudden urges for chocolate from him?

She really didn't think she could deal with a cranky Nick. An irritated Nick was bad enough. No, if he got worse she was going to grab the first bimbo she saw and throw her his way. She'd do anything to avoid Nick getting crankier.

"Jamie?"

"Huh?"

"I said we could go after this if you want to," he said, looking up long enough to send her a frown.

### A Reclusive Heart: A Hollywood Heart's novel

"Oh, okay. Thanks," she mumbled, feeling giddy. Who knows maybe by this time next week she wouldn't be a virgin. That would be fantastic. She was also sure that having experienced the act first hand would probably benefit her writing. If anything she should have sex for her job. Yes, she definitely owed it to her readers to go out and have sex.

* * * *

"Nick!"

He looked up from his computer and nearly groaned. A half hour ago he realized that someone fucked up and double booked them next week and he'd been trying to figure out how to fix it. He'd just come up with a solution that would work for everyone, meaning him, when the banging started.

Shouldn't she be off working? he wondered as he pulled on a pair of jeans. Then again, she probably had another question about her computer. Granted, he thought he'd covered everything during the two hours they spent setting her new computer up, but maybe he missed something.

"Nick!" she yelled again.

"What?" he demanded as he opened the door to find the little recluse hugging her laptop tightly to her chest and looking close to tears.

"I broke my computer."

"Did you drop it?" he asked, already taking the computer from her hands to inspect it.

"No," she muttered, sounding miserable.

He threw her a curious look as he took her computer over to the couch and placed it on the coffee table. He opened the lid and felt his eyebrows jump as pop up window after pop up window featuring sex in various acts kept popping up on the screen.

"What the hell did you do?" he asked, already having a pretty good idea that she'd downloaded a virus.

"Research," she mumbled pathetically.

"What?" he asked absently as he did his best to stop the attack.

She mumbled something that he didn't quite understand. "What was that?" he asked as he opened and ran the anti-malware program he'd installed only hours ago.

"I said I was watching sex for research," she said, shocking the living hell out of him.

"You were watching porn?" he snapped. "What the hell kind of research requires you to watch porn?" he demanded as he stood up and walked over to his computer, half afraid that she'd done something to his computer.

"That's personal," she said, trying to sound firm, but the woman just didn't have a clue how to pull it off.

He ran the malware scanning program on his computer and was just about to go recheck her computer when a thought occurred to him. This morning he spotted a peculiar file in her folder and at the time hadn't thought much about it, but now he did. He clicked the file open and received his second shock of the night as he quickly read through the list.

"What are you doing?" Jamie asked, sounding nervous and for good reason.

Holy shit, was she serious? He looked over the list again as dread shot through him. Yes, she was. She'd made a list, started to do the items on the list and was curious. He'd bet everything he had that brown bag she'd hugged to her chest this morning hadn't been tampons. His damn recluse had bought condoms and was now watching porn.

## A Reclusive Heart: A Hollywood Heart's novel

She wanted to try new things. Hell, he'd encouraged her to try new things so that he had something to hold over her head and now it seemed as though she taken it one step further. His little recluse was getting ready to start a little sex revolution.

For a moment he wondered how she planned on approaching him about helping her out with this, but then realized that she hadn't planned on approaching him at all. She didn't want his help. For everything else he was fine, but he wasn't good enough for this. No, for this his little recluse planned on approaching a strange man and trusting him not to hurt.

He glared up at her as she shifted nervously in front of her computer as she wrung her hands together. Although she was a sexy little thing now and he wouldn't have minded a go between her legs he'd decided that she was off limits. He also had a firm rule about touching virgins, he didn't.

Virgins were too much work, too much drama and he didn't care enough to introduce them to sex patiently. When he had sex he wanted to get off. He didn't really care about anything else and he sure as hell didn't care about making things perfect for a woman. He got them off and that was enough in his book. It was the main reason he decided not to act on his attraction to the little recluse even though he thought she was developing a bit of a crush on him and he knew he could have had her on her back within seconds if he wanted, but damn.....

She really didn't want him. She wanted a stranger and that was not the reason why he surged to his feet and suddenly found himself glaring down at her. It wasn't. He was concerned for her because she was doing something stupid. That was all.

"Are you out of your fucking mind?" he snapped, grabbing her by her arms and giving her a rough shake. "Do you have any idea what could happen to you by going around and letting some guy fuck you?"

She winced, from his crude words or the tiny shakes he was giving her he didn't know or care. Didn't she realize she could catch something? Get pregnant? Or worse, go home with some asshole that got his thrills by beating the shit out of women? Didn't she realize how stupid this was?

"T-that's why I was doing research, you jerk!" she snapped back, surprising them both by the expression on her face. "I don't know anything about sex and have no one I can ask!" she said, getting good and mad as she pulled her arms back only to give him a good shove.

"I'm sick of not knowing! I want to have sex! I want to know what it feels like to be with a man and if I want to have sex with a thousand men then that's my business, buddy!" she said, giving him a good shove. "And if you don't like it then......then......then that's too darn bad!" she said, giving him a final shove that knocked him back onto his ass on the edge of the bed.

She turned to grab her computer and storm off when he found himself saying something he knew he'd regret. "I'll teach you."

## Chapter 11

Was it possible to die from mortification? Jamie was pretty sure she was about to find out. Did he just offer her sympathy sex? Admittedly she didn't know much about sex, but she didn't think she wanted some guy having sex with her because he felt bad for her.

She wanted what the heroines in her books got from their men, passion and desire. She wanted a man who couldn't keep his hands off of her, not a man who was willing to take one for the team.

"Um," she cleared her throat uncomfortably, "no thanks. I'll just stick to videos and books."

His eyes narrowed on her as he got to his feet. "I meant," he bit out tightly, "that I'd help you, not that I would sleep with you, Jamie."

"Oh..........," she said, thinking it over before asking, "Why?"

"Why what?" he snapped, looking agitated as he walked over to her computer to check something.

"Why do you care?"

"I need you healthy and whole to do this tour, Jamie," he explained, keeping it short and sweet, but she got the point. He was only offering to help her for his job, not because he cared. It was foolish, but she couldn't help but feel a little hurt and disappointed that he didn't care.

Maybe that was for the best, she decided. If they kept a professional distance she'd feel more comfortable about asking him questions. If they were friends she'd feel a little awkward and embarrassed with some of the questions that she was dying to ask.

"Okay, where do we start," she asked brightly, ignoring his scowl as he gestured for her to sit on the couch.

Trying to hide her nerves, she quickly sat down, at the far corner of the small sofa. Nick sent her a questioning look, but said nothing as he turned the television on and went to the pay-per-view menu. When he scrolled down a list of titles that could only belong to adult movies she gasped and lunged for the remote.

"What the heck are you doing?" she demanded as she did her best to steal the remote away from him before he could do something that would embarrass them both.

"I'm helping you go through your list," he said, holding the remote just out of reach as he selected a movie.

"Oh my god!" she gasped. "They'll know!"

"Who?" he asked, frowning.

"Everyone!"

"That I watched a skin flick?" he asked, frowning.

"Yes!" she hissed as she shot a nervous look at the door, half expecting someone to break down the door to yell at them.

"No one's going to care as long as I pay for it and besides, no one will know you watched it, Jamie. This isn't your room," he pointed out.

"Oh," she mumbled, thinking it over and realizing that he was right. As long as no one said anything, no one would have to know that she'd watched this with him. Maybe it would be for the best to have him help her with this, just the learning and asking questions part. For the rest she'd find a willing man who wanted her, which she hoped wouldn't be too difficult because she was really ready to have sex soon.

Well, if they were going to do this then they needed to do it right, she thought as she rushed out of the room.

"Where are you going?"

## A Reclusive Heart: A Hollywood Heart's novel

"To get my notebook!" she yelled over her shoulder as she opened the door and ran out.

"You're kidding, right?"

* * * *

Nick shot a look over at his little recluse as she scribbled something else down on her notebook and couldn't help but sigh. She hadn't been kidding after all. Fifteen minutes into the movie and the woman hadn't stopped writing for more than a second.

"Doesn't that hurt?" she suddenly asked.

He followed her gaze to the television and nearly groaned when he realized what she was asking. "No, it doesn't," he said tightly, shifting on the couch, again, which sadly had nothing to do with the brunette giving head in the movie and everything to do with the little recluse sitting by his side taking notes.

"It doesn't hurt when her teeth glide over it?" she asked, looking entranced with the action as he struggled not to imagine Jamie on her knees in front of him doing exactly that. What the hell had he been thinking to offer to help her with this?

He really was an idiot.

Any other man would have shoved the woman out the door, but instead of doing that he'd offered to teach her about sex. Now he was stuck sitting here sporting the hardest erection of his life and wishing like hell that he hadn't offered to put himself through this hell.

"Why is she moaning when he's not even touching her?" she asked, sounding curious.

"Because it's a movie," he said, shifting again before reluctantly adding, "And some women enjoy the act."

"Really?"

"Yes," he said tightly, praying the movie would end soon and he'd be able to get her the hell out of here so he could relieve himself, again. For almost two weeks he'd been forced to seek relief from his hand as she drove him crazy and wonder why the hell the little recluse affected him like this.

She was cute, pretty and had a great body, but he'd seen better, but no other woman left him hard and aching like her. The only explanation he had for this temporary insanity was the fact that she was forbidden fruit and virginal, untouched. He nearly whimpered when his cock jumped at the thought.

This was hell.

"I don't think he's doing that right."

"What?" he asked, refusing to look over at her, knowing that his poor dick didn't need a visual.

"She looks bored and, um, well, his tongue is barely touching her," she pointed out.

He looked back at the screen and cursed softly as he watched the man go down on the admittedly bored looking woman. Normally that was something he liked to skip with a woman. It was too intimate and he sure as hell didn't trust any woman enough to do that. He might like one stands, but that didn't mean he liked to take chances. Growing up with the type of women that he did he knew damn well what could happen. It also didn't hurt that he didn't like doing that for a woman and didn't have much of an interest in doing it.

Until now.

Now he wanted to do if for Jamie. Hell, who was he kidding? He wanted to do it for *him*. He wanted to strip her naked, lay her on the bed and lick between her legs where he knew he'd find her soft, so damn soft and wet. He'd take her with his tongue, but not like this idiot was doing, and he'd make damn sure that she wasn't bored. Until she screamed his name he wouldn't stop licking her, sucking her, fuck-

## A Reclusive Heart: A Hollywood Heart's novel

"I don't think I want some guy doing that to me," she muttered, sounding disgusted.

He just barely stopped himself from telling her that he damn well was going to do it to her and she damned well was going to like it when he remembered that he was going through a momentary lapse of sanity. She was a shy little recluse who didn't know the game and was so far from his type that it wasn't even funny. He liked his women practiced, who knew what they wanted in bed and most importantly how to give him what he wanted. Jamie didn't know shit and was going to be completely dependent on whatever guy she took to bed to introduce her to sex.

Why the idea of being the one to teach Jamie how to fuck had his poor dick twitching, he would never know, but he wished like hell that it would stop. He rubbed his hands over his damp face and had to wonder when he broke out into a sweat. Probably about the same time he thought about Jamie's lips wrapped around his dick, he thought, shifting, again.

"Wait, why is he putting his-"

Whatever she said was lost on him as his eyes shot to the screen. He felt is eyebrows arch impossibly higher as he dove for the remote.

"Wait, I wanted to see that!" Jamie grumbled, but he didn't care. A man could only take so much.

"It's time for bed," he blurted out as he swiped up a magazine off the bureau and held it discretely in front of the huge tent in his pants.

"What?" Jamie asked, shooting a nervous look between him and the bed. The fact that she didn't look excited over the idea did not piss him off.

It didn't.

"I meant that I'm tired and that we're going to have to call it a night," he explained tightly.

"Oh," she mumbled, shoulders slouching as she stood up, hugging her notebook to her chest as she headed for the door only to pause halfway there and worry her bottom lip. "You're still going to help me, right?" she asked softly as she stared down at her feet and he just barely stopped himself from going over to her and taking her into his arms.

He was not a hugger, damn it!

"Yes," he gritted out, knowing that the sooner he helped her get laid the better. No, scratch that. The sooner *he* got laid the better.

Maybe he should head downstairs to the hotel bar and pick up a woman. No, he couldn't do that since there was absolutely no way that he was going to last that long. The damn woman had him panting and ready to burst and she hadn't even touched him.

"Are you okay?" she asked, moving to take a step closer as she ran her eyes over him with obvious concern.

"Great. Fine. Never been better," he said quickly as he ushered her towards the door, making sure to keep the magazine firmly in place. "I'll look over your computer and get it back to you tomorrow," he said, opening the door and pretty much shutting it her face.

"Okay, goodnight," he thought he heard her mutter, but didn't really care.

He dropped the magazine, reached down and undid his pants and had himself in hand as he quickly made his way to the bathroom. He slapped his hand flat against the wall above the toilet, closed his eyes and thought about Jamie's face. Never in his life had been this turned on by one woman and he sure as hell never pictured a woman's face while he jerked off. Now he couldn't help but moan as the image of her sweet face caused his balls to tighten. He didn't even finish the second stroke before his legs threatened to give out and a long groan escaped him.

"*Jamie,*" he heard himself growl in ecstasy.

## A Reclusive Heart: A Hollywood Heart's novel

He dropped his hand away and flushed the toilet, panting harder than if he'd just done thirty minutes on the treadmill and stumbled back from the toilet, wondering what the hell was happening to him. She shouldn't be affecting him like this. He didn't want her. Okay, that was bullshit. He *shouldn't* want her.

She was his responsibility and definitely not his type, but he couldn't help but like the idea of holding her in his arms or kissing her, something he didn't usually like but did to get a woman to spread. With Jamie he just wanted to kiss her just to kiss the little recluse. His arms actually ached from the urge just to hold her.

This was so damn wrong. If he didn't need J.L. Lewis so damn much he'd either walk away or fuck her to get it out of his system, but he did. J.L. Lewis was the key to his success. Once he was done with her no one would care that he was the bastard raised by whores. He was going to make a name for himself, but he needed her to do it and sleeping with her would only screw up his plans.

He was going to have to keep his damn hands to himself and his dick in his pants around her. It didn't matter how much he wanted her, because he wanted what J.L. Lewis could give him a whole hell of a lot more.

## Chapter 12

"You know what?" Jamie asked, trying to pull away from Nick, but the big jerk wouldn't let her go. "I've changed my mind. Having sex is overrated. I'm more than happy to remain a virgin. *Very happy*," she stressed as he ignored her and dragged her into the store.

As soon as the door closed behind him with a soft little chime he pushed her in front of him where she got her first look inside a lingerie store. There was lace and silk in every color and style imaginable and she had absolutely no idea about what to buy, how to figure out her size and in some cases how to wear the tiny contraptions. This was all wrong. She might be passably pretty now, but she was in no way sexy enough to wear any of the pretty things in front of her. It was flannel pajamas for her, she decided as she tried to make a run for the door, but the infuriating man wouldn't let her go.

"Behave," he whispered as a pretty redhead in a sexy silk camisole and short skirt walked over to them. She ran an assessing eye over Jamie, barely biting back a frown before her eyes shifted to Nick and widened in pleasure right along with a coy smile.

"May I help you?" she asked Jamie, but her eyes were on Nick.

"That would be great," Nick said in that deep sensual voice he used on everything female. Well, every female except for her, she thought with a small sigh as she tried to make another run for it, but the darn man wouldn't let her go.

The woman's smile became knowing as she sent Nick a welcoming look. Did the woman not see her? For all the woman knew she could be his girlfriend, his fiancé, or his wife. Okay, that was really pushing it, but it was still really rude.

"My friend could use some help if you have a moment?" Nick said, placing his hands firmly on her shoulders to keep her in place. Why wouldn't he just let her run away?

## A Reclusive Heart: A Hollywood Heart's novel

The woman reluctantly looked at her and did a wonderful job of pulling back her frown. With a slight nod she gestured for Jamie to follow her. When she just stood there Nick gave her a gentle shove in the woman's direction and forced her to move her butt. She shot him a glare over her shoulder, but of course he just ignored her death glare and kept pushing her towards a whole new level of embarrassment.

They followed the redhead into a back fitting room decorated in pastel colors, several oversized chairs, mirrors and three changing rooms. She watched as Nick walked over to one of the chairs and sat down and thought that perhaps she should do the same thing when the woman began manhandling her.

"Hey!" Jamie gasped when the woman wrapped a measuring tape around her chest. Before she could shove the woman's hands away she measured Jamie's stomach, hips, and one thigh, leaving her blushing and irritated. Of course she decided to take her irritation out on Nick by sending him a glare, but he was already busy reading a magazine so she gave up scowling and tried to figure out how she was going to get out of this.

Apparently she wasn't.

"What are you interested in?" the saleswoman asked.

Jamie opened her mouth to tell her anything flannel when Nick answered for her. "Soft colors and nothing too bold," he said in a bored tone.

"Virginal?" the woman asked, making Jamie gasp. How the heck did she know?

"Yes," Nick said in that same bored tone as he continued to read.

"I'll see what I have," the woman said, throwing Nick one last look of longing before she reluctantly left the room.

Jamie opened her mouth to tell the man that if he was bored then he could darn well go wait in the car while she did this, but the saleswoman chose that moment to walk back into the room, carrying a huge selection of silk and lace. Something about the woman's flushed cheeks told her that she probably ran around the store and grabbed anything and everything so that she could come back to ogle Nick. For his part, Nick just sat there thumbing through a magazine on fashion.

"Try these on and we'll see what we have to work with," the woman said, shoving several items in Jamie's hands and absently gesturing for her to go change.

Knowing there was probably no way to get out of this now, Jamie accepted her fate and walked to the first changing room. She wasn't too surprised when she saw the saleswoman sit down in the chair next to Nick. Resigning herself to being ignored, she walked into the changing room and decided just to get this over with. The sooner she picked out what she liked, the faster she could put this nightmare behind her.

The first one was white silk with lace trimming. It seemed harmless enough, so she quickly undressed, leaving her underwear on and tried on the beautiful nightie. She turned to look in the mirror only to discover that there wasn't a single mirror in the small room. Well, that was kind of dumb, she thought as she wondered how she was supposed to know what it looked like.

"Have you tried something on yet?" Nick asked, sounding impatient, which was a little shocking since he was usually cool as a cucumber whenever a woman was around, again not when it was just her. She didn't seem to count.

"Yes, but there isn't a mirror in here," she explained, looking down at herself and twisting and turning as she tried to see if it looked okay.

There was a long suffering sigh that she knew all too well. "Use the mirrors out here," Nick said, well, more like ordered.

"With you out there?" she asked, worrying her bottom lip nervously.

## A Reclusive Heart: A Hollywood Heart's novel

"Of course. How else am I supposed to help you if I don't see what you're wearing?" he pointed out and she just barely stopped herself from reminding him that she didn't in fact want his opinion about this.

In fact, she specifically told him that she didn't want his help with this matter. As soon as they finished the interview with the local paper she'd told him that she was going to Wal-Mart to pick out some lingerie. For a moment he'd only been able to stare down at her in that intense way that made her self-conscious and fight the urge to apologize to him. When the urge to apologize to him became too much he grumbled something, grabbed her arm, and practically dragged her to their rental car.

"I'm waiting, Jamie," he reminded her and she was about to refuse when it occurred to her that having a man like Nick help her pick out sexy lingerie would probably cut out half the stress. She wouldn't have to worry if it made her look fat or frumpy because Nick would tell her. He would never hold anything back because he was afraid that he'd hurt her feelings because he didn't care. How that was a good thing she wasn't sure, but it was an advantage, one she'd be foolish to ignore.

Taking a deep breath and praying that she didn't do something like pass out, she opened the door and walked out of the room. She looked over at Nick to find him taking his time from looking up from his magazine. When he did, he placed the magazine on his lap as he ran an assessing eye over her. He gestured for her to turn around and with a little sigh of annoyance she did just that only to come to a sudden halt when she spotted herself in the mirror.

Wow........

The nightie looked so beautiful and delicate. It put her breasts and figure on display without being obscene. It was really rather pretty, sweet and sexy all at once.

Nick cleared his throat. "It looks nice. Why don't you try on another one?" he suggested as she looked back to find him grabbing another magazine and ignoring the one on his lap. Apparently he lost his interest in fashion and the saleswoman wanted to kill her if that glare was any indication. Frowning, she returned to the dressing room.

Ten nighties later they were walking out the door and the damn stubborn man was holding her bags firmly in front of him so that she couldn't take them and carry them. Every time she went to grab her bags he stepped away, glaring down at her as if she'd slapped him or something. Finally she gave up and was content to ride in silence as he drove them back to the hotel.

"What's on the agenda tonight?" he asked as he pulled onto the highway.

"I thought I'd have a drink in the hotel bar and find a man to kiss," she said casually, shooting him a sideways look and noting the way the back of his knuckles were turning white as he clenched the steering wheel tightly. She was just about to ask him what was wrong when her cell phone rang.

She pulled her phone out of her pocket and sighed when she saw that it was her mother calling. Her mother didn't call often, but when she did it was usually to brag about Caitlyn or whine about some injustice done to Caitlyn. As much as she'd like to send the call to voicemail she couldn't. Her mother would have a fit and the call would be ten times worse for Jamie. Resigning herself to a half hour rant about the perfection that was her sister, Jamie answered the phone.

"*Where do you get off humiliating us like this, young lady?*" her mother demanded before Jamie could say hello, stunning her and leaving her a little confused.

"What are you talking about?" she asked, sure that her mother was mistaken since she hadn't done a single thing that should humiliate her family.

## A Reclusive Heart: A Hollywood Heart's novel

"*You know darn well what I'm talking about, young lady! I'm talking about that smut that you publish! I have never been more humiliate than I was today when Macy Powers showed me the magazine article that talked about your erotic novels,*" she said with open disgust and Jamie tried not to wince, but she couldn't help it.

Well aware of the man beside her, Jamie turned as far as she could away from him, almost huddling into herself as she quickly explained, "They're not erotic novels, mom."

"*Don't you dare lie to me, young lady. I flipped through one of those horrible books that you write and I found inappropriate material in it! Do you have any idea how embarrassed I was? Do you even care that you've humiliated your poor sister, hmm?*"

"I-" she started to explain, but of course her mother cut her off.

"*I cannot believe this is how you wasted the college education we provided for you! Do you have any idea how hard your father worked to send you to college and this is how you repay him?*" she demanded and it took everything she had not to remind her mother that they hadn't paid a cent for her college education. That was Caitlyn and she hadn't even bothered to graduate or really attend for that matter.

By the time that it was her turn to go to college, her parents told her there was no money for her because they had used up all the money they set aside for Caitlyn to "find herself." When she flunked out of three private, expensive, colleges her parents decided that Caitlyn had worked too hard and simply needed time off which they paid for. Jamie on the other hand had worked her butt off and put herself through college. She graduated top of her class and never regretted one second of it because that experience showed her that she could do anything even if no one else thought that she could.

*"I cannot believe you pulled this petty juvenile stunt. Was it for attention or just to embarrass your sister? Are you really that petty that you can't be happy for your sister? You really felt it was necessary to humiliate her like this?"*

"Mom, this has nothing to do with-*hey!*" she gasped, startled when her phone was suddenly yanked from her hand. She turned around in time to see Nick end the call and shut the phone off before he tossed it onto the backseat.

"You just hung up on my mother," she said, more shocked than anything.

"I know."

"She's going to be mad," Jamie said, worrying her bottom lip even as her stomach coiled tightly in guilt.

It didn't matter that she hadn't been the one to hang up or that she hadn't done anything wrong, she still felt guilty. Her mother always made her feel bad about everything. When she was a kid it was so much worse because she truly believed everything her mother said. She'd become so racked up with guilt that she'd end up making herself sick. When she moved out things slowly got a little bit better and she realized that her mother was laying everything at her feet even things that she had no control over and hadn't done.

Unfortunately knowing that her mother overreacted didn't help her stomach. She couldn't shove away the sense of dread over what her mother would do now. Would she leave messages of her crying? Give Jamie the silent treatment? She wasn't sure what passive aggressive nonsense her mother had in store for her and really shouldn't care, but she did. She couldn't help it.

"Do you want to go see if we can rent a bike and hit the road for a few hours?" Nick asked.

## A Reclusive Heart: A Hollywood Heart's novel

She gave him a forced small smile as she shook her head and murmured, "No, thank you." Even though she'd rather do that than sit in her room feeling guilty she couldn't. She hated when her mother was mad at her, probably because it felt like another rejection. She knew her mother had too much power over her, but she couldn't help it. Maybe by the end of this tour she'd figure out how to deal with her, but it hadn't happened yet.

A few minutes later they were in the hotel lobby waiting for the elevator when Nick reached over and took her hand into his and gave it a small squeeze before letting it go, startling her. She looked up at him to find him scowling down at her. Great another person she'd pissed off. This day was just getting better and better, she thought.

"There's nothing wrong with your books, Jamie. They're great. They're not trash and they're certainly nothing to be embarrassed about. I don't know what's going on in your family, but I can guarantee you that you didn't embarrass your family. If anything your mother and sister are probably jealous," he said with a shrug as if what he just suggested wasn't ludicrous. Her mother and sister would never be jealous of her. They were beautiful, popular, and married while she barely had anyone that she would consider a real friend, kind of okay looking now and didn't even have a man interested in her.

Still.......

"Why do you think they're jealous?" she found herself asking.

Nick simply shrugged as he gestured for her to step into the elevator before him. "I know women," he simply said and she found that she couldn't really argue that point, but sadly it didn't really clear the matter up for her.

"Meaning?" she prompted when he didn't add anything else.

"Meaning," he said as he pressed the button for the fifth floor, "that she wouldn't be making a huge deal out of this if she wasn't jealous. For whatever reason your mother and sister are too petty to be happy for you. They're upset about the amount of attention that you're getting so they're trying to tear you down a bit to make themselves feel better," Nick said, stepping out of the elevator next to her as she thought that over.

Was it possible? she wondered as she walked past Nick's door and pulled out her keycard. It did seem that they acted this way every time anything good happened for her. They also went well out of their way to make her feel bad for it and did whatever they could to shine the light back on themselves. Not that she cared. She really didn't like attention, especially all the attention that she was receiving on this tour. The only reason she was sticking it out and not running for the hills was her contract and the "List."

Well, both lists.

Thanks to this tour she was trying new things and learning about herself. She'd worked really hard to get to this point and maybe, just maybe it was time to stop allowing her family to make her feel like garbage. Maybe she should.....should.....

Her thoughts kind of drifted off as her brain registered the feel of Nick's mouth on hers. As she tried to figure out what was happening he reached up and gently cupped her face in his large hands. His lips moved tenderly against hers and she couldn't help but relax against him. The kiss was tender, sweet and did funny things to her stomach and it was also perfect. She honestly could not have hoped for a better first kiss.

He pressed one last kiss against her lips before pulling back. She opened her mouth to say something only to find her mouth covered with his again, this time with a pained groan that had her toes curling.

"Don't let them bring you down, Jamie," he whispered against her lips before pulling back.

## A Reclusive Heart: A Hollywood Heart's novel

"What was that for?" she asked in a daze as she fought against the urge to throw herself at him for another kiss.

"Now you don't have to worry about going out tonight for a kiss. Go relax, take a hot bath and get some work done," he said, taking the keycard out of her hand and opening the door for her and giving her a gentle shove inside the room before closing the door and leaving her slightly confused.

It didn't take long to figure out that he'd done that to get her mind off of her family drama. It was kind of sweet, but the fact that it had been done out of pity and probably to get her to focus back on work kind of spoiled it, but not enough to stop her from smiling as she went about doing exactly what he asked her to do.

## Chapter 13

This was sure to be an awkward moment, Nick decided as he stood outside of Jamie's door. What the hell had he been thinking last night? He had no business kissing her, but even knowing that he couldn't force himself to regret doing it. As much as he would love to say that he did it for her, he knew the kiss had been for him.

All day yesterday he'd struggled against the urge to reach out and touch her, hold her and kiss her and when she looked so damn miserable standing in front of her room yesterday he couldn't help himself. He'd kissed her. It wasn't wild or out of control, but it had been the most pleasurable kiss of his life. The kiss had been simple and controlled, but still managed to leave him hard and aching for her.

He'd shocked even himself by walking away from her last night when everything in him screamed to take her to bed. It would have been easy. She was desperate to lose her virginity and for the first time in his life he was more than eager to take it. He'd never wanted a virgin before her, but he wanted her. He wanted to be the first man to touch her, taste her and take her until she could barely scream his name and that was why he walked away from her.

Jamie was not the screw and leave kind of woman. She was the type of woman any man, besides him, could happily do forever with. She might think that she can handle having sex with a man and never see him again, but he knew her well enough by now to know that wasn't the case. She might be able to go through with sleeping with a man she didn't know the first time, but he knew the moment it ended she would be wracked with guilt. If the guilt that she slept with a guy didn't get to her then the loneliness afterwards would.

This type of life wasn't for her. She needed to wait for a guy that loved her and wanted to take care of her. Wasting her virginity on some loser she met at a bar was only going to cause her pain. He couldn't let her do this and it had nothing to do with the fact that he didn't like the idea of another man touching her.

## A Reclusive Heart: A Hollywood Heart's novel

He knew he was just worried about her because he felt responsible for her in a way and that was why he didn't like the idea of some asshole touching her. It had nothing to do with jealousy because he didn't get jealous. When she announced that she was going to hit a bar last night to get that first kiss and he wanted to put his fist through something it was because he didn't want to see her hurt.

It was his job after all to make sure that she was safe. He had no problem teaching her about sex, especially if it kept from doing something stupid like trusting some asshole. He'd teach her and discourage her from doing anything stupid. She was a timid little thing so he didn't think it would take all that much to get her to stay clear of men while they were on tour. When they got back he would ask Dana if she knew any decent available men for his little recluse. Of course, he would have to meet them first to make that they were good enough.

Before he could do any of that he was going to have to break her heart. He wasn't looking forward to it, but it had to be done. There was no doubt in his mind that the little recluse probably thought that last night meant more than just a kiss between friends. She probably had her heart set on the two of them becoming involved, but that couldn't happen. He didn't do relationships and she shouldn't accept anything less.

With a sigh, he knocked on the door. He really had no idea how to do this without hurting her. He'd never cared before about letting a woman down, but his little recluse was his responsibility and he was surprised to realize that she was indeed becoming a good friend. He'd let her down gently. It really was the least that he could do for her.

Jamie opened the door and he prepared himself for her tears, but all he got was a warm smile. Of course she'd be happy to see him, he realized, feeling like an idiot. She probably spent the entire night doodling his name all over her notebooks and imaging what their kids would look like. It was sad, cute, but sad.

"Hey, Nick," she said, smiling. "I'm so glad that you're here."

He couldn't help but sigh. Of course she was happy to see him. Maybe it would be best to quickly explain that last night's kiss had meant nothing. Sure, he'd be destroying all her hopes and dreams, but it was for the best.

"I'm starving," she said, walking past him as she pulled the door shut behind her. "I was just about to head downstairs and grab something to eat. Do you think that we have time to grab breakfast before the signing?" she asked as she headed for the elevator.

"I think we should talk about something first," he said quietly as he tried to think of a way to break it to her without breaking her heart. Sadly, he just didn't see any way around it. He was going to break her heart, but he'd do it quickly. It surprised him that he actually cared if he hurt her, but he figured that was because he genuinely cared about her, another surprise, but one that didn't matter at the moment.

"Okay," she said, pulling her beautiful strawberry blond hair up into a messy bun. "But can we talk while we walk? I'm starving," she said, pressing the elevator button.

"It's about last night," he said as they stepped into the elevator. When she frowned up in adorable confusion at him he added, "About the kiss," he said, knowing it was for the best to get it over with, but hating that he was about to hurt her. Maybe they should return to her room for this talk. He didn't want his little recluse embarrassed when she broke out in tears.

"What about it?" she asked, looking so damn pretty at that moment that all he could think about was kissing her, but that would just send the wrong message.

"I just wanted to make sure that you understood why I did it," he said, inwardly wincing when she smiled. Oh god, did she expect a declaration of love? That would never happen. Maybe they should go upstairs after all, he thought just as the elevator doors opened to the lobby.

### A Reclusive Heart: A Hollywood Heart's novel

"I know why you did it and I should thank you. That was really sweet, Nick. You're a good friend," she said, reaching out and giving his arm a quick squeeze.

For a moment he could only stare after her as she walked across the lobby. It took the elevator doors shutting to snap him out of his shock. That was it? Seriously? He'd given her, her very first kiss and it meant nothing to her, he thought with disgust as he shoved the doors open and went after her.

It didn't mean anything to her? Well, that was fine because it meant less than nothing to him. He was relieved, glad even, that she didn't misconstrue that kiss to mean more than it really was. As long as they were both on the same page then everything was fine, just fucking peachy.

\* \* \* \*

"Are you okay?" she asked as she took her water from Nick.

"Peachy," he said tightly.

"You wouldn't be so crabby if you'd eaten breakfast," she pointed out quietly as he glared down at her.

"I am not cranky," he bit out, narrowing his eyes on her.

"No, of course not. My mistake," she said, barely managing to bite back a smile as that glare intensified. When she started to think of his glares as cute she didn't know, but they were. It really had been silly to be intimidated by this man. He might come off as a jerk, but he really was a big sweetie pie.

"Damn straight," he said, running his eyes over the large crowd that had gathered to meet her. The bookstore manager had booked them for only three hours, but she had a feeling they wouldn't be getting out of here until after dinner time.

"Do you think we could do something off the list tonight?" she asked, trying not to sound too eager, but it was difficult. She'd wanted to do this for years, but never had the guts to try. Now that she had Nick she was excited to go for it.

"Which list?" Was his voice hoarser than a minute ago? She wondered if he was getting sick. If he was, they would have to put off her plans for another night. She'd be disappointed, but she'd get over it.

"The original list," she said, stepping out of the way as one of the cashiers carrying a large cardboard sign with a picture of her books on it walked past her.

"Oh," he said, looking a little disappointed.

Well of course he was disappointed, she realized, feeling like an idiot. He hadn't been with a woman since this tour started and was probably hoping that they'd hit a bar or a club so that he could rectify that. The realization that he wanted to be with another woman hurt so she shoved the thought away, knowing that it wouldn't do her any good to wish things were different.

They were two completely different people and nothing she said or did would ever change that. When this was all over she doubted that she'd see very much of him. Maybe they'd share a laugh while they waited for the elevator together, but she doubted there would ever be anything more than that. Right now she was going to focus on what they did have, a friendship of sorts.

When the manager, a short woman with thick glasses and a nervous smile, removed the red ribbon that kept the people in the line forming in front of the small table they set up for her, Nick pulled her chair out and gestured for her to sit down. Biting her lip, she did just that, hoping that the large breakfast she ate before coming here would help settle her nerves.

## A Reclusive Heart: A Hollywood Heart's novel

She'd been doing this for about a month now and although she thought she was improving with making small talk with her readers and not freaking out, it was still stressful for her. The only times she found herself relaxing was when Nick was close by. Thankfully, he'd been staying closer the past couple of weeks, probably to make sure that she didn't scare off the fans, she thought as she sat down and took a quick sip of water. Out of the corner of her eye she watched as Nick spoke to the bookstore manager, but was thankfully still close enough that she didn't feel like panicking.

Six hours later everything was still fine. Nick wasn't too far away and the fans had been great. A few made her nervous, but that was mostly because they treated her like a freak of nature. Okay, maybe freak of nature was a bit of an exaggeration, but that's how she felt when they wouldn't stop gushing and going on and on about how excited they were to meet her. It was flattering, but it also made her really nervous. She preferred it when her readers didn't make a big deal out of meeting her. She liked meeting them and hearing what they had to say about her books, but the gushing was a little unnerving. Several times Nick had to step in and calmly get the over-enthusiastic fan to move along.

As she said goodbye to the sweet woman who'd given her a copy of her family's cookie recipe because Jamie mentioned on her Facebook page the other night that she was dying for a homemade cookie she noted the young college guy behind her. Her eyes shot to the trio of guys waiting for him near the Sports section. They kept gesturing for their friend to move up in line.

Why were they holding cameras? she wondered as he finally moved up in line and stood in front of her. He cleared his throat nervously.

"Um, J.L. Lewis?" he said, sounding unsure.

"Yes?" she asked, wondering if he was here to get her autograph for his girlfriend or mother. That was the reason most of the guys used when asking for her autograph, but a few of them she suspected were closet romance novel junkies. Something about this guy told her that wasn't the case.

Before she could wonder what he was doing he reached over and grabbed her hand, yanking her to her feet and had his mouth plastered against hers, surprising the heck out of her and everyone in line if the startled gasps and nervous chuckles were any indication. Just as fast as it happened it was over.

What the heck just happened, she wondered as her eyes landed on Nick and widened. He was kneeling in front of the table and it wasn't until he pulled his arm back that she realized what he was doing.

"Stop!" the guy on the ground cried as Nick pulled back his fist and punched him again.

"Oh no," Jamie mumbled, scrambling out from behind the table to stop him, but before she could get close enough to stop him the guy's friends were there trying to pull Nick away. Nick didn't bother to look back as he shoved them away and focused his attention on the guy on the floor.

"What the hell is wrong with you?" the blonde guy with a buzz cut demanded as he tried to yank Nick back. "It was just for a frat scavenger hunt. Let him go!"

Nick ignored him and focused on the guy throwing wild swings as he tried to fight Nick off. A few connected with Nick's jaw, but if they hurt it didn't show. Having had quite enough of this nonsense, Jamie shoved two of the college kids who were in the way and did the only thing she could think of at the moment.

She launched herself onto Nick's back.

"Get the hell off of me!" he snapped, trying to gently shrug her off even as he moved to punch the guy again.

"No!" she said, wrapping her legs around his waist in an attempt to use her weight to throw him off.

"Jamie!" he snapped, pausing mid-punch to try and shrug her off again, but she wouldn't budge.

## A Reclusive Heart: A Hollywood Heart's novel

The guy on the floor took the opportunity to make a run for it with his friends not far behind him. With a growl of frustration, Nick got to his feet to go after them, but apparently he refused to do it with her still on his back.

"Get off!"

"No!"

"Get the hell off my back so that I can go kick his ass!"

"You already did!" she pointed out and then added. "He left bloody and crying! Is that not good enough for you?"

He paused briefly and shook his head as he reached back to pull her off, but she refused to let go. "*Jamie,*" he growled out in warning. Once upon a time that would have sent her screaming for the hills, but not anymore. He wouldn't hurt her. She knew that, but just in case he decided to get even with her for this little stunt she made a mental note to hide all her chocolate.

"Um, excuse me?" the bookstore manager said, grabbing their attention.

With a sigh, Nick turned so that they were both facing the woman, who looked a little freaked out. Not that Jamie could blame her. She just hoped the woman didn't call the cops on Nick because she had absolutely no idea how to bail someone out of jail and she really had no interest in learning how.

"I'm afraid I'm going to have ask you to leave," she said much to Jamie's relief. She really hadn't liked the idea of Nick becoming some guy's "special friend" for the night.

## Chapter 14

"Go. Away," Nick bit out tightly, but the damn woman refused to leave. At least she was on the other side of the door, he decided, otherwise he'd be tempted to strangle his little recluse.

"You can't still be mad!" she said in exasperation. "I eventually got off your back."

He paused mid-sip of his beer and glared at the door. "You didn't get the hell off my back until I was in front of your door!" he snapped.

"I had to make sure that you wouldn't do anything stupid," she pointed out and he barely stopped himself from storming over to his door, ripping it open and kissing the hell out of her.

Now *that* would have been stupid.

Perhaps not as stupid as attacking some dumb kid in front of a group of J.L. Lewis' fans at a signing, he thought with a groan. What in the hell had he been thinking? He'd never lost it like that and certainly never over a woman. Several of the women he'd taken out over the years received attention from other men and he hadn't cared at all. He didn't get jealous, never cared enough to, but today he'd been ready to kill the little bastard.

For any other client he would have simply pulled her away and signaled for either store security to handle the guy or the manager. There was no way he would have taken a chance screwing up his career for anyone. He'd worked too damn hard to get where he was and wasn't about to let anyone come between him and what he wanted.

### A Reclusive Heart: A Hollywood Heart's novel

All his plans went to hell the moment he saw another man kiss her. All he could think of at the time was that another man was touching his little recluse. Even as he grabbed the guy, he knew what he was doing and that it could very well be the end of his career, but he hadn't given a damn. All that mattered was taking care of Jamie and if he hadn't been so furious at the time the realization would have probably worried him like it did now.

"Are you going to let me in?" she asked, sighing heavily with annoyance and sounding so damn cute that he had to stop himself from smiling.

"No."

There was a brief pause before she said, "If you do I'll tell you about the new book I'm writing and the big surprise," she said brightly, probably hoping to lure him into letting her in and pestering him.

"I don't care," he said, surprising even himself. As her editor he should care. The woman's books were a goldmine and he'd be an idiot not to find out what she was working on so that he could prepare an advertising campaign, but at the moment he simply didn't care.

The only thing he cared about at the moment was getting his head clear, perhaps getting drunk as he tried to figure out how to explain to this whole thing to Rick in the morning when he called up to chew Nick's ass out for the pictures that were no doubt already making the rounds on the internet.

"You're really not coming out of there?" she asked, sounding disappointed.

"No."

"Are you sure?"

"Yes!"

"Fine," she said, sighing unhappily. "I guess I'll just go without you."

He didn't bother responding as he took a sip of his beer. She could go out on her own for one night. She'd be more than fine. Besides, he doubted that she was doing anything dangerous. Knowing his little recluse, she was probably getting around to the little karaoke item on her to do list that had made him want to cry. Actually, if she was hitting a karaoke bar then he definitely wasn't going with her, he decided, taking another sip of his beer.

"Okay, but if you need me I'll be at Extreme Tattoo on Elm Street. I'll be back later," she said brightly as he choked on his beer.

* * * *

"What do you think of that one?" she asked, pointing to a skull with snakes coming out of its eyes to make Nick laugh, but the man only glared down at her.

He'd been doing it for the past hour. Well, actually for the first twenty minutes he argued against her going through with this, but this was something that she wanted to do and wouldn't let anyone talk her out of. For years she toyed with the idea of getting a tattoo, but her family's disapproving attitude and her inability to stick up for herself held her back. After the phone call from her mother she decided that she was done letting her family's expectations, needs, and wants dictate her life. This was her life and she was going to start really living it.

It also didn't hurt that over the past month she'd learned to take chances and enjoy her life. Before this tour she only dreamed of doing things like riding on a motorcycle or trying out paintball, but now that she did them she couldn't help but want to do all of those other things that she'd been curious about over the years. She was still nervous. Not that she'd admit that to Nick, but she was glad that he came with her tonight. She only wished that he'd lighten up a bit.

"This is permanent, Jamie," he reminded her, again.

"That's the whole point, Nick," she said, walking over to the picture of the tribal tattoo that she'd chosen ten minutes ago. It was black, intricate and beautiful and she couldn't wait to have it on her body.

## A Reclusive Heart: A Hollywood Heart's novel

"I really think that you should take some time and think this over," he said as he ran his eyes over the artwork on the wall.

"I've been thinking about doing this for years, Nick. It's not like I'm making some drunken impulsive decision," she pointed out.

"Then what would one more week hurt?" he asked, still not looking at her. She'd noticed that since he opened his door to try and stop her from doing this that he wouldn't look her in the eye, or at her face for that matter. She didn't know what was wrong and wasn't going to stress herself out trying to figure it out.

"Are you ready?" the tattoo artist names Bret asked as he gestured for her to come with him.

She didn't even hesitate when she said, "Yes," and followed after him. She ignored Nick's muttered curses and focused on getting something she'd always wanted.

This was going to be great!

* * * *

"Ow! Owie!" Jamie cried out, but thankfully didn't move.

It was bad enough that she was going through with this asinine plan, she didn't need a fucked up tattoo on top of everything. He really wished she'd listened to him, but the damn stubborn woman wouldn't listen to reason. Tattoos on women were tacky and he hated the idea of her marring her body with one. It didn't matter how sexy the woman was, tattoos always turned him off. Then again maybe it was for the best that she was getting something done to her that would repulse him, he decided as Jamie squeezed his hands tightly.

"I think he's almost done," he said soothingly even as he prayed that it was the truth. His damn legs were cramping up, but he refused to let her hands go out of fear that she would bolt and screw up the tattoo.

"That's what you said an hour ago!" Jamie said accusingly as she squeezed her eyes shut.

"It was ten minutes ago, Jamie. It only seems like an hour ago because you're in pain," he explained as gently as he could while Jamie continued to mutter a combination of "ow" and "owie."

"Almost done," Bret thankfully said.

Nick didn't bother looking at her tattoo as it was being drawn on. He'd still been too upset that she was doing something this stupid. He still couldn't believe she was getting it on her lower back, right above her ass and yeah, when the guy had her drop her pants and panties halfway down her ass he looked and drooled.

She really had a beautiful ass. It was round, soft and groan worthy, but the damn woman decided to ruin the scenery with a tramp stamp of all things. No doubt by next week he was going to have to take her to have the damn thing removed.

"All set," Bret announced.

Jamie cracked one eye open. "Are you sure?"

"Yup."

With that, Jamie was off the table and righting her clothes even as she walked stiff legged to front of the store to pay the man.

"Don't you want to look at it?" Nick asked, frowning when the stubborn woman shook her head and kept moving.

With a sigh he followed after her, making a mental note to pick up chocolate on the way to the hotel since there was no doubt that she was going to need it.

\* \* \* \*

## A Reclusive Heart: A Hollywood Heart's novel

"What now?" he asked wearily as he opened his door and found his little recluse shifting nervously in front of him wearing a baby blue tee shirt and another pair of those damn flannel pants that he shouldn't find sexy, but did.

"I can't get the bandage off. It's been more than two hours and I'm supposed to wash it now with a little bit of antibacterial soap," she said, holding up the small bottle of liquid hand soap, "and gently wipe it, but I can't reach the top corners of the bandage."

Pinching the bridge of his nose as he wondered when this horrible day would end, he stepped to the side and allowed her to come in. The sooner he got this over with, the sooner she'd leave and he could return to staring at the television as he tried not to think of all the bullshit that waited for him tomorrow.

"Where do you want to do this?" she asked, looking around the small hotel room.

"Get on the bed, Jamie," he said, gesturing lazily towards the double bed.

"O-okay," she said nervously as she put the soap and tube of ointment she'd been carrying onto the edge of the bed and carefully laid across the bed on her stomach.

When she didn't move her shirt and pants out of the way so that he could get to the tattoo, he resigned himself to the task. He paused by the bed and pulled his shirt off before it got ruined by the ointment.

"I have to move your clothes out of the way," he explained even as he reached for her tee-shirt. Thankfully she had enough sense not to argue and even raised up a bit to help him with the task. He pushed it up until it reached her underarms and then reached for her flannel pajama pants, careful not to touch the bandage and hurt her.

When his fingers brushed against her surprisingly firm ass he had to take a deep breath to get his breathing under control. He was supposed to be doing her a favor, not ogling her ass, he reminded himself as he pulled her pants and panties down, revealing move of her ass.

"*Mercy*," he hissed softly at the sight.

"What?" Jamie asked, moving to turn over, but he stopped her by placing a hand on her back to keep her right where she was.

"Nothing. I'm going to take the bandage off now. Try not to move," he said, reaching for the corner of the large white gauze pad as he prepared himself for the splash of cold water that he tattoo would douse his lust for her.

Five minutes later the bandage was removed and his damn cock was straining in his pants to get to her. Of course it would turn him on if it was on his little recluse, he thought dryly as he gently cleaned the black tattoo that he couldn't help imagine tracing with his tongue. As soon as it was clean he applied the ointment that would protect it and washed his hands.

By the time he stepped out of his bathroom he expected to find Jamie dressed and scrambling for the door, but instead he found her right where he left her. Wondering what was wrong since his little recluse by all rights should have yanked her clothes back into place the second he announced that he was done, he walked over to her and couldn't help but smile when her cute little snores reached his ears.

He considered waking her up and sending her to her room, but then decided against that. The poor thing was exhausted and probably wouldn't have the energy to walk back to her room. At least that's what he told himself as he gripped the bottom of her pant legs and carefully pulled them off her. Then he readjusted her pretty light green panties to cover her bottom and frowned down at her shirt.

## A Reclusive Heart: A Hollywood Heart's novel

With the ointment on her back, her shirt would stick to her new tattoo and he wasn't sure if that would damage the tattoo. Plus the guy told her to leave it exposed to air whenever she could. Not knowing what else to do, he reached down and worked her shirt off, careful not to wake her or roll her onto her back. When that was done he turned up the heat, dropped his pants and joined her on the bed, preparing himself for a long night of torture as the object of his desire lay less than six inches away practically naked.

As he started to doze off with a rather painful erection, he couldn't help but wonder if this was hell.

## Chapter 15

As she slowly woke up she couldn't help but wonder why she was naked. Then Bret's instructions from the night before ran through her head and she remembered that she planned on sleeping in the buff for the first time in her life to save her tattoo from being ruined. It had also been on her list, well the mental portion of her list, to try out and she had to admit that it wasn't all that bad. She could totally see why people slept like this.

When she moved to turn over all rational thought left her brain as her eyes landed on Nick, no, correction, a half naked Nick. She felt her eyes widen in appreciation at the sight that he made. When her eyes landed on his normally styled and neat blond hair she couldn't help but smile. The mussed look looked really good on him. It gave him that sexy bad boy look with a touch of sweetness that she found endearing.

She ran her eyes over his handsome face, down his neck, over his well defined biceps, chest and abs only to land on his gray boxer briefs and stayed there. As much as she'd love to look away at the moment she couldn't. This was her first up close look of that area. Granted it was covered by his underwear, but that wasn't stopping her from getting an eyeful at the moment.

Wow......

Were all men that big? she wondered as she watched in utter fascination as the large thing in his underwear started to get bigger until it strained against the material and the large pink tip pushed itself out from beneath the waistband of his boxer briefs. For a moment she laid there, helpless to move or even breathe.

## A Reclusive Heart: A Hollywood Heart's novel

Actually, now that she saw one, well part of one up close and personal, she was a little frightened. There was no way something like that was going to fit inside of her. It was physically impossible and it helped her realize that she really wasn't ready for sex. Correction, she was pretty sure she was ready for all the other stuff, just not the actual sex part. She didn't want to do that yet. Not until she was comfortable about being intimate with a man and if she had to look forward to being split in two by a monster like that the first time it would be a long time before she had sex.

It would probably be better if she learned how to please a man before she actually had sex just in case she was bad at it. She should probably find a man that she trusted to introduce her into sex, but the problem was that she didn't know any man that would be interested in that job. The only man she trusted enough to do that with unfortunately was the same man that didn't see her as anything more than a job.

Sure they were friends right now, but she seriously doubted he'd bother acknowledging her when this tour was over. She was far from being his type and as much as she'd love to say that she wasn't interested in him, she couldn't lie. She was. Even if it was just a short affair she would love to be with him. Nick was exciting, sweet in a cranky way that she found endearing, handsome, and probably the sexiest man she'd ever seen. It really was too bad that he'd never be interested in her because she would love to-

She lost her train of thought when Nick's warm lips brushed against hers as he cupped her jaw with one hand. When she gasped in surprise he took advantage and slid his tongue into her mouth. The idea of some guy's tongue in her mouth never appealed to her before. Then again, she'd never imagined Nick doing this to her, but now that he was, she found that she rather liked it.

Unable to help herself, she reached up and cupped the back of his head, sliding her fingers through his thick hair as she tentatively slid her tongue against his. His growl excited her so she slid her tongue against his again. It wasn't until he dropped his hand from her face and wrapped his arm around her to pull her tightly against him that she remembered that she was currently topless.

She stilled at the alien sensation of having her breasts plastered against a man, but it didn't last long. Soon she was pressing back against him, moaning as her hard nipples slid over his warm firm chest and through the sparse crisp hair the covered his chest. Her enjoyment lasted until she suddenly found herself on her back with Nick lying on top of her and one hand on her breast. As good as it felt to have him on top of her and touching her, it also scared the hell out of her.

"Nick, stop," she said, hating the way her voice trembled.

Not even a second later, Nick stopped and was off of her and she couldn't stop her sigh of relief which caused him to frown.

"What's wrong?" he asked as he reached over to brush the hair out of her face.

She opened her mouth to calmly explain the situation, but instead found herself blurting out, "I don't want to be torn in two." As soon as the words were out of her mouth she groaned out of embarrassment, covered her face with her hands and since that wasn't enough, she buried her face in the pillow all while praying that he forgot that she was there and went about his business. But of course it didn't work out that way.

"Care to explain," he said, pressing a kiss to her shoulder.

She mumbled into her pillow.

"Sorry, I didn't catch that," he said, sounding amused.

With a sigh, she turned her head slightly and repeated it. "I said I don't think I'm ready for sex." With that announcement she buried her face back against the pillow and prayed for a quick death.

## A Reclusive Heart: A Hollywood Heart's novel

"I know," he said, pressing another kiss to her shoulder.

She moved her hands away from her face and turned to lie on her side, facing him, careful to cover her breasts with her arms. "You do?"

"Yes," he said, moving closer to her as he laid his hand on her hip and pressed a quick kiss to her lips. "I'm well aware of that fact, Jamie."

"Oh," she said, frowning.

"But that doesn't mean that I don't want you," he explained, making her blush and fight back a rather pleased smile. That is until he added, "You're the type of woman who needs to be in a solid relationship with a man before you give up that kind of trust and I'll never be him," he said gently.

"I know," she reluctantly admitted on a sigh. As much as she wanted to try sex, and she did as long as she wasn't split in two, she also had to admit that she just couldn't sleep with anyone. She wished that she could, but she had too many trust issues to be able to do something like that. She wondered if Nick realized that since the beginning of this agreement.

"What I can give you," Nick said, pressing another kiss to her lips, "is fun."

"Fun?" she repeated, too curious to pretend otherwise.

"Mmmmhmm," he said, leaning in to press a kiss to her lips again almost as if he couldn't help himself, which pleased her greatly. She liked the idea of a man like Nick wanting her, even if it meant nothing. "We can enjoy each other during this tour," he said, cupping her chin between his fingers and gently giving her a nudge to look into his eyes, "but you need to understand that this isn't going to lead anywhere, Jamie. I can't be the kind of guy that you need. All I can offer you is a little no strings attached fun and I'm not sure that would be enough for you."

Jamie thought about what he was saying as she absently snuggled closer to him, needing his warmth. When he pulled her the rest of the way she laid her hand against his warm chest. "So what you're saying is that you're not looking for any sort of commitment and that I shouldn't expect one from you, because you don't want a relationship, but you're willing to spend time together during this tour," she said, summing it up.

He nodded slowly. "I can't promise that this will even last to the end of the tour, Jamie. I don't do relationships and even that might be more than I can handle. If we do this I need to know that you understand everything going into this or we can't do this, Jamie. We work together and I don't want any drama at work. Do you understand?"

"Meaning I shouldn't expect anything or get upset if you lose interest tomorrow," she said, shoving away her disappointment. She was on this tour to experience things and if she only had one day with Nick then she would simply treasure the experience and move on. She knew he wasn't the type of guy to settle down and she wasn't going to expect it.

Nick sighed heavily as he leaned in and pressed a kiss against her forehead. "I'm sorry, Jamie, but that's all I can give you."

"Okay," she said, deciding that she wasn't going to worry about tomorrow, but enjoy him now. "Just understand that sex is not an option," she said, knowing that without sex he would lose interest a lot quicker.

"That's fine," he said, slowly smiling. "There are other things that we can do," he said even as he leaned in to kiss her again.

"Other things?" she asked against his lips, too curious to focus on the kissing.

"Mmmmhmmm, other things," he murmured against her lips as his hand slid between them and cupped her breast. "A lot of other things," he said softly as he gently guided her onto her back.

## A Reclusive Heart: A Hollywood Heart's novel

"B-but no sex," she reminded him even as her body trembled.

"No sex," he repeated smoothly as he leaned in and kissed her again.

Lying on her back like this, she felt exposed and had to grab the floral comforter to stop herself from covering herself up. She'd never been very comfortable with her body and having a man like Nick, who'd probably been with more beautiful woman and probably found her lacking, made her even more nervous.

"Beautiful," Nick said as he teasingly traced his fingers up and down her stomach. It was only then that she realized that he'd stopped kissing her. Worrying her bottom lip, she glanced to the left to find him kneeling by her side as he ran hungry eyes over her body. The way he looked at her, made her feel warm and helped ease some of the tension out of her body.

That tension came right back when he ducked his head and took one of her sensitive nipples into his mouth and suckled, hard. She gasped as she reached up instinctively to push him away, but then she realized that it felt really good and didn't want him to stop. Not sure what to do while he gently ran one hand over her stomach and down her leg while he licked and sucked her breast, Jamie decided that since this might be her only chance with him that she was going to do some touching of her own.

She reached out with her right hand and slowly ran her fingers through his hair, loving the way it felt, but more importantly, encouraging him to keep going. It felt so good. Never in her life had she experienced anything that felt better. A moment later that opinion changed when he released her left nipple to work on her right nipple just as his fingers lightly brushed over her panties, making her gasp.

When he did it again she fought against the urge to shut her legs together tightly and forced herself to open her legs wider. His growl of approval sent waves of pleasure through her nipple and straight down between her legs and she couldn't help but moan and run her free hand over his back. He felt so good beneath her hand.

"You're soaking wet," Nick said tightly as he cupped her through her panties, making her arch into his touch. From everything she'd read she knew that was a good thing, but that didn't stop her from being embarrassed.

Her embarrassment didn't improve in the next second when his hand snaked beneath her panties and he teasingly traced her wet slit with his fingertips. Writing about sex hadn't prepared her at all for this, she suddenly realized. She'd used what she'd learned from reading romance novels to create the sex scenes in her books and now realized that they hadn't been adequate, not at all. She wrote about the mechanics of the act, but had never truly expressed how it felt to be touched by a man, but now she knew. She really couldn't help but think that doing this with Nick might actually improve her writing. Of course when he ran the pad of his finger over her clit and traced her core she decided to stop thinking and just feel.

Nick kissed and licked his way back up to her mouth. This kiss was different from the others. It was wild, hot and intensified the pleasure between her legs. When he suddenly reached back and caught the hand that had been exploring his back by the wrist and lowered it, she became a little nervous. Maybe he didn't want her to touch him. Was she supposed to just lie here while he explored her?

The selfish part of her didn't have a problem with that, but the other part of her, the curious part, wanted to explore, touch and learn him. This was something new for her and she knew she wouldn't be satisfied in just lying here. She needed to-

"Touch me," he pleaded softly against her lips as he brought her hand between his legs and placed it against the straining erection in his underwear.

## A Reclusive Heart: A Hollywood Heart's novel

Not needing to be asked twice, she ran a hand slowly, cautiously over his cloth covered erection and as much as she liked it she needed more. When she reached the buttons on the front of his underwear she quickly undid them and reached inside and couldn't help but moan when her hand came in contact with something hard as a rock and hot. She took a steadying breath as she wrapped her hand around his erection, noting the silky smooth feel of his skin and slowly pulled it out.

She didn't need to see it to know that it was large, very large. When she went to wrap her hand around it she discovered that she could barely do that because it was so thick. That pretty much confirmed her decision to hold off on sex for now. There was just no way she was going to be able to lie there with this thing coming after her, she decided as she began to explore him.

"Don't stop," Nick said against her lips before he pulled away and sat up, putting that monster between his legs right above her chest.

For a moment she could only stare at the large, dark pink almost purple appendage in her hand, but then Nick just had to go and slide a finger inside of her. He groaned as he slowly worked his finger in and out of her and it wasn't long before she was running her hand up and down his length as she moaned softly in pleasure.

As he worked his finger inside of her, she was torn between watching that and what she was doing to him. When several drops of liquid seeped out of the tip of his penis she looked up to find him watching her intently. Using her curiosity, she pushed aside her nervousness and pulled his erection closer as she tilted her head to the side, never taking her eyes off of him, and licked the drops of liquid away.

His bucked hard in her hand and worked his finger harder and faster in her as his thumb came into play and gently pressed against her clit. She continued to work her hand down his shaft, but now she couldn't help but lick and suckle the large head. He tasted so good that she couldn't help it.

"That's it, baby," Nick said, groaning.

She couldn't help but moan when he shifted slightly so that the bottom of his shaft near the head was pressed against her hard nipple. It felt so good. Every time she stroked him, his erection brushed against her nipple, sending wave after wave of pleasure through her body until she was left half-sobbing/half-moaning as she rolled her hips, riding his finger as she licked and stroked his erection almost wildly.

Just as she thought that she couldn't take anymore her body suddenly tightened and exploded into what felt like a million pieces. She was barely aware of her screams of pleasure or his. The only thing she knew was that she never felt anything that good. That is until the hot liquid shooting across her sensitive nipples set her off again.

Suddenly she found her hand empty and Nick's mouth back on hers as he slowed his movements between her legs. He swallowed her content little moans as her hips slowly came to a stop, leaving her panting content and weak. He pressed one last kiss against her lips before pulling away.

"Go get cleaned up. We have to leave for the airport in an hour," he said absently as he tucked himself back in his underwear and headed for the bathroom, leaving her feeling a little used and unsure, but then she reminded herself that it would be stupid to expect anything else.

This just might be their only experience together and she wasn't going to wreck that by feeling anything but the pleasure he'd just given her. Although she really hoped they did it again, she thought with a content little sigh as she began her search for her clothes and apparently a wash cloth.

## Chapter 16

"Aren't you cold?" Nick asked through clenched teeth as the asshole standing next to him checked Jamie out instead of the airport's arrival board like he should be doing.

He sent Jamie's sexy tattoo another glare. Why the hell was she walking around with her jeans low on her hips and her shirt ending just below her breasts like that? She should only be wearing those types of things when he was around, which brought him right back to why he was pissed.

After fooling around with Jamie this morning he should have grown bored immediately, especially when he realized that was all he would ever get from her. They could fool around for months and she would probably never let him between her legs. Jamie was a good girl whether she wanted to be or not. Fooling around with him was one thing, but losing her virginity to him was quite another.

Even knowing there was no chance in hell to slide into heaven he couldn't stop thinking about her. He wanted to touch her and make her come again, but this time while she screamed his name and he sure as hell wanted her to touch him again. It had been the first hand job he'd received since he was a kid and undoubtedly the best. He'd never come so hard in his life and he knew that if she ever fully took him into her mouth it would probably kill him.

"No," Jamie said, looking around and not bothering to look back at him, which was probably a good thing since he couldn't seem to tear his eyes away from her tattoo and ass. "It's warm in here and we're going to Georgia so I doubt I'll be cold."

He sent a glare at her ass before he forced himself to look away. "Too much sunlight isn't good for your tattoo," he reminded her, hoping she'd just take the damn hint and cover up before he had to break the jaw of the bastard practically drooling next to him. What the hell was wrong with this asshole checking Jamie out when she was clearly with him?

Maybe the asshole didn't know that Jamie was with him, he decided since the damn woman was a good five feet in front of him instead of by his side where she belonged. He threw the bastard a glare as he stepped up to Jamie's side and threw his arm around her shoulders. Jamie threw him a curious look but didn't say anything.

Smart woman.

Right now he was torn between kissing the hell out of her and spanking that sweet ass of hers. This was all her fault. He shouldn't be feeling like this. In fact, he hated feeling like this. Instead of standing here with her, he should have followed through with the brush off he'd automatically started this morning and right now he should be flirting with the hot stewardess that kept shooting him welcoming glances.

*What in the hell was wrong with him?*

"Are you still cranky?" Jamie asked.

"I'm not cranky," he bit out even though he was feeling pretty damn cranky at the moment.

"Uh huh," she said as she looked around the busy airport until her eyes landed on the small cafe. "Well, while you're doing whatever it is that you're doing I'm going to get something to drink and eat while we wait to board."

Before he could stop the damn woman she was stepping out from beneath his arm and heading over to the cafe. He of course took note of every guy that stopped what they were doing to stare at her ass. That was *his* ass they were all staring at and he wasn't having it. Until he was done with her that was his ass to enjoy and he was damn well going to enjoy it, he decided as he stalked over to her and took her back into his arms where she damn well belonged.

At least for the moment.

\* \* \* \*

## A Reclusive Heart: A Hollywood Heart's novel

"Where are you going?" Nick asked as she headed towards the front exit of the large convention center.

She gestured towards the door where most of the fans were heading. "To grab a taxi and head back to the hotel," she said, frowning since he was the one that said they were ready to leave.

Nick gestured towards the back exit of the building. "The *RNL* was so pleased by this year's turnout that they decided to treat you to a limo for the night," Nick explained as they walked towards the back exit.

Jamie wondered if this was going to be the moment he chose to clear the air between them. Even though she'd already figured it out for herself it would be nice to hear it from him. It wouldn't be the first time that she heard the rejection speech, but it would probably be the most painful one. She wasn't looking forward to hearing it, but she knew this morning that it was possible that this little love affair of theirs wouldn't last throughout the day. She already had her experience with him and she wasn't going to ruin it by being sad about it ending before it really begun.

"Here we are," Nick said, gesturing to a sleek black limousine parked less than ten feet from the door.

Jamie sent the driver, an older man with short brown hair a polite smile as she accepted his help into the limo. Once she was inside, she of course had to look around since it was her first time in the back of one these things. There was a lot more room than she thought there would be. There was plenty of room to seat eight adults comfortably, a flat screen television and even a mini bar in the sidewall. Being given the kiss off by Nick would definitely be memorable, she thought with a frown as she watched a black divider suddenly sliding up, cutting off her view of the front seat and the driver. Privacy was probably for the best. She'd really hate to have anyone witness this.

"Come here," Nick suddenly said, drawing her attention from the mini cans of Coke to the backseat where he was lounging as he pulled his tie loose. When she hesitated, he reached over and grabbed her hand and gave it a little yank until she was up and somehow found herself straddling his lap.

"Much better," Nick said, sounding pleased as he pushed her hair away from her neck and he leaned in.

Her eyes closed of their own accord when his mouth landed on her neck and his hands on her bottom. "Um, what's going on?" she asked, wondering if perhaps she'd misread his crankiness. She did seem to make him especially cranky lately.

He chuckled against her neck and holy heck did that feel good. "What does it look like I'm doing?" he asked teasingly as he readjusted her on his lap until she found the bulge in his pants pressed tightly against the spot that ached for him.

"Um," she said, licking her lips as she tilted her head back to give him more room to work, "confusing the heck out of me."

"What exactly are you confused about?" he asked, grabbing her bottom and grinding her against him. The move robbed her of the ability to speak so she had to contend herself with just grabbing onto his shoulders and holding on for dear life when he did it again.

"Uh, nothing?" she said, not really sure what the question was or more importantly what the answer should be. Not that it mattered, she decided a moment later as he slipped one hand down the back of her pants while the other one slid beneath her shirt and bra to cup her breast.

This was heaven, she thought with a moan as she ground herself against him. She leaned down and kissed him as she moved frantically on his lap, desperate for the release he'd given her that morning. When she found it, he swallowed her screams and she swallowed his curses.

\* \* \* \*

### A Reclusive Heart: A Hollywood Heart's novel

"Everything is canceled," Nick announced as he tossed his cell phone on top of his open suitcase. "The signing and the interviews have all been canceled thanks to this storm," he explained unnecessarily.

The truth was, Jamie hadn't been looking forward to braving this weather and for the past hour had been contemplating faking her own death to get out of it. She didn't know what was worse, the thunder and lightning, the buckets of water was being poured down from the sky or the hail that occasionally snapped against the hotel window. The only thing she knew for certain was that she didn't want to go out in it.

One good thing came out of this horrible day, she got a day off. Granted, she couldn't do anything fun. They'd be stuck in their hotel rooms all day. If it got too boring she could always grab her laptop and head downstairs to the bar and have lunch. She had been planning to hit a bar tonight since they hadn't had the chance to and she was dying to try it and not chicken out like she had at the club. With Nick by her side it should be a lot easier.

Speaking of Nick......

She looked up from the file she was working on to run an appreciative eye over the man as he sorted through folders stacked on top of the desk. Maybe they could use this time to try out a few more things. After the incident in the limo last night they hadn't had a moment to rest, relax, or more importantly, at least to her, to do it again. Thanks to him, she'd been up half the night aching for him. She used those hours wisely and got some work done. She finished editing a novel, finished her **chapter** early in her secret little project, and finished three **chapter**s of her latest Vampire of the Heart novel. Now that she had some time she would like nothing better than to-

"I guess we'll use this time to get some work done," Nick announced, bursting her bubble as she watched him loosen his tie and sit down behind the desk without looking her way.

"Fine," she grumbled, knowing she was pouting, but not caring. She moved to sit on the small couch, but decided that if she wasn't expected to leave this hotel room then she wasn't going stay in this pretty, but uncomfortable, suite. "I'm going to change into something more comfortable to work in then," she said, heading for the door connecting their rooms and eager to change into her flannel pajamas and order a hot fudge sundae from room service.

Nick didn't say anything as she left the room and she didn't expect him to. When he was working, it was pretty much impossible to distract him. Maybe she'd head downstairs to the bar now instead of waiting for lunch. She walked over to her bag to grab her flannel pajamas when the light pink and baby blue shopping bag that she'd forgotten about caught her eye.

Worrying her bottom lip, she shot a look over her shoulder at the closed door and then back to the bag. Could she really do this? Curious to see if she could make Nick lose his cool she decided that yes she really could. With an excited little giggle, she grabbed the bag and ran into the bathroom.

\* \* \* \*

When Jamie walked into the room he didn't bother looking up from his computer. He needed to figure out a few backup plans just in case this bad weather followed them on their tour. He was just about to ask Jamie how she felt about hitting Texas when a flash of white caught his eyes. Not really thinking much of it, he looked up and nearly choked on his tongue at the sight before him.

Before his mind fully registered the fact that Jamie was wearing the short white silk and lace number that made him harder than steel at the store, he was getting to his feet and tearing off his tie and shirt. When she bent over in front of him to pick something up off the coffee table he stumbled when he got his first look at her bare ass. If he hadn't already been hard that would have done it.

"Get on the bed and spread your legs," he bit out, uncaring that he was barking orders at her or that she was still new at all of this. He wanted her and he was damn well going to have her.

## A Reclusive Heart: A Hollywood Heart's novel

He could have kissed her when she did exactly what he asked without any hesitation. When she laid back on the bed and spread her legs, he noted the blush that crept up her cheeks, but he was helpless at the moment to reassure her that everything would be okay when the only thing he could focus on at the moment was the neatly trimmed moist curls between her legs. He toed off his shoes and dropped his pants, uncaring that were going to get wrinkled.

His underwear was barely pushed off by the time he crawled onto the bed and buried his face between Jamie's legs. The sharp cry of pleasure she released when he swiped his tongue over her clit pleased him so he did it again and again as he ran his hands all over her silk encased body. By the time she started screaming his name he was on top of her, grinding his erection between her wet slit and he taking her mouth in a hard brutal kiss that she eagerly welcomed.

The moment he came he realized that they wouldn't be getting any work done today. The realization would have normally pissed him off, but today it only pleased him.

\* \* \* \*

He gritted his teeth and forced himself to breathe as the torture continued. Just as she took the tip of his cock into her mouth and began working him into a frenzy she'd stop and tested his control. She'd been doing this for twenty-three minutes and ten seconds now.

When she shyly asked him if she could take him into her mouth he'd nearly groaned wondering if Christmas had come early for him this year. It felt like years since he first imagined her sucking on him, but in reality it had only been a few weeks. This morning when she showed up in his room in that barely there teddie he'd hoped and prayed that she'd do it, but had absolutely no intentions of forcing the issue. So when she offered all he could do was lie there dumbly and nod like an idiot.

He didn't even question her need to work under the covers as she did it. Truth be told, watching the shape of her head move beneath the pale green sheet while she worked him turned him on even more. Just then she decided to up her game by licking him from his balls to the tip and he had to stop himself from arching his back and silently demand that she take him in her mouth again. When she licked him again he felt himself relax. That is until she stopped, again, and shifted around.

Jamie mumbled something, but he was too focused on the painful erection between his legs to pay attention. When she licked only to stop again he had enough. He really couldn't take any more and wondered why she hated him so damn much to torture him like this. When he pulled the sheet away he received his second surprise for the day.

She had one hand wrapped around the base of his cock as she frowned down at her phone. "I can't tell if I'm doing this right," she mumbled as she stared at her phone.

With a shaky hand, he reached out and took the phone away from her and nearly groaned when he realized that his little recluse was watching an instructional video on her phone. The fact that she wanted to please him touched him in a way nothing else had. In that moment it didn't matter that she had him hard enough to cause pain. All that mattered was his little recluse.

He tossed the phone to the side and reached out and cupped her face. "Anything you want to do will please me, Jamie. You don't need that," he said, struggling to beg her not to continue with the start and stop torture. He didn't want to hurt her in any way and he sure as hell didn't want to make her feel bad. He would lie there for the rest of the night while she tortured him if that's what she needed.

## A Reclusive Heart: A Hollywood Heart's novel

"Okay," she said, sighing as she straightened her shoulders and set back to work. This time she took pity on him and didn't stop. Actually, she didn't stop until he was shouting out his release and begging her to stop sucking on his poor abused cock. When she finally released him with a small little pout he couldn't help but laugh as he pulled her into his arms and kissed her. She snuggled contently in his arms. As he drifted off, he couldn't imagine a more perfect way to end the day.

## Chapter 17

"Where have you been?" Nick asked when Jamie showed up with only two minutes to spare.

"Nothing," she said, shifting nervously as she looked everywhere but at him.

He narrowed his eyes on his little recluse as she shifted nervously as she hugged that large bag she dared to call a purse tightly against her chest. "I asked you where you've been, not what you've been up to," he pointed out as they stepped to the side as one of the camera men rushed past them.

"Oh.....,um," she mumbled, but didn't really answer him. He knew she was nervous about doing her first on camera interview and really didn't expect much at the moment. He had hoped that he'd have time to calm her down. In fact, he'd planned on pulling her into one of the dressing rooms and doing everything he could to help her relax, but the damn woman had made other plans this morning and told him that she'd meet him here.

Which brought up an interesting question, what had she been up to?

Judging by the way she was shifting with nervous energy, avoiding making eye contact, and hugging her bag in a death grip, he was afraid he knew exactly what the little recluse had been up to. With a sigh, he snatched the bag away from her and opened it, ignoring her protests as he pulled out five large bars of Belgium chocolate and glared down at his little recluse.

"You promised that you'd avoid sugar this morning," he said accusingly as he shoved the chocolate back in the bag and held it away from her.

She swallowed nervously as she reached for it. "You don't understand! I need it!"

He shook his head even as he grabbed her hand and led her deeper into the studio. "No, what you need to do is get your cute little ass into makeup and then do this interview."

## A Reclusive Heart: A Hollywood Heart's novel

When Jamie gasped in outrage he couldn't help but smile. "But I need it! Please, Nick! Chocolate soothes me!"

He threw her a disbelieving look over his shoulder, but didn't slow his pace as he continued to drag her over to makeup. "You're like the Energizer Bunny when you have chocolate, Jamie. If you want some chocolate you'll have to get through this interview otherwise I'm throwing it out," he threatened, knowing that if he took her chocolate anywhere near a trash can that she'd probably try to kill him.

"You wouldn't dare!" she hissed out and he didn't bother to answer her as he maneuvered her around a large group of people and planted her ass in a tall chair.

"Here she is," he announced to Margaret, the makeup specialist who'd been hitting on him since he showed up an hour ago to make sure that everything was set up for Jamie's interview.

"Thanks, Nick. You're such a sweetie," Margaret said, placing her hand on his arm and giving it a little squeeze as she sent him another inviting smile. His eyes shot over to Jamie to see how she was reacting to the other woman's obvious come on, but the damn woman was still sending the bag in his hands looks of longing.

Did he want her jealous? No, not really, but some kind of reaction would be nice since he couldn't help but want to kill every bastard that got within speaking distance of her. He felt his lips twitch as Jamie tried to discretely reach out and take the bag from his hand.

"This is just getting sad," he said, sighing as he moved the bag further away.

She looked up at him with sad puppy dog eyes as her lower lip began to quiver and he just barely stopped himself from chuckling, which she probably wouldn't appreciate. Instead, he shook his head and her shoulders slumped in defeat as she let out a cute little sigh.

"Miss Harris?" one of the production assistants said in greeting as she approached Jamie. "My name is Carla. Is there anything I can get you?"

Jamie immediately perked up. "Yes, um, is there any chance that I could get some chocolate? It helps settle my nerves," his little recluse said, lying her adorable ass, that he planned on focusing on tonight, off.

Carla smiled. "I believe we can arrange that."

"No," Nick said, cutting the woman off before she did something they'd all regret later. "No chocolate for her whatsoever," he said, earning a killing glare from Jamie, but he didn't care.

Chocolate was Jamie's drug of choice and unfortunately for her she didn't seem to handle the sugar very well. She got wired, then cranky, then sleepy and when she woke up from her chocolate induced nap he usually had to wrestle more chocolate out of the addict's grasp before she could make it to the toilet hugging phase, which was probably his least favorite of the phases.

"Then can I have a Coke, please?" she asked, sounding hopeful.

Sugar and caffeine? No, that would never work.

"She'll have water," he said, thankful that the assistant knew better than to listen to Jamie.

When Jamie sulked in her chair he of course ignored her even as he made a mental note to order a huge ice cream sundae for her later. The woman was a little sugar addict and thankfully could be bought easily. Actually, now that he thought of it he should probably hunt down something sweet to give her once her interview was over. He could give her the chocolate in her handbag, but judging by the looks that she was shooting the bag the little junkie had already reached her limit for the day.

"So what do you say, Nick?" Margaret asked, making him realize that he'd missed everything she said while he'd been smiling like a fool at his little recluse.

## A Reclusive Heart: A Hollywood Heart's novel

"Hmm?" he asked, barely able to take his eyes away from Jamie as Margaret fussed with Jamie's hair and makeup.

"She wanted to know if you'd like to go over to her house after this so that she could cook for you," Jamie explained casually, not sounding upset at all, but judging by the hurt expression on her face she didn't like the idea one bit. Why that made him happy, he didn't know, but it was nice to know that he wasn't the only one that got jeal-

"Actually," Jamie said brightly as she sat straighter in her chair, "why don't the two of you go discuss your dinner plans," she said smoothly as she reached out and snagged her bag out of his hand, "and I'll just sit here and wait to be called for my interview."

His eyes narrowed on her as he felt a tick start beneath his left eye. "You'd sell me out like that? Over *chocolate*?" he said with obvious disgust.

She shrugged as she held the bag tightly to her chest and let out another cute little sigh. "It's Belgium chocolate," she said as if that explained it all. That explained nothing. It also pissed him off that she clearly chose chocolate over him.

He reached over and tore the bag away from her, earning a little gasp of horror that he refused to find adorably sexy. "Just for that, you aren't getting this chocolate back until tomorrow."

"B-b-b-but," she stuttered, reaching for it but he simply stepped back.

When she realized that she wasn't getting it back she went back to slumping in her chair. He thought he heard her mutter, "Big jerk," but he decided to ignore it since that was most likely the chocolate withdrawal talking.

"Are you busy tonight, Nick?" Margaret asked as if the little odd conversation hadn't just happened. Then again she was probably used to weird conversations in this line of work.

He should take the woman up on her invitation. She wouldn't drive him crazy or have him drooling after her like some kid. In fact, he was pretty sure he'd have her out of her panties and beneath him within two minutes of walking through her front door, but unfortunately for him the thought of touching her left him cold. The only woman he wanted was coming down from a sugar high and would probably require some babying later tonight when the stomach ache hit. What the hell happened to him when he'd rather spend the night cuddling a cranky woman than fucking a willing one?

"That's a very sweet offer, but unfortunately we have to work tonight and then catch an early flight in the morning," he said, giving the woman his most charming smile and hoping it was enough.

"Maybe next time you're in town," she said, giving him that coy smile that promised all sorts of naughty things between the sheets. Since this thing with Jamie would be over by the next time he swung through Virginia for work, he didn't see any reason why he shouldn't accept.

"That sounds like a great idea, sweetheart. How about you give me your number so I can give you a call the next time I'm in the area," he said, forcing his eyes away from his little recluse as he told himself that he had no reason to feel guilty. He never felt guilty for living his life and he sure as hell wasn't about to start now.

\* \* \* \*

"We're ready for you, Miss Harris," one of the assistants said, gesturing for her to join Andrew Jameson, the show's host, on stage.

She decided not to keep her promise to Nick and hunt him down for last minute advice since he'd just given her the kiss off and joined Andrew on stage. Out of the corner of her eye she saw Nick try to discretely gesture for her to walk over to him, but she ignored him and plastered what she hoped was a friendly smile on her face and sat down in the small leather chair next to Andrew.

## A Reclusive Heart: A Hollywood Heart's novel

The man was in his mid-thirties, handsome and the look he gave her slightly appeased the hurt Nick had caused not even twenty minutes ago. She still couldn't believe that he'd hurt her like that. She knew that they'd never have a lifetime together, but the last few days had been wonderful, especially yesterday when they spent all day in his bed, but apparently she'd been wrong. Well, she'd enjoyed it but obviously he had not.

If he had, he wouldn't have been making plans to meet up with another woman right in front of her. The least he could have done was taken her aside beforehand and given her the brush off. Finding out like that hadn't exactly been pleasant.

"It's so nice to meet you, Miss Harris," Andrew said warmly as he reached over to take one of her hands into both of his.

"It's nice to meet you too, Mr. Jameson," she said, easily returning the smile.

"Please call me Andrew. From what I gather this is your first on camera interview. Just relax and pretend the camera's not there and you'll be fine. I'm also assuming that you would prefer to be called J.L. Lewis during the interview?" he asked, still holding her hand she might note.

She risked a quick glance over to where she'd last seen Nick and was a little surprised to find him glaring at their hands. Considering he'd just basically made plans to have sex with another woman she thought he had a heck of a nerve to look pissed that another man was touching her. After this they were going back to a strictly professional relationship. She didn't even want help with her list and come to think of it, maybe it was time just to bite the bullet and have sex. It sure as heck would stop her from pining after him and it would help shred a little more of the old Jamie away for good.

"If you're ready?" Andrew asked, reluctantly releasing her hand as he sat back in his chair.

Was she?

Yes, she was and not only for this interview. It was probably childish, but tonight when she found a man to take to bed she was going to make darn sure that Nick knew that she was doing it. Not that he'd care since he'd probably be having sex with another woman and couldn't care less that she moved on and she had. It was just a few days. Nothing major. She could move on just as easily as he had.

"Thank you for joining us this evening, J.L. Lewis," Andrew said, letting her know that they'd begun recording the interview.

"Thank you for having me," she returned easily, surprising herself. Maybe this wouldn't be so bad afterwards.

After a few minutes of basic questions he moved smoothly into her personal life. "So tell me, is there a Mr. Lewis in the picture?"

With a soft chuckle she shook her head, "No, I'm not married yet."

"Is there any special man in your life?" he asked and she wondered if that was interest she noted in his expression.

She couldn't help watching Nick out of the corner of her eye as she answered, "No, there's no special man in my life." The area Nick stood in was dark, but she could have sworn he made a move to come closer, but stopped himself at the last moment. Wishful thinking on her part, she realized.

"I wanted to tell you how profoundly sorry I was about the news that came out this morning. I'm sure it was a bit of a shock that your family came forward and shared the rather personal information. I'm actually flattered that you chose KJK to share your thoughts on the matter," Andrew said, confusing the heck out of her.

"I'm sorry. I'm afraid that I don't know what you're talking about," she admitted.

He frowned at the admission as he sent someone to the side a questioning look. Seconds later a young man wearing large headphones came halfway onto the stage and handed Andrew a thick newspaper before quickly scurrying away.

## A Reclusive Heart: A Hollywood Heart's novel

"I'm sorry. I thought you knew," he said, sounding truly sorry as he handed the newspaper over to her.

Dread filled her stomach as she reached over and accepted the newspaper. When her eyes landed on the large black print stamped across the top she felt the air in her lungs rush out of her as if she'd been hit with a two by four.

"You didn't know about this?" Andrew asked.

"No," she said hollowly as she ran her eyes over the article title once again.

At least now she knew why she'd always been treated differently and why she never felt like she belonged, at least where her mother was concerned because the woman she believed to be her mother wasn't. According to the paper, she was the product of an affair that her father had with his secretary and was of course deeply ashamed of. He had no knowledge of Jamie's existence until she was dropped off at his door when Jamie was four years old.

Why?

Why would they do this to her? Why couldn't they have just told her this? Did they really need to make this a public announcement? Then Nick's words came back to her and she realized that to her mother, well, really the woman who'd tolerated her existence, hated that she was in the spotlight and wanted it for herself. Jamie could care less about that. The only thing that mattered to her at the moment was that she was truly alone in this world.

## Chapter 18

"Open the fucking door, Jamie!" he shouted, pounding on the door.

"Go to hell, Nick!" she snapped back, shocking the living hell out of him. There was no doubt that she wanted to tell him off, but he hadn't expected her to actually do it. No matter how much he pissed her off, and he did that on a daily basis, she usually mumbled her way around it.

But not today.

Then again, she did have liquid courage in her room right now. He was going to kill the bellhop for bringing it to her. It was the last damn thing that she needed on a day like this and now that she had it and plenty of it apparently, she was probably going to do something incredibly stupid and make the news that they'd only received hours earlier a hell of a lot worse.

He wasn't sure who he wanted to kill more right now, the asshole who pretended to be sympathetic as he captured Jamie's reaction to the news on camera, or her so called family who'd just shoved her to the wolves. Actually right now he was pretty fucking pissed at the people working below him who should have been on top of this and given him a head's up.

They should never have walked into that mess. He should have known first thing this morning and been given all the information so that he could have prepared Jamie. Instead they'd walked right into that little mess and by now the video clip of Jamie finding out that she was the result of an illicit affair between her father and secretary was all over the web.

The only good thing from this nightmare was that Jamie somehow managed to keep it together during the rest of the interview. Once it was over she was polite to the asshole he wanted to deck and walked out with her head held high. Unfortunately she took off before he could talk to her and holed herself up in her hotel room and wouldn't let him in.

## A Reclusive Heart: A Hollywood Heart's novel

He wanted to hold her, comfort her, shake her for not letting him do all those things when the interview was over, but most of all he wanted to know that she was okay. He needed to feel her in his arms and know that she was all right.

"Let me in, Jamie," he said even as he pulled out the card he managed to talk the front clerk out of.

"Go away, Nick," she said, sounding stressed and there wasn't a doubt in his mind that she was. He didn't think of her as his little recluse for nothing. She didn't have many close friends in her life and now it seemed that she didn't have any family either.

It took a few well placed phone calls, but he discovered that they'd sold the story for a hefty sum and were already booked with some of the bigger talk shows to share their story. Of course, most of those talk shows were more interested in getting Jamie to come give them her side of the story and when he made sure that she was calm and ready he'd talk her into it. It would be good for her to clear the air not to mention good publicity for her books.

When it became painfully obvious that she wasn't about to open the door he decided that he wasn't going to wait any longer. He opened the door and stepped in and made another mental note to throttle the bellhop for this bullshit. He rubbed his hands down his face warily as he took in the empty candy bar wrappers, snack cake wrappers and empty cans of Coke strewed around the double bed where his little recluse sat with her legs crossed as she downed another Coke.

His eyes shot over to the nightstand overflowing with more junk food to the coffee table with four ice buckets filled to the top with ice and fresh Cokes. Realizing that the damage was already done, he grabbed a Coke and paused by the little table of junk food and grabbed a packet of Twinkies and kicked off his shoes before he sat down on the bed next to Jamie.

"I'm not speaking to you," she said quietly, not bothering to take her eyes away from the television that unfortunately was playing a chick flick. The hell he put up with to do his job, he thought as he ripped open his Twinkies. When she reached over and grabbed one of his Twinkies he simply sighed and started in on the other one.

Normally he didn't touch sweets. He'd never been big on them probably because that's all he had to eat when he was a kid. His mother and "Aunts" hadn't exactly been up to date on parenting one-o-one and hadn't thought that a growing boy might need more than fake juice filled with sugar, chips and microwave pizza to live on. The only times he got a real meal were when he went to school or when he stole it.

When he was old enough to work he took jobs busting tables at restaurants mostly for the free meals. Once he got the hell out of his mother's house and into a dump of his own he'd refused to live off junk food. He put his student meal plan to good use and kept two jobs during the school year so that when he no longer had the student cafeteria as an option he wouldn't have to eat shit to live. Since then he rarely ever indulged in anything sugary or sweet since it usually brought back sour memories, but with his little recluse he found himself simply enjoying the occasional treat.

"What's the game plan?" he asked after a few minutes.

Jamie raised her Coke. "I'm going to have another one of these, take a shower, head downstairs and find a guy to help me out with the next item on my list," she said calmly and he knew just knew that she was close to breaking down. Any other woman and this would have been the point where he made his excuses and left the room, but this was his little recluse and he couldn't leave her.

He just couldn't.

"So, I take it you're ready for sex," he said casually even though he felt like screaming at the stubborn woman for even thinking about letting another guy touch her.

## A Reclusive Heart: A Hollywood Heart's novel

She was *his*.

At least until he got over this weird obsession with her and he would, eventually. For right now he enjoyed being with her, laughing with her and doing absolutely nothing with her. It made the not having actual sex part worth it, which was crazy. He normally didn't waste his time on a woman if she wasn't going to put out, Dana excluded, but for her it was well worth it.

"You're not ready for sex yet, Jamie, and if you go do this now you're going to feel worse in the morning," he calmly pointed out.

For the first time since he entered the room she looked at him. "Oh, and I suppose you're an expert on when people are ready for sex? How old were you when you lost your virginity?"

"Twelve," he said flatly.

"Twelve?" she repeated in disbelief.

He nodded as he took another sip of the Coke that now felt like acid in his stomach. "It was a thirteenth birthday gift from my mother. She asked one of her friends to do the honors," he said, not really sure why he was talking about this when he usually made it a point to pretend that his childhood never happened. He sure as hell never shared any of the gory details with anyone and never planned to, but with Jamie he felt comfortable telling her. Maybe it was because he knew that his little recluse wasn't into gossip. Whenever people were gossiping around her, she seemed really uncomfortable and always excused herself even if that meant she had to go stand in a corner all alone.

"I-I thought you said you were twelve," she mumbled.

"I was. She had no idea how old I was. The only reason she knew it was my birthday was because the school sent home a general birthday announcement and she just happened to read it," he said with a shrug as if it had been no big deal.

At the time he'd been ecstatic that his mother was showing him interest. All day she called him her "little man." They even celebrated his birthday. It wasn't much, beer, chips and video games. When eight o'clock rolled around his mother and her friends were drunk enough that they actually thought popping his cherry that night was called for. When his "Aunt" Judy took him by the hand and his mother handed him a condom and smiled at him he hadn't wanted to disappointed them. Two minutes after the most humiliating experience of his life Judy patted his cheek and told him the next time would cost him fifty dollars.

There hadn't been a next time with Judy or any of his mother's friends. He stayed clear of hookers and strippers. He might use strippers when he needed to convince a vendor to give him what he wanted, but he wouldn't touch one with a ten foot stick never mind his-

"And you think that experience makes you an expert on when someone is ready?" she demanded, sounding agitated, angry and so damn hurt that his heart actually ached for her.

"No," he said, shaking his head as he turned to look at her. "I just know that you're not ready for this, Jamie, and rushing off to do this because your family hurt you is only going to cause you pain. Don't let them push you into something that you'll only regret later."

"This has nothing to do with them!" she snapped, quickly climbing off the bed and away from him. "I'd already decided to do this before I found out," she announced, surprising the hell out of him. She'd decided to sleep with him? That was actually kind of flattering and apparently all his damn dick needed to hear before it took notice and stood at attention.

"Then why didn't you talk to me about it before?" he asked, climbing off the bed and setting his empty can on the coffee table.

"Because it had nothing to do with you!" she snapped in irritation as she practically stomped out of the room, leaving him there to process her words and when he finally did he went after her.

## A Reclusive Heart: A Hollywood Heart's novel

He found her already naked and climbing into the shower. "What the hell do you mean it had nothing to do with me? How could it not have anything to do with me?" he demanded, grabbing her by the arms and yanking her away from the shower so that she couldn't avoid this conversation.

"Exactly what it sounds like," she said, yanking her arms away and turning her back on him as she climbed into the tub.

"Bullshit," he snapped, stepping in behind her, uncaring that was getting his clothes wet. "This morning you couldn't get enough of me and then all of a sudden you're ready for sex and looking elsewhere? I'm not buying it, Jamie. So why don't you tell me what the fuck is going on here."

"Nothing is going on," she said evenly as she pushed him to the side and climbed out of the tub. She stalked out of the bathroom naked and wet and he was right behind her.

"Then do you mind letting me know what I did exactly to piss you the hell off?" he demanded, grabbing her hand and forcing her to turn around to face him.

"Are you serious?" she demanded, taking a step closer to glare up at him.

"Deadly. One minute you're just as hot for me as I am for you and now you're telling me that you're ready for sex, but only if it's with another guy," he said, taking a step forward and backing her up until the back of her knees hit and the bed.

"I don't understand your problem, Nick. You're the one who ended things this morning. I'm just following your lead and moving on."

"What the hell are you talking about? I didn't end things with you," he said, somehow resisting the urge to grab her and give her a good shake. What hell was she thinking? He couldn't stop thinking about her and she thought he was done with her? Not even by a long shot.

"Then what exactly do you call making plans with another woman right in front of me?" she demanded, looking so damn hurt and alone that he wished like hell that he hadn't been a moron. "I call that ending things, wouldn't you?"

"No, I call it a moment of stupidity, Jamie. I don't want to be with her," he explained slowly. When she snorted and moved to step past him he cupped her damp face in his hands to stop her. "It was a reflexive thing for me to say, Jamie. I wasn't thinking at the moment. Since I knew the next time I came here this tour would be over I didn't think much about making a promise that I didn't plan to keep. Trust me, if I wanted her I wouldn't be here. I threw her number away as soon as I was done talking to her."

"Why didn't you go home with her tonight?" she asked so softly that he nearly missed it.

"Because she wasn't you, Jamie," he said, leaning down to brush his lips against hers to offer some comfort.

The second his lips touched hers he needed more from her, needed her. He knew it was the same for her. Whatever this thing was between them it left them helpless to fight it. Simply touching her and kissing her never seemed to be enough. He could never seem to get close enough to her and always wanted more.

She sighed a little hungry moan into his mouth as she frantically worked at the buttons on his wet shirt while he reached between them and struggled with his equally soaked leather belt and pants. His zipper was barely down before they were on the bed. He settled himself between her legs even as he raised himself up so that he could slide a finger inside of her only to find her soaking wet.

It never failed to make his blood boil to discover just how turned on his little recluse could get. When she rolled her hips to ride his finger he was forced to release his poor cock from his wet underwear to relieve some pressure. She felt so good and so damn perfect.

## A Reclusive Heart: A Hollywood Heart's novel

When she wrapped her legs around his waist he didn't even question it. He just went with it even as his brain screamed for him to back the hell off and give her space. She was upset and for good reason and he knew that he should back off. She wasn't thinking clearly, but he wanted her so damn badly that he couldn't think straight. That always happened around her. As he settled between her legs, he prayed that she wouldn't regret this later, but he just had to be sure.....

"Is this what you want?" he asked against her lips, pressing the tip of his cock to her core and nearly groaning in pleasure as hot liquid coated him.

"Yes!" she hissed out as she wrapped her arms around his shoulders and deepened the kiss until he couldn't take anymore and pushed inside of her.

He let out a load groan as he swallowed her small cry of pain as he broke through the evidence of her innocence and buried himself to the hilt. Once there he forced himself to stop. It didn't matter that this was the wettest, hottest and tightest hold he'd ever experienced. The only thing at the moment that mattered was his little recluse. He had to make it good for her and judging by the way her body went rigid he knew that she wasn't enjoying this nearly as much as he was.

Not thrusting into her body was one of the hardest things he'd ever done, but for her he suffered through it as he slowly kissed her back to the point where she needed this, needed him. When she rolled her hips experimentally against him he knew she was ready. He slowly pulled out, groaning at the sensation of a thousand wet tongues licking his cock and pushed back in.

His pace never increased and his thrusts were gentle as he took her. It was the most erotic experience of his life. He'd never taken a woman like this, never. Whenever he took a woman to bed it was always a fuck and nothing more. He'd also never taken a woman without a condom and that thought was just registering in his mind when he felt her tighten around him. Instinctively he wrapped his arms around her to hold her tightly against him. When she shattered around him he lost control and with three deep, hard thrusts he was joining her, barely bighting back a curse at the biggest fuckup of his life and silently praying that this didn't come back and bite him in the ass later.

When the last spasm tore through him, he rolled over onto his back and pulled a panting Jamie with him. A moment later when the haze of pleasure began to wear off he felt the change in Jamie almost immediately. When she tried to pull out of his arms he held her tighter. She wanted to escape what happened and she couldn't any longer. It was time to give into the grief of what her family put her through. When the first sob finally broke through, his arms tightened around her and didn't relax until the last sob left her body hours later and she fell into an exhausted sleep in his arms.

After he was sure that she was asleep he carefully crawled off the bed. He walked into the bathroom and shut off the shower and gave Rick a call asking him to cancel their plans for the day. Rick didn't need to ask why and for that Nick was grateful. With that done, Nick walked back into the room and looked down at his little recluse as she curled up into a ball on her side. He bent to grab his shirt only to discover that he didn't want to leave her.

Deciding not to question his need to stay at the moment, he quickly pulled off his now damp clothes and threw them over the shower rod before joining Jamie in bed. Once he had her back in his arms something inside of him calmed and found himself falling into a deep peaceful sleep.

## Chapter 19

"We need to talk," Nick announced when she made the mistake of opening her eyes. That of course was also the moment her stomach decided to inform her that it was quite angry with her. Actually, the way it was tightening and twisting let her know that it hated her.

One look around the room at the empty junk food wrappers and empty soda cans reminded her exactly why her stomach was no longer on speaking terms with her. She pressed a hand to her stomach as she slowly, ever so slowly climbed off the bed and headed for the bathroom. Thankfully Nick didn't argue when she shut the bathroom door in his face so that she could relieve herself.

The moment that he heard the sink faucet turn on, he decided that she'd had enough time and walked into the bathroom. Thankfully the man was a saint and started the tub for her while she brushed her teeth. Once she was done, she walked slowly to the tub, sending him a small smile of gratitude as he helped her into the tub, sat down and sighed with relief as the hot water pooled around her stomach and eased some of the aches.

She was never going on another junk food binge as long as she lived, she decided as she laid back in the tub. When Nick handed her a bottle of water she had to stop herself from asking for a Coke since she knew that would probably earn her a glare so she accepted her water and took a small sip, praying it wouldn't set off her already too sensitive stomach.

"Jamie, we really need to talk about last night," Nick said, looking adorably sexy with his hair mussed and a sexy five o'clock shadow painting his face.

"Okay," she said, wincing when her stomach sent up a warning not to talk so much. She was done with sweets. From now on she was sticking to tasteless, bland food that didn't give her cravings or stomach aches.

"We didn't use a condom last night, Jamie," Nick started to say, reminding her of the other thing she'd done last night.

She'd had sex!

Really great, fun sex and it hadn't been pity sex or even sex with a stranger. It had been with Nick and he'd been sweet, gentle and so good that just thinking about it made another part of her ache. She wondered if her stomach would be okay if she had sex again, because she definitely wanted to do that again.

Her mind chose that exact moment to remind her that she broke out in sobs pretty much after the deed was done. The memory was pretty mortifying and she decided that she was going to just go ahead and drown herself now. Nick stopped her with an exasperated sigh and a hand. He gave her elbow a gentle nudge to sit up and when she did, he shocked her further by lathering up his hands with her bar of lemongrass soap and began to wash her.

"I wanted to tell you that I am clean. I've never had sex without a condom before and I always get tested," he paused mid wash to meet her eyes and stress, "Always."

She nodded slowly, wondering if this was his way of asking her if she was clean. She opened her mouth to reassure him that she was when she remembered that he was well aware of her virginal status last night and probably realized that she was clean as well.

"If it will make you feel better I'll go out today and get tested again, but I want you to know that it has been several months since I had sex and I've been tested since," he explained.

"Okay," she said, nodding and not really sure what else there was to say.

When he became quiet she got a little nervous. "Is there something else?" she asked, trying not to worry. She hoped this wasn't the moment he chose to let her go or worse tell her that she sucked in bed, because if that was the case she was more than happy to keep trying until she got it right.

## A Reclusive Heart: A Hollywood Heart's novel

"Are you on birth control?" Nick asked grimly, looking less than pleased with the idea of having a baby.

"Oh," she said, feeling like an idiot. Of course they should talk about birth control. Thankfully it was of those things she had covered. "Yes, I've been on birth control since I was fourteen," she announced, trying not to laugh when the announcement noticeably startled him.

She decided to take pity on him and explain, "My periods were too irregular so the doctor thought it would help me."

He nodded, looking relieved as he returned to washing her. "I guess that's one less thing to worry about," he said quietly.

"I guess," she agreed, worrying her bottom lip as she tried to sort through the other things that she didn't have a choice but to worry about.

Actually, now that she thought about it, she wondered if her little monthly problem was something that she inherited from her birth mother since her mother, well, the woman she thought was her mother, she reminded herself sadly, didn't have that problem and neither did Caitlyn. It also reminded her that she had about a thousand questions that she wanted to ask her father. She also wondered who her real mother was and where she was now.

The one thing that she couldn't help but wonder was what was so wrong with her that her mother gave her away. It was more than obvious, at least to her, that she must have done something bad. According to the paper she'd been four years old by the time she went to live with her father. She wanted to find her mother and ask her what she'd done to make her so angry that she'd give her away to a father who ignored her and a woman that made it obvious that she wasn't welcome and she had to do it in person.

It was bad enough that she had to find out about the origin of her birth with the rest of the world by newspaper and the internet search she'd done last night when she arrived back at the hotel. She didn't want to have this conversation over the phone. She wanted her father to look her in the eye when he explained why he'd never told her and he decided it was okay for the rest of the world to find out about her birth before she did.

This might very well be the last time she spoke to her father since it was more than obvious that he didn't want her around. Part of her hoped that he'd break down and apologize for her crappy childhood and promise to make it up to her, but she wasn't some naive girl. She'd always known that she didn't belong and didn't expect things to suddenly change now that everything was out in the open.

"Nick?"

"Yes?" he asked, not taking his eyes away from his work as he cleaned her back.

"I know this is last minute, but I need a few days off to figure some things out," she said, hoping that he could get her out of her obligations since she didn't want to have to put this off for another day.

His hand stilled on her back. "Is it about us?" he asked casually, a little too causally she noted.

"No," she answered honestly. Whatever was going on between them wasn't worrying her at the moment. She knew this wasn't going to last so she decided not to stress out about it, much. There was no question in her mind that he was going to break her heart when he became bored with her and decided to move on. When it happened she would deal with it, but right now she had other things to worry about.

"You're going home to see your family?" he asked, running his hand down her back again.

## A Reclusive Heart: A Hollywood Heart's novel

"Yes, I don't want to put it off and I really don't want to find out anything else secondhand," she explained, praying that her family didn't share anything else with the media. She still couldn't believe that they did that to her.

"Okay, I'll go with you," he said, surprising the heck out of both of them judging by the startled look on his face.

She simply gave him a polite smile as she looked away. He hadn't meant to say it and she had no plans to hold him to it. When she got back if he wanted to continue with their relationship then that was fine with her and if he didn't......

She was going to need a heck of a lot more chocolate and Coke to get through it.

* * * *

"You really didn't have to come," she said, again as he pulled into the long driveway of a large white two story house with an attached three car garage. One look at the well kept home, manicured lawn and upscale neighborhood let him know that their childhoods had been worlds apart. Why that bothered him he didn't know.

"I wasn't about to let you face this problem alone," he said as he stepped out of his car. When the words rushed out of his lips this morning no one had been more surprised than him by the offer, but once he thought about it, he realized that she was going to need him. More importantly, he realized that he'd go crazy waiting for her to return to him and he'd be too damn worried about her to focus on getting any work done. This really was for the best, he decided as he walked around the car to open Jamie's door. It was then that he noticed the cameras.

Paparazzi.

Fucking perfect, he thought as he took Jamie's hand and walked her to the door. She'd barely finished pressing the doorbell when the door was practically ripped open and an older woman in her fifties with dark brown hair, a tad too much makeup and designer clothes grabbed Jamie and pulled her into her arms.

Nick looked over in time to see dozens of cameras go off while several more men and women ran to the sidewalk to join in the feeding frenzy. When he turned around he noted that the woman was still holding on to Jamie even though Jamie was rigid in the woman's arms. He also noted the smug smile on the woman's face as she watched the paparazzi go nuts.

Having had enough drama for one day thanks to this woman whom he was assuming to be her "mother", Nick smoothly pulled Jamie away and waited for the older woman to invite them in. With a fake smile the woman did just that. As soon as the door was closed behind them the smile was gone and a look of utter disdain took over the woman's features as she gestured for them to follow her.

He gave Jamie's hand a squeeze as they followed the woman through the foyer to a room with double doors. When the door opened, he spotted an older man with graying red hair sitting on small sofa, sipping a glass of what appeared to be whiskey as he spoke with a younger man and a woman who was obviously this woman's natural daughter judging by her coloring and pinched expression when she spotted Jamie. When her eyes shifted to him they widened in surprise before they turned calculating.

The woman was beautiful, classically so with a partisan look and it wasn't too hard to see that the woman had been pampered every day of her life. Remembering how his little recluse used to look it wasn't too difficult to figure out that Jamie hadn't been and the reason behind it. Her mother wanted her real daughter to have all the attention and she'd made damn sure of it at Jamie's expense.

He looked over at the man by her side just in time to see his expression when his eyes landed on Jamie and he did a double take. His eyes lit up when he spotted Jamie and Nick didn't appreciate the way the man ran his eyes over his little recluse. The smile he sent Jamie's way also didn't please him.

## A Reclusive Heart: A Hollywood Heart's novel

"Jamie," the man said, getting to his feet and walking over to greet her, "you look great." When the man pulled Jamie into a hug he barely stopped himself from shoving the asshole aside and telling him keep his hands to himself. Something in his expression must have given away his feelings on the matter because when the man looked at Nick, he noticeably blanched and stepped away from Jamie.

"I don't believe we've met," he said, reaching out to shake Nick's hand. "I'm David, Caitlyn's husband."

"Nick, Jamie's boyfriend," he said before he realized what he was saying, but once it was out he decided that he rather liked it, especially if it let this asshole know that he had a claim on Jamie.

David noticeably started as he looked between him and Jamie as if he just couldn't believe it. The looks the other women were sending their way pretty much said it all. They didn't think very highly of Jamie. The fact that her father and sister didn't greet Jamie also said it all.

He took Jamie's hand into his and entwined their fingers. It was then that he realized that she was trembling and that her hand was ice cold. Without waiting for an invitation, he walked Jamie over to the love seat across from her sister and sat down, pulling Jamie into his side. He put his arm around her as he tried his best to give her the support that she needed, but he wasn't sure what to do.

This was the first time he ever tried to be there for a woman and he didn't want to mess this up. Jamie needed him and normally that thought would have scared him, but he had to admit that he rather liked being there for her. He didn't think he would, but he liked being needed by her. Any other woman and he wouldn't bother.

"I suppose you're here because of the story," her father said instead of acknowledging his youngest daughter.

"Yes," Jamie said firmly. "As much as I would like to know why you leaked the story to the press instead of talking to me about it, I'm more interested in my mother."

He noticed the older woman didn't protest or get mad that she referred to another woman as her mother. Then again, it was more than obvious that Jamie was just a means to get attention at the moment. He didn't need to be a psychic to know that it had been this woman's idea to leak the story. She probably felt the attention was owed to her for raising her husband's unwanted bastard child.

"We really don't know much about her," Jamie's father said, taking a sip of his drink before he reached into his jacket and pulled out an aged envelope and handed it over to Jamie. "She left when she was just a few months pregnant with you. Then when you were four she left you on our doorstop with only a copy of your birth certificate."

"She didn't leave a reason why she left me?" Jamie asked, sounding hurt but trying not to show it.

"I'm afraid that's all we know," her father said, sighing heavily.

"Henry, you should tell her," Mrs. Harris said, earning a glare from the man.

"Tell me what?" Jamie asked, shifting in her seat anxiously.

"Barbara," Henry said tightly in warning.

"She has a right to know," Barbara said, carefully smoothing her hands down her blouse and skirt as she turned her attention to Jamie. "I'm afraid when we searched for her we discovered that she'd passed away."

He felt Jamie's reaction like a physical blow. "Did she have any family?" she asked in a hoarse whisper.

"No," her father said with a firm shake of his head. "I'm afraid that she was all alone in this world."

## A Reclusive Heart: A Hollywood Heart's novel

Like Jamie.

Like him.

No, he realized a moment later. That wasn't true. He had a great job and good friends that more than made up for what he lacked in family and Jamie had him. At least for now. But he'd make sure that she was taken care of even after his feelings for her faded. She was a great woman and deserved better than this.

"Is there anything else I should know?" Jamie asked, looking both hopeful and weary.

Her father didn't even hesitate when he said, "No," causing Nick's bullshit meter to go off the charts.

## Chapter 20

"I love you," Jamie sighed heavily as she settled back against the hill of pillows she'd piled on her bed and hugged the pint of double chocolate, caramel and fudge swirl ice cream to her chest.

This was exactly what she needed after the day she just had. Admittedly, it had been a strange one. She woke up with a sugar hangover, remembered she'd had sex, was pampered by Nick before he whisked her off to the airport and then probably had the last visit with her parents that she would ever have. Now she was back in her own bed in her own apartment with a week's supply of junk food and absolutely no intentions of working.

She picked up her can of Coke and just because she could, she took a long deep sip of the bubbly sugary drink that she craved day and night before setting it back down on her nightstand. After taking a big bite of her ice cream and wincing with a few "owies" from brain freeze she focused her attention on the first chick flick she'd started and couldn't imagine life getting any better.

It was good to be her, she decided, grabbing a handful of M&M's and munching on them as she pondered her current situation. She wouldn't have to worry about money for quite some time. Her books were selling like crazy. She had a great job, plenty of junk food, and sole ownership of the remote control. The cherry on the icing of course was that she was no longer a virgin. Life really did not get better than this, she thought warily as she downed another handful of peanut butter M&M's and threw a look of longing towards her cell phone.

When it didn't chime to let her know that someone was trying to reach her, she shot a look at the clock. It was ten o'clock at night and obviously Nick was taking their return as a pause in their tour, or rather technically an end to it. Right now he was probably between the legs of some hot model, laughing about how bad she was in bed, she thought with disgust as she took another huge bite of ice cream only to drop the spoon back into container to grab her poor head as she fought back against the dreaded brain freeze.

## A Reclusive Heart: A Hollywood Heart's novel

"I leave you alone for a few hours and this is what you do?" Nick said from somewhere in the vicinity of her doorway, but she was too busy squeezing her eyes shut to look.

"Brain freeze?" he asked, sounding amused.

Instead of answering him, because at the moment that was kind of impossible, she settled for nodding. When she felt him remove the carton of ice cream from her lap she contemplated murder. The telltale sound of her M&M's being removed had her opening one eye to glare at the man.

He just ignored her as he quietly worked on removing her junk food away from her. Her eyes shot to the large paper brown bag on her nightstand that was giving off the most delicious scents and she decided to forgive him for daring to go near her junk food.

"What are you doing here?" she asked once her brain freeze vanished.

"Making it easier on you," he said, as he unloaded white Chinese food containers.

"Making it easier for me to do what?" she asked, frowning.

"To make me breakfast in bed of course," he said with a wink as he shoved a carton of chicken lo mein in her hand.

"Well, then I'm afraid you're in for a huge disappointment because I can't cook," she told him casually as she fought against a pleased smile. She couldn't believe that he was here never mind planning on staying the night. It was easily the sweetest thing anyone had done for her.

Wow, that thought was kind of depressing so she shoved it aside and focused on the man ejecting her DVD. "Hey! What are you doing? I was watching that!"

"I brought dinner that means I get to pick the movie," he said, shrugging as he kicked off his shoes, grabbed a carton of food and joined her on the bed.

"Then I should still get to pick the movie since I was eating dinner when you got here," she pointed out innocently, loving the little glare he sent her way.

"I'm going to pretend that you didn't just call that insane pile of junk food dinner," he said, settling in closer as the movie started.

"Oh, but I did and I was planning on devouring a box of Krispy Kreme donuts for dessert," she said, laughing when his scowl returned.

"Okay," he said, sighing heavily as he moved a few inches away from her, "we're no longer speaking."

"You're such a baby," she said, rolling her eyes as she reached over and stole a forkful of honey chicken from his carton.

With a long suffering sigh, he held his carton out to her as she moved closer to him. When she was less than an inch away from him he threw his arm over her shoulders and brought her closer. For the next half hour they sat like that, sharing their food and watching a really horrible action comedy, but Nick seemed to enjoy it and she enjoyed being with him so she was content to sit back and watch the movie.

When they were both done she collected the rest of the cartons and brought them out to the kitchen. By the time she came back, Nick was wearing only his underwear as he lounged back on her bed. The sight of his half-naked well muscled body did a lot to ease the tension left over from her day. It took her only a second to decide to join him. Biting back a smile, she walked over to her bureau and pulled open the top drawer she decided to use for her lingerie. When she went to reach for the baby blue number Nick suggested she buy, her hand brushed against the envelope her father had given her.

## A Reclusive Heart: A Hollywood Heart's novel

She hadn't bothered to open it. There was no point. Her mother was dead and the mother she thought she had didn't want her and neither did her father. At least this explained why they never seemed to want her around, because they hadn't. She was a constant reminder of what her father did and on some level she actually felt bad for her mother. It must have been painful for her to see the physical reminder that her husband had betrayed her every day. She wasn't sure she could handle something like that, but she knew she would never take it out on the child.

"Have you looked at this?" Nick asked, placing a hand on her hip as he reached around her and slowly took the envelope from her.

"No," she said, forcing a smile as she shook her head. She hadn't seen the point of torturing herself with something that would never be. Maybe a few years from now when this whole thing didn't make her feel like crying she would open it and find out her mother's real name, but for right now it was too much for her to handle.

"Do you mind if I take a look at it?"

"What for?" she asked, turning to face him.

"I might be able to hunt down a picture or a lost relative," he suggested.

"Oh." She hadn't thought about that, but it would be nice to know what her mother looked like since her father hadn't exactly been forthcoming with the details. After they'd announced that her birth mother was dead they'd practically shoved her and Nick out, but of course her mother and sister made sure to give them a tearful goodbye from the front door and wish her luck on her tour for the paparazzi.

"I'll take care of it tomorrow at the office," he said as he placed the envelope on top of her bureau. "I did tell you that we're expected at the office tomorrow to go over the tour so far, didn't I?"

"No," she said, smiling when he winced. "But that's fine."

He leaned in and gave her a quick, too quick, kiss. "About the office......"

"I know that I have to keep my dirty little hands off of you," she said, sighing heavily. "I'll try, but it will be difficult," she teased.

"You have no idea," he said roughly as he leaned down and took her mouth in a passionate kiss.

It wasn't long before he was tearing her clothes off and she was sliding her hand beneath the waistband of his boxers and stroking him. When she was left in nothing but her panties he grabbed them and ripped them clean from her body, startling her and sending her arousal into overdrive. It was as if he'd thrown gasoline on the fire and she couldn't get enough of him.

Somehow she found herself sitting on the edge of her bureau with her legs spread and his tongue sliding inside of her as she buried her fingers in his hair. Eventually she was forced to grab the back of the bureau as he took her roughly with his mouth. When his fingers joined his tongue she couldn't hold back. Within seconds she was screaming his name until her voice was hoarse.

Before the last ounce of pleasure drained out of her body he was standing in front of her and slamming his way home as he took her mouth in a hungry kiss that had her panting and screaming for more in seconds. She wrapped her legs around his waist and her arms around his neck, desperate to be closer to him. When he stumbled away from the bureau, she let out a surprised little squeal that had him chuckling even as he slowly ground himself inside of her.

"What are you doing?" she asked, licking her lips hungrily as he moved his mouth down to her neck and suckled in that naughty little way of his that drove her crazy.

"I'm making love to you, baby," he said huskily against her skin seconds before they were falling.

## A Reclusive Heart: A Hollywood Heart's novel

She landed with a startled gasp on her back across the bed with Nick still firmly in place. He buried his face against her neck as his right hand came up and cupped her breast and he rolled his hips slowly against hers. She loved the way he touched her, looked at her and made her feel, but most importantly she realized as he shifted until he was on his elbows looking down at her that she just plain loved him.

As he stared into her eyes she had to fight the urge to cry at the tender expression on his face. She reached up and cupped his face and drew him down for a kiss. He would never know how much she loved him, she thought sadly.

"Jamie, oh god, *Jamie*," he groaned against her lips as she fought against the urge to tell him how much she loved him. It was a difficult battle, but somehow she won. As much as she would love to tell him how she felt she knew that he'd be running for the door before the last word left her mouth so she would have to settle for whatever he could give her and hope like heck that it didn't kill her when he finally walked away.

\* \* \* \*

"Oh, I'm sorry. Did I wake you?" Jamie asked with that innocent smile that he loved as she readjusted herself on his lap.

He shook his head, fighting back a yawn as he watched her bite her lip as she slowly slid down his morning erection. A loud groan escaped him as his hands shot out to grip her hips and gently guide her so that she didn't hurt herself. How in the hell had he lived this long without morning sex? There really was no better way to wake up, he decided as his little recluse gripped his forearms to steady herself as she moved back up his shaft.

Her eyes closed in pleasure as she licked her lips and he knew he'd have to make damn sure that he was around every morning to start his day off like this. He'd never had morning sex before, early noon sex, yes, but not first thing in the morning sex. That probably had something to do with the fact that he made it a point to leave as soon as he was done. Sticking around usually sent the wrong impression to the woman he slept with like he cared or even remembered her name. With Jamie he more than cared.

"You can go back to sleep if you want. I promise to be quiet," she said on a soft little moan that had his cock twitching inside of her.

"But if I go back to sleep I won't be able to do this," he said, adjusting his hand so that his thumb was able to tease her clit.

Jamie gasped as she laid one hand over his as she slowly rode him. "It would probably be best if you stayed awake then," she agreed as she did this little twist and drop thing that had him sucking in a breath and struggling not to throw her on her back and fuck her until she couldn't move. When she did it again he arched his back and let out a loud groan.

As much as it killed him he decided to lay back and let his little recluse have her fun. That didn't mean he couldn't help her reach the point of screaming his name a little faster to put him out of his misery. He wasn't a masochist after all.

\* \* \* \*

Jamie's warm smile when he stepped out of her bathroom made him wish that they could call in sick today, but they had too damn much to do. Well, he did. His little recluse needed to go over some things with Rick and work on her books. They still had a month of tour dates to complete and there was so much that he wanted to show his little recluse. He couldn't wait to get back on the road with her.

She walked over to him and lightly ran her fingers down his silk tie before standing on her toes to press a kiss against his cheek. "I love your hair," she said, smiling as she walked past him to the door.

## A Reclusive Heart: A Hollywood Heart's novel

He barely stopped himself from telling her that he knew that she liked it this way or that he'd given it a mussed look for her since it would just make him look like an idiot. Never before had he cared what a woman thought or wanted, but he found himself eager to please his little recluse. It was funny how making her happy, made him happy. Not that he was going to look too far into that, because he wasn't.

As he headed for the door, he grabbed his briefcase and the overnight bag he'd thrown together last night. He followed after his little recluse only to come an abrupt halt when he found her shifting nervously in front of some guy wearing cheap cologne that smelled like Windex and the expression of a guy who hadn't gotten laid in decades.

"You can't do this," Jamie said, holding up a white piece of paper.

"I just did, lady. When you moved in, I told you that I didn't want any problems and for almost two months I've had to deal with crowds, people breaking in and weirdos. I'm done. I want you out by the end of the week!" the man snapped, moving to walk away, but his little recluse scrambled to catch up and cut him off.

"A week? I won't be here. I have to go back on tour. Can't we make some sort of compromise?" she suggested, almost desperately.

The man stubbornly shook his head as he walked past her. "I'm sorry, Miss Harris. I really am, but I've put up with too much nonsense over the past month and I've gotten one too many complaints about you," he said, surprising the hell out of Nick. People complained about his little recluse? Bullshit.

"But I didn't do any of those things! You know Mrs. Brigs has a hearing problem and Mr. Ames thinks the government is stealing his thoughts! Please don't do this!"

"A week, Miss Harris, and I want you out," he said, getting the final word in before he disappeared through the stairwell door, leaving Jamie standing in the hallway, looking defeated with her little shoulders slumped.

"I think you're going to have to move, Jamie," he said, switching his bag into his other hand so that he could put his arm around her shoulders.

"I know," she muttered unhappily as he steered her towards the elevator. "Do you think Rick will let me out of a few events so that I can find a place and move?" she asked, sounding hopeful.

He sighed heavily as he pushed the call button. "I'm sorry, Jamie, but we already pushed the dates as far back as we could without breaking any contracts."

"Oh," she muttered, her shoulders slumping even further.

"I tell you what, sweetheart," he said, giving her a little nudge when the elevator doors slid open and she remained standing there, looking lost and so damn sad that he ached to pull her into his arms and hold her all day, but they needed to get to work. "I can arrange for someone to rent a house for you and even hire movers to move all of yours things. How does that sound?"

"Will it allow cats?" she asked, perking up at the idea.

"You have a cat?" he asked, wondering how he missed it.

"No."

"You want one?"

She scrunched up her face endearingly as she shook her head. "No, I can't stand them."

"Then why do you care if they allow cats?" he asked, fighting back a chuckle.

"I just like to keep my options open," she said, shrugging.

As he followed her onto the elevator he wondered why he loved it when she drove him crazy.

## Chapter 21

"Oh my god, I can't do this," Jamie groaned as she watched in horror as a large group of paparazzi descended on her vehicle.

Why had she told Nick that she didn't need him to follow her to work? Because she hadn't wanted to come across as clingy or needy that's why. Somehow she'd managed to escape the small group that waited for her outside of her apartment building, but that was probably only because they knew exactly where she was going to end up. There was no way she was going to survive this without sugar, she realized as a swarm of people surrounded her car and started taking pictures.

For a moment, she considered calling Nick and begging him to come rescue her, but she decided that at some point she'd have to figure out how to deal with this by herself and what better time than right now? She took a deep breath and when that didn't give her the confidence that she needed to move her butt she took another one and grabbed her purse.

Trying to appear confident and relaxed, she slowly shut off her car and opened the door. The paparazzi backed up and gave her plenty of space to step out of her car, probably hoping that she'd do something really stupid or embarrassing, but the joke was on them because she wasn't going to-

*Oh, darn it*, she thought as her purse somehow tipped upside down and spilled its contents all over the black pavement, leaving her with no choice but to drop to her knees and hurry to grab everything before they found anything embarrassing. Not that she had anything embarrassing in her purse, she thought as she grabbed a handful of butterscotch discs and shoved them back into her bag. She was pretty sure she'd learned that lesson a month ago and had cleaned out her purse since that little incident in the bathroom. The only thing they'd find now was a used paperback book, her wallet, candy, and-

"I see you believe in safe sex, Miss Harris," a man said mockingly as he held up the box of condoms she'd bought weeks ago and unfortunately forgot about.

She felt her cheeks burn as what had to be a hundred cameras clicked as the big jerk held the box of unopened condoms in front of her face. Clearing her throat, she took the box back, trying not to wince when she heard more clicks, and shoved them in her bag. "Yes, it's, um, very important," she mumbled pathetically, getting to her feet and fighting back the urge to make a run for it.

When she made it to the front of the building she nearly sighed in relief. That is until the large security guard held up a hand stopping her. "Employee pass or guest name," he said firmly.

"Oh," she muttered, trying to ignore the clicks as she searched through her bag for her employee pass only to come up empty handed. "I...I think I lost it."

"I'm sorry, ma'am, but I can't let you in the building without an employee pass."

"Did you get fired?" one of the paparazzi demanded as Jamie struggled to figure out a way to get inside and away from the cameras, but all their questions and the constant clicking of their cameras made it difficult to think at the moment.

"How did it feel to find out that your mother wasn't really your mother?"

"I hear your family couldn't wait to get rid of you," another one said, hitting a little too close to home.

"Please, I work for Rerum Publishing. If you call Rick Edwards or Nick Quinn they can vouch for me," she pleaded quietly as the crowd began to close in tightly around her.

"I'm sorry, ma'am," the guard said, gesturing for her to step away from the front door. "But I have strict orders not to let in anyone without a pass or who isn't on the list," he said, holding up a clipboard.

## A Reclusive Heart: A Hollywood Heart's novel

She opened her mouth to ask him to check for her name, but realized that she wouldn't be on the guest list. If she wanted to get in the building she was going to have to call Nick. She opened her purse even as the large man herded her away from the building and the paparazzi descended on her. After a quick one minute search she realized that her phone wasn't in her bag.

"When did they fire you?"

"Probably after they realized your books sucked."

"Need help? Guess you can't call your family," someone shouted.

Jamie hugged her bag to her chest and tried to walk away, but they wouldn't let her. Anytime she tried to move away they shifted to block her. When she tried to fake left and go right she was knocked down and before she could get back up, she found about a dozen people standing over her, yelling questions that she'd rather not think about as they documented her humiliation.

She tried to stand up, but no one would budge an inch, forcing her to curl up into herself and bury her face against her knees as they continued shouting their questions and knocking into her as they shoved each other to get the perfect shot. She was stepped on, kicked, humiliated and screamed at she couldn't help but wish that she had some chocolate and Nick's arms around her as the first embarrassing tear streamed down her cheek. Thankfully, she had her face buried against her knees so the cameras missed it, but that didn't stop them from trying to get some kind of a reaction from her.

\* \* \* \*

"I'd love to make you dinner tonight, Nick," Mandy, Sandy or was her name Chrissy? said as she leaned in a little too close for his comfort, forcing him to sit back in his chair and shift away from her as he shot the empty chair by Rick's side another glance.

Where the hell was she?

She should have been here by now. In fact, she should have been here an hour ago, but the woman was a no show. He called her apartment, thinking that she'd run back because she'd forgotten something, but she hadn't picked up. She wasn't answering her cell phone either and now he was really starting to worry about her.

"Nick?" the woman said with a hint of a whine to her voice when he didn't answer her right away.

"I have to catch an early flight in the morning," he said absently as he turned to shoot another glance at the boardroom's closed double doors.

"That's okay. I don't mind giving you a ride," she said in a husky whisper that left absolutely no doubt in his mind about what she really meant.

"Not interested," he said, not even bothering to soften the blow as he sent another questioning look to Rick, who wore a grim expression as he shook his head. Great, his little recluse hadn't called Rick to let him know why she was running late.

"What do you mean you're not interested?" the woman demanded, but Nick was barely paying attention to her as he stood up and headed for the door. He didn't need to look back to know that Rick was right behind him.

"The morning meeting is canceled. Please return to your duties," Rick said as Nick pulled his phone out and tried to call Jamie one last time.

"Are you sure she was coming in today?" Rick asked as they stepped in front of the elevator.

"Positive," he said, hitting the call button repeatedly with a little too much force.

"Any idea what could be keeping her?" Rick asked.

## A Reclusive Heart: A Hollywood Heart's novel

"Not a clue," he said, regretting leaving her on her own. He should have insisted that she drive with him, but he hadn't wanted to give the office gossips anything to talk about.

"Fuck this," he snapped when the elevator didn't move fast enough. He made his way to the stairwell, glaring at anyone that got in his way. Three minutes later they were downstairs in the busy foyer, searching for her.

"Do you see her?" Rick asked.

"No," he said, barely biting back the urge to put his fist through a wall. Where the hell was she?

"Let's check outside," Rick said, already heading in the direction of the glass doors. As they moved to step outside the two large guards Rick had posted at the door stepped aside, revealing a large group of paparazzi going nuts not twenty feet from the building.

"Police are on their way, sir," one of the guards informed Rick, but the man didn't seem to be listening as he moved towards the crowd.

A feeling of dread twisted Nick's stomach as he followed after Rick. When he heard some of the questions being yelled he moved faster, shoving anyone that got in his way aside as he fought to find his little recluse. When he finally found her, he felt his heart break and his teeth grind.

"Please just leave me alone," she begged, her voice breaking on a sob as she buried her face against her knees.

He didn't hesitate as he bent down and scooped her up in his arms. At first she went rigid and moved to push away from him, but then she looked up and saw him and her body relaxed as she buried her tear soaked face against his shirt.

"Is this your boyfriend?"

"Are you using her for her money?" a woman demanded as she snapped their picture. Nick ignored them all as he shouldered his way through the crowd. Rick stepped in front of him and cleared the path.

When they reached the front doors one of the large guards noticeably swallowed. "She didn't have a pass and wasn't on the list," he explained.

"Did she ask you to call us?" Rick asked in a cold, even voice. When the man nodded, Rick didn't even hesitate in saying, "Then you're fired." It probably saved the man from a trip to the hospital. That and Nick wasn't about to put his little recluse down.

As Jamie trembled in his arms he followed a very somber Rick to the elevators.

"Are you okay?" he asked softly, wishing for Jamie's sake that everyone would stop staring at them so that she could calm down.

"I-I could really use some chocolate right about now," she said softly, sniffling.

"I'll hunt down the biggest chocolate bar I can find. How does that sound?" he asked soothingly as he stepped into the elevator after Rick.

She sniffled as she thought it over. "C-can I have two?"

"Yes."

"A-and a Coke?" she asked, sounding hopeful, but no less pathetic as she continued to sniffle and shake in his arms.

He sighed heavily as he pointedly ignored the questioning look Rick was sending their way. "Fine, you little sugar addict. You can have a Coke."

"Can I have two?"

"No," he said, knowing that she'd regret consuming that much sugar at once.

## A Reclusive Heart: A Hollywood Heart's novel

"You're mean," she grumbled even as she snuggled closer in his arms.

"Uh huh," he said, adjusting her in his arms as he waited to arrive at their floor.

"Take her to my office," Rick said, but Nick had no intention of listening to the man. He wanted to take Jamie to his office where he could take care of her.

"I'll take her to mine. We have a few things to go over," he said, hoping Rick would just drop it and let him have some time with his little recluse.

"I need to talk to her about a few things," Rick stubbornly pointed out.

"We can talk about them in my office," Nick argued just as his little recluse started to struggle for freedom in his arms.

"Um, guys? I can walk to my own office," she said, drawing his attention. He looked down at her tear streaked face and noted the deep blush burning her cheeks. Of course she was embarrassed, he realized feeling like an idiot.

His little recluse embarrassed too damn easily. He also knew how hard she tried to blend in and go unnoticed and being carried in the office by him wasn't going to help. With a great deal of reluctance, he set her down on her feet.

"Better?" he asked, pushing her loose hair back behind her shoulders.

"Much better," she mumbled, hugging her bag tightly to her chest.

He watched as she threw Rick a nervous look. "Is there a morning meeting?"

"No, not this morning," Rick said, giving her a reassuring smile.

"Alright then," she said, straightening up as the elevator came to a stop. "Then if either of you gentlemen need me, I'll be in my office," she said, shifting anxiously as she let out a slow breath.

She was nervous and there was nothing he could do for her. He hated this. He hated having to pretend that he didn't care just to protect both of their reputations, but if he still wanted to have a job at the end of the day, then he had to do it. He was her editor, technically her boss and sleeping with her was more than enough to get his ass canned.

If he lost his job for fucking one of the clients his reputation wouldn't be worth shit and he'd never work in this field again. He loved his job and what he did. He sure as hell didn't want to start over again, but more importantly, he didn't want to leave his little recluse to fend for herself. She needed him and as long as he was around, he was going to protect her.

When she stepped off the elevator only to look around nervously, he had to stop himself from smiling since he knew that she wouldn't appreciate that one bit. He stepped off the elevator to joined her and waited a moment by her side for her to admit that she was lost, but of course she was too damn stubborn to admit that so he gave a strand of her beautiful strawberry blond hair a gentle tug to get her attention.

"Your office is down that hall," he said, gesturing to his right.

"I knew that," she said with a stubborn nod as she took off in that direction, hugging her bag tightly as she went. He sighed heavily as he watched her occasionally jump out of the way of someone who wasn't watching where they were going and he knew without seeing her face that she apologized each and every time. It seemed they still had a few things to work on, he thought as he moved to follow her only to come up short when Rick stepped in front of him.

"We need to talk," the man said, not looking pleased at all.

## Chapter 22

If she didn't get a fix soon she was pretty sure she was going to die, Jamie thought as she shifted restlessly in her too firm leather chair as she tried uselessly to focus on the word document in front of her. She was supposed to be writing. Well, she assumed that's what she was supposed to do since no one had told her differently. She was already caught up editing other writer's manuscripts so that really left her with nothing to do but write.

She checked her inbox, hoping that she'd find an email telling her that it was her to turn to write the next **chapter**, but so far nothing. This was the first time she'd ever collaborated with someone on a book and she had to admit that it was pretty fun. The story was enjoyable and she was really enjoying the experience. It was a challenge, one she loved and hoped to do again.

After another minute, she realized that staring at her inbox wasn't exactly going to help so she returned her attention back to the **chapter** that she was working on, but her mind kept drifting to what happened outside not even an hour ago. As hard as she tried, she couldn't stop thinking about the things they'd said to her. Nick had warned her about the paparazzi and how cruel they could be to get what they wanted, but it hadn't prepared her at all.

She really needed some chocolate and a Coke, but so far she hadn't been able to track any down. When she asked around, her questions were met with stares of horror and comments about carbs and diets. How could any woman function without chocolate? she wondered again. It really was unnatural.

After a quick search of the vending machines on the floor and the break room she discovered much to her horror that everyone had been telling the truth. There wasn't one single morsel of chocolate to be had. For all of ten seconds she considered sneaking out of the building and hitting the convenient store she spotted down the street, but she really didn't want to deal with reporters again.

A small knock at her door had her sitting up and nearly sighing with relief. Nick said he was going to find some chocolate for her and since he knew the lay of the land a heck of a lot better than her, she figured that he'd have better luck finding some chocolate and hopefully that was him bringing her the much needed sustenance.

"Come in," she said, trying not to look too eager, for the chocolate or the man, she wasn't sure which one she needed more.

When a pretty, tall brunette stepped into her office carrying a cardboard box she did her best to hide her disappointment. The woman placed the box on the corner of Jamie's desk and with a smile explained, "This is all the mail we picked up from your apartment building while you were on tour."

"It's all my mail?" she said, nearly pouting. Not only was there a lot of mail to sort through, but she had been kind of hoping that there was also some chocolate in there.

"Yes, Miss Harris. Is there anything else I can do for you?" the woman asked with a polite smile.

"No, no thank you," she mumbled, not at all looking forward to the task of sorting through all of it. Thankfully she'd set up her checking account to automatically pay all of her bills so she didn't have to worry about those. As the woman quietly left she pulled the box closer to her, dreading every minute of this chore. She hated sorting through junk mail.

Not even thirty seconds into the boring chore she came across a letter. There was no return address, but at least it wasn't junk mail. She opened the letter and felt the air rush out of her lungs as her eyes widened. With a shaky hand she put the letter aside and practically dove through the rest of the mail, looking for any more letters. She found thirty-five letters in total, each one more gruesome and detailed than the last.

## A Reclusive Heart: A Hollywood Heart's novel

Having absolutely no idea what to do, she placed the letters that made her sick to even look at into the box and headed out of her office, hoping to find Nick. He would know how to handle this, she decided as she tried to shove away the urge to drop the box and finally make a run for it.

* * * *

"How's the tour going?" Rick asked as he handed Nick a glass of iced water.

"It's going well," Nick said, wondering when the man was going to get to the point. He didn't have to wait long.

"That kid isn't going to sue," Rick said as if Nick had really been worried. The kid got what he deserved for attacking Jamie. As far as he was concerned the kid was lucky to still be walking.

"He attacked her," Nick simply said.

Rick nodded his agreement. "I've seen the pictures, but from what I understand it was part of a frat house scavenger hunt. He wasn't trying to hurt her."

"I don't care what it was for. He had no business putting his hands on her," Nick explained calmly even though the memory of the asshole putting his lips on Jamie's left him feeling anything but calm.

"You don't think that you took things a little too far? You broke his jaw, Nick," Rick said, sighing heavily as he sat in the chair across from Nick.

Nick met his friends eyes as he asked, "If it had been Dana would you have done anything differently?" he asked, knowing the soft spot the man had for Dana Pierce. She was a sweet woman that they both cared deeply about. He also knew the man viewed her as a sister. When Rick didn't answer, but instead clenched his jaw tightly, he had his answer.

"Was there something else you wanted to discuss? I need to get back to my office and go over the rest of the dates to make sure there are no last minute surprises," Nick said, not bothering to wait for the man to speak as he stood to leave. He had too much shit to do to sit here twiddling his thumbs.

"Have you slept with her?" Rick asked bluntly, taking him off guard.

"What the hell are you talking about?" he asked, sitting back down.

"Jamie. I need to know if I should have someone else work with her."

"Do you have a problem with her work?" Nick demanded.

Rick frowned. "No."

"Do you have a problem with my work then?"

"No."

"Then I don't see how it's any of your business what we do in our spare time," Nick said, refusing to lie and belittle what he had going on with Jamie to save his own ass. If they fired him, and he prayed that didn't happen, then he'd go with her and watch out for her during the rest of this tour and hopefully when it was finished he'd have another job. One thing was for certain, he wasn't ready to lose Jamie.

Not yet.

"It's not that simple and you know it, Nick. We have that particular policy for a reason and I'm afraid that I can't look the other way. You're going to have to end things with her and I'm afraid I can't allow you to continue overseeing this tour," Rick said grimly.

## A Reclusive Heart: A Hollywood Heart's novel

He would still have the job he busted his ass to get, but he would lose Jamie, he realized. They were never going to last past this tour. This had been a fling, a wonderful, earth shattering fling, but nothing more. They could still be friends and he'd see her whenever she worked in the office and he was in town, but that was all. He would no longer be allowed to touch her, kiss her or hold her ever again because she would be off limits to him.

As he stood up, he couldn't believe how easily the decision came to him. For years, he wanted nothing more than to get his name out there, make a better life for himself, and erase every last memory of his childhood. When the best opportunity of his life came, he fucked it up by sleeping with his little recluse. He could either keep his job and he knew that it wouldn't be long before he came across another chance to make a name for himself or he could keep the best thing that ever happened to him.

It surprised him that he didn't have to think about it. "Then I quit," he said, walking towards the door with every intention of grabbing his little recluse and taking her home where he planned on losing himself in her arms for the rest of the day.

"You're serious?" Rick said, coming to his feet.

"Deadly," Nick said without any hesitation.

"She really means that much to you?" Rick asked, sounding more than just a little curious.

"She means everything to me," Nick said, closing in on the door. "I'll be out within the hour and just so you know, I plan on going with her for the rest of the tour. I'll stay out of whoever's way that you send to take over for me, but I'm not leaving her."

Rick's chuckle brought him up short. He turned around to glare at the man. "What the hell is so funny?"

"I can't believe the day the mighty Nick Quinn got brought to his knees by a woman finally came," Rick said, shaking his head ruefully and grinning hugely.

"She didn't bring me to my knees," Nick ground out. "I care about her and want to keep her safe."

Rick waved his comments of which actually pissed him off more than the man's laughter. "Relax you're not fired."

"I quit," he pointed out.

"I chose to ignore it," Rick said with a simple shrug. "But you should know that I've decided to send someone with you for the rest of the tour."

"I don't need a babysitter, Rick," he said, shocked at how relieved he was to still have a job.

"I know you don't. Even though I'm not entirely comfortable with this situation I'm going to trust that you know what you're doing," he explained and Nick just barely bit back his wince.

He had no idea in hell what he was doing. He'd just tried to quit his job for a woman he didn't plan on seeing past next month. What the hell was wrong with him? This wasn't like him and he couldn't help but blame his little recluse for it. If she hadn't made him fall in-

No, no, no, he was not in love with her. He liked her a lot, but it sure as hell wasn't love. It was great sex and he enjoyed her company, nothing more. Maybe he'd been spending too much time with her. It might be best if he stepped back from her, but then he realized that he didn't much care for that idea.

Maybe this didn't have to end once the tour was done. They could be friends, good friends and when the need arose they could have no strings attached sex, often. It wouldn't be anything permanent, just two good friends who had great sex whenever they wanted, wherever. This could work, he realized as he walked back over to the large sitting area and sat down.

## A Reclusive Heart: A Hollywood Heart's novel

The only problem as far as he could see was convincing Jamie that this was a good idea. He really didn't see a problem with that. She loved spending time with him, had an insatiable appetite for sex and didn't expect anything from him. There would probably come a time when she started to date and when that time came......

No, that wouldn't work for him either, because the thought of his little recluse being touched by another man didn't sit well with him so they were going to have to figure out something else. He liked being with her and actually liked thinking of himself as her boyfriend so maybe they'd continue with that for a year or two until they worked each other out of their systems or got bored. That made more sense than torturing himself by allowing another man to get near her.

"I'm sending Holly to help. J.L. Lewis' popularity is skyrocketing. Thanks to her family's antics more people are curious about her. We've already had calls from venders demanding more books as well as interviews. Your already tight schedule is about to become a little tighter to accommodate this demand and to make sure that everything goes smoothly I'm sending you help," Rick explained as Nick took the chair across from him. Damn if he couldn't see the logic in what the man was saying. Of course there was just one thing that he wasn't sure about.

Who the hell was Holly?

Before he could ask, Rick's door swung open and his little recluse came storming into the room, holding a cardboard box in front of her. She didn't look too happy, but when her eyes landed on him she looked decidedly less than pleased.

"Is everything okay, Jamie?" Rick asked, getting to his feet when she approached them.

Instead of answering him, she shoved the box onto his lap and glared accusingly at him. "You promised me chocolate, you big jerk," she snapped and hell if he couldn't help but grin. The woman was a sexy little thing that entertained him on so many levels.

"I got you chocolate and some Coke, Jamie, but Rick ate it," he said with a helpless shrug.

"Wait, what?" Rick asked, looking like a deer caught in headlights as Jamie turned her cute little temper on him.

"You ate my chocolate?" Jamie asked as she glared up at the much taller man. It was actually interesting that his little recluse couldn't stop apologizing to people for screwing *her* over, but mess with her sugar obsession and she'd rip someone's throat out.

"I-I-," Rick stammered helplessly as Jamie's lower lip began to tremble.

*Ah, shit.*

His little recluse needed a fix and soon. He knew the signs quite well at this point. As he stood up he wondered if perhaps they should look into a chocolate rehab center for her, but he knew she wouldn't last twenty-four hours without something sweet.

"I tell you what, Jamie," he said, shifting the box under his arm as he put his other arm around her shoulders, "why don't we take you out for a nice big hot fudge sundae and you can tell us what's in this box," he said in a soothing voice.

"You're patronizing my needs again," she sighed, but thankfully that lower lip stopped trembling.

"Are you trying to tell me that you don't want a nice big ice cream sundae?" he asked, already knowing his little recluse would never be able to refuse sugar.

"That's not what I'm saying and you know it, but I don't think you should bring that box with us," she said, moving away from him and towards the door.

"Why not?" Rick asked, stepping up beside him to peer down at the box with him.

## A Reclusive Heart: A Hollywood Heart's novel

"Because half of those letters contain explicit sexual content and the other half are death threats."

## Chapter 23

"Come on, Jamie. It's time to get up," Nick said in a soothing tone as he pulled her to her feet.

"Go away. I'm tired and I hate you," she muttered, trying to pull away from him so that she could cuddle back up in her seat and go back to sleep, but he wouldn't have it. The horrible man didn't seem to care that it was barely one in the morning. In seconds, he had her back on her feet and was nudging her off the plane.

"We'll be at the hotel in a half an hour and then you can go back to sleep, okay?" Nick said in that same tone that he probably thought would make her nod and do whatever he asked when it just made her want to nod off.

"Mr. Quinn is right, Miss Harris. Once we get to the hotel you can rest until the book signing this afternoon," Holly, the woman who now made them a trio for the rest of the tour, said from somewhere ahead of her, but she was too busy struggling to keep her eyes open to look for the woman.

Not that she thought the woman would be very hard to find. With stunning red hair, exotic style, and way too much perfume she was kind of hard to miss. Since her ticket was a last minute booking, Holly had been forced to sit several rows away from them, but unfortunately that wasn't enough. The woman's perfume invaded the cabin space and within minutes a lot of people, including Jamie, were complaining about having a headache.

If Nick tried to force her to share a room with the woman she was going to revolt. She'd pay for her own room, because there was no way she could stay in the same room with the woman and that perfume. She could be the nicest woman in the world for all Jamie knew, but she just couldn't take being trapped in a room with that eye stinging perfume. It was not happening.

"You're doing great, Jamie. Just hang in there and we'll be at the hotel soon," Nick said after they collected their luggage and headed for the front entrance.

## A Reclusive Heart: A Hollywood Heart's novel

"I don't need a pep talk," she muttered, biting back a yawn as she readjusted the duffle bag over her shoulder, "I need sugar, lots and lots of sugar," she grumbled, wishing that he would at least let her get some before they left, but the infuriating man decided about twelve hours ago that he was going to turn into Super Overprotective Man, which of course meant keeping an eye on her and depriving her of her beautiful much needed beloved sugar.

Then again, she couldn't really blame him since those letters had freaked her out pretty badly. She still couldn't believe someone who didn't know her could hate her so much. When she showed the letters to him and Rick she'd been kind of hoping that they'd laugh it off and tell her that it was a joke, but the looks on their faces when they read the first one told her that it was anything but a joke.

Within minutes, Rick had been on the phone with the police and Nick wouldn't let her out of his sight, not even to use the bathroom. When she couldn't hold it a minute longer he made her use the men's room so that he could stand guard. He thought she was kidding when she told him to sing so that she could use the bathroom. She hadn't been. Besides learning that the men's bathroom had less traffic than the women's room, she also learned that Nick had a very sexy singing voice.

That of course didn't make up for the fact that she hadn't had sugar in nearly twenty-four hours. She wasn't hypoglycemic or anything, but very much addicted to sugar at this point in her life and if she went too long without something sweet she got cranky, very cranky. This morning Nick had been sweet enough to make her breakfast, a straightforward breakfast of eggs, bacon and wheat toast that didn't fulfill her sugary needs. She meant to pick something up on the way to work, but never got the chance. Once the guys saw the letters she never got her hot fudge sundae either or any food for that matter.

"She's going to fall over," she mumbled just as her poor stomach growled viciously for a little attention. As soon as they reached the hotel she was going to order some food and grab some sleep. Her new game plan was to sleep until the very last minute possible instead of spending the customary hour with Nick going over things. If he didn't like that then that was too bad. She was a tired cranky woman in need of sugar and he was the big jerk denying her, her fix.

"How much shit does she need?" Nick asked as he reached over and grabbed the duffle bag that was giving Jamie so much trouble. He threw it over his already occupied shoulder before taking her now free hand into his.

They watched as Holly directed the man carting all eight of her bags towards the waiting line of taxis. Jamie realized that they wouldn't be heading home for four weeks, but eight bags was a bit of an overkill, especially since they would be moving around a lot. While Holly's bags were loaded into a taxi, Nick signaled for a different taxi and had their things thrown in the back.

"Nick!" Holly said brightly, waving to get Nick's attention.

With a small groan that had her smiling, he looked over at the woman. "I thought that it might be a good idea if you and I shared a taxi so that we could go over a few things," Holly said casually, but there was no doubt in Jamie's mind that talking was the last thing the woman wanted to do with Nick.

It wasn't too difficult to figure out that the woman was interested in Nick. What heterosexual woman in her right mind wouldn't be? He was incredibly sexy, handsome and charming. It seemed that she wasn't the only woman to notice.

He opened the taxi door and gestured for her to get inside. She barely held back her disappointed sigh as she resigned herself to riding to the hotel alone. "We'll meet you at the hotel," Nick said as she closed her eyes and settled in for what she hoped was a short ride.

"Okay," she said around a loud yawn.

## A Reclusive Heart: A Hollywood Heart's novel

"Okay, what?" Nick asked as he sat down next to her and took her hand into his.

She opened her mouth to explain that she thought that he was riding with Holly, but she was too damn exhausted to try. Instead, she curled up next to him and forced her eyes to stay open during the blessedly short ride.

It seemed like minutes later she was leaning against the wall near their things while she watched Nick check them all in. She was waiting to see how many rooms they had before telling him that she was getting her own room. She didn't want to hurt Holly's feelings unnecessarily by flat-out refusing to bunk with her.

Holly just stepped into the hotel foyer followed by a man pushing her bags on a trolley when Nick walked over to Jamie. He handed her a keycard and one to Holly as she joined them.

"So we get our own rooms," Jamie said, hoping that she didn't sound too hopeful.

Nick shook his head as he reached down and grabbed his bags. "No, I'm afraid all of our original reservations still stand. Two of us are going to have to double bunk," he announced and she wasn't too busy trying to find a tactful way around it to notice the look Holly sent Nick. She knew the minute she was out of earshot that the woman was going to offer to share a room with Nick.

That wasn't happening. She might be a pushover, but that didn't mean that she was going to stand by quietly while some woman made a play for her boyfriend, she was-

Utterly shocked that she thought of him as her boyfriend.

Even though he'd referred to her himself as her boyfriend a few times she hadn't given it much thought mostly because she didn't want to get her hopes up, but she realized that it was true. For the first time in her life she had a boyfriend. She ignored the fact that that little bit of information was kind of pathetic and focused on the here and now and right now there was another woman interested in her man.

Although she wasn't the down and dirty cat fight over a guy kind of girl that didn't mean she was going to stand back while another woman made a play for Nick. She'd simply take the woman aside and explain to her that-

"Miss Harris and I will be sharing a room," Nick announced, shocking the woman and putting the matter to rest as far as she was concerned, which was a good thing since Jamie really didn't think she would have had much energy to explain anything to the woman at the moment. "We'll see you in the morning. Have a good night, Holly," Nick said, grabbing Jamie's bag and throwing it over his shoulder once he had all of his things.

"Wait! You can't do that!" Holly yelled after them.

"Goodnight," was all Nick said as he ushered Jamie onto the elevator. Just before the elevator doors closed she saw the look of fury on the woman's face and thanks to growing up with Caitlyn, knew the woman was going to make her life a living hell.

Great, she thought dryly as the elevator doors closed. That's all she needed to make her life perfect.

\* \* \* \*

"I could have rented my own room," Jamie mumbled as she stepped out of the bathroom, drying her damp her and wearing a pair of light pink flannel pajama pants and a tiny white tee shirt that had his blood simmering.

## A Reclusive Heart: A Hollywood Heart's novel

"They were sold out for the night," he lied. "It was either share a room with me or with Holly," he explained, noting the pinched look on Jamie's face at the suggestion. Not that he could blame her. The woman was incredibly annoying and that perfume of hers was strong enough to peel paint. She was also the last person that he wanted to tag along on this tour.

When he realized who Holly was, he took Rick aside and told him to pick someone else. Unfortunately there was no one else. Correction, he could have had her replaced for this tour if he'd been willing to wait another couple of days, but he hadn't been.

After seeing those letters he wanted to get his little recluse the hell out of there as soon as possible and for damn good reason too. The reason of course was the death threats. It wasn't uncommon for celebrities and authors to receive death threats from unhappy fans and psychos. He knew that she'd no doubt receive more over the years, but these letters were alarming.

Not only did they go into graphic detail about how the psycho wanted to kill Jamie, but the letters were all addressed to Jamie, not J.L. Lewis. That probably wouldn't have been entirely alarming since her family took it upon themselves to give away her real name, but that had only been a few days ago. The letters dated back a month ago before anyone knew her real name. The other concern of course was that none of the letters had been sent through the mail.

There wasn't a single postage stamp on any of the death threat letters which meant that whoever wrote them had them hand delivered to the building. Thankfully, Jamie's landlord decided to throw her ass out, otherwise he'd probably be having a hell of a time convincing her to move out. All of her things, her personal items like her computer, clothes and toiletries were being moved out of her place at that very moment. He'd convinced her to donate all of her furniture not because he really thought it was a nice thing to do like he claimed, but because it allowed the movers under Rick's direction to get in and get the hell out without tipping anyone off about what they were doing.

They had a month left of this tour and he hoped the police were able to find the sick fuck before it was time to go home. If they didn't, some things were going to have to change and he was afraid those changes were going to push Jamie back into a corner and she'd go back to being afraid of her own shadow. It was only because they'd kept certain details from her that she wasn't panicking right now. He'd just have to keep her distracted with work and other things in the meantime.

"Please tell me they have room service," she mumbled in a sexy little whiny voice that had him smiling.

"They do, but the kitchen closed down an hour ago," he explained as he grabbed his bag of toiletries and headed for the bathroom.

"Of course it did," she said, dropping the menu back on the small rectangular coffee table and plopped down on the couch with a sigh.

The knock at the door had him biting back a smile. He ignored Jamie's questioning look as he tossed his small bag to her and headed for the door. When he opened it and spotted the bellhop, he stepped to the side so the man could roll the cart into the room.

With a polite smile, the bellhop unloaded the two covered trays onto the coffee table and rolled the cart back towards the door where Nick stood waiting. He slipped the kid a hundred before shutting the door. That was one thing he learned long ago, in places like this money and position were everything. There wasn't anything that he couldn't get by greasing the wheels a little. It also didn't hurt that the manager's wife was a huge fan of J.L. Lewis and Nick promised him a set of signed copies if he opened the kitchen for his little recluse.

"What's all this?" Jamie asked, shooting the covered trays a curious look.

"This," he said, walking over to her and lifting the tray even as he bent to kiss her, "is dinner, sweetheart."

"Is that double fudge cake?" his little sugar addicted asked on a gasp.

## A Reclusive Heart: A Hollywood Heart's novel

He chuckled as he set the cover down. It figured that she'd focus on the cake instead of the large plate overfilled with stuffed chicken breast, cranberry sauce, mashed potatoes, dressing that were giving off a mouth watering aroma and had his stomach growling, reminding him that he hadn't eaten since breakfast.

"It's actually triple fudge with real Belgian chocolate and chocolate mousse in the middle," he said, chuckling when she let a little reverent gasp of pleasure.

When she picked up her fork and went for the cake, he wasn't too surprised. "I'm going to grab a quick shower before I eat. Try to eat some real food too, Jamie," he said as he stepped into the bathroom only to come to a halt and add, "and don't touch my cake, woman!"

"I won't!"

Of course she lied, he thought with a chuckle as he raised the lid off his food ten minutes later and found his cake plate empty. His little addict seemed satisfied at the moment with her sugar intake and was now focused on her actual dinner. Since he'd actually ordered the second slice for her, he didn't say anything as he dug into his own food.

When they were done, he placed the trays outside of his room just as Holly was opening her door across the hall. Her eyes widened in pleasure when she saw him and then narrowed when they ran over his bare chest and unbuttoned jeans. Without a word she slammed her door shut and he resigned himself to a call from Rick in the morning. Not that he cared what the man said. With some sick fuck after Jamie he wasn't letting her out of his sight. Rick could bitch all he wanted and it wouldn't change a damn thing.

He shut the door and walked back into the room as Jamie was climbing under the covers. He waited until she was settled before shutting the lights off and dropping his jeans and underwear before joining her. Before his head hit the pillow she was curling up next to him. It wasn't long before he realized that she'd ditched her pajamas and was naked, just the way he liked her.

Neither spoke as he found her mouth with his and gently rolled her onto her back. When he slipped a finger inside of her, he found her wet and ready which was a good thing because he was too tired to stretch this out tonight. He wanted it hard and fast and he gave it to her.

The louder she screamed, the harder he slammed into her and when she dug her nails into his ass he quickened his pace until he thought the damn bed would break. After she came the first, second and third time he didn't slow down, but instead gave her everything he had. When he couldn't hold back any longer he pulled back and turned Jamie onto her stomach before covering her body from behind. He slammed into her as he wrapped his arms around her, gripping her breasts tightly in his hands as she drenched him in her arousal. Her walls tightened impossibly further around him seconds before she was screaming his name.

His balls tightened almost painfully as he felt himself harden further inside of her. As her walls clenched mercilessly around him he pinched her hard nipples, forcing her into another screaming orgasm that robbed him of his own. He buried his face in the pillow as he roared her name.

Afraid that he was hurting her, he rolled over onto his side and pulled her with him, still inside of her. Moments later they were both falling into a deep satisfying sleep and he realized that he never wanted to let her go.

## Chapter 24

"Oh god," Jamie muttered, panting hard as she braced her hands on the tiled wall behind her and looked down.

Nick winked as he leaned forward and slowly ran the tip of his tongue between her slit. It felt so good, but it wasn't enough. She needed more. She needed him.

Taking a deep breath, and praying that her legs didn't give out, she somehow managed to step away from Nick and moved into the middle of the large bathroom. She looked over her shoulder to find him getting to his feet to come after her and that's when she did the most brazen thing of her life.

She got down on her hands and knees and offered him up a view that she hoped he couldn't resist. It was funny how she'd only been having sex for less than a week and she couldn't seem to get enough. Maybe she was playing catch up, she thought as she felt him grip her hips and rub the tip of his penis over her bottom.

He slid a finger inside of her as he continued to tease her bottom with the large soft velvety tip of his erection. The combined sensations had her panting harder and desperate for release as she pushed her hips back and rode his finger. He released an approving growl that had her mumbling incoherently and begging him to take her. When she felt his finger slide free and the tip of his erection take its place she nearly wept with joy.

The loud banging at their door had her near frustrated tears. When the banging didn't stop after a minute, Nick moved away from her, cursing up a storm that was pretty impressive. When he left the room she decided to stand up to make it easier for her to attack him and have her dirty little way with him before someone else could interrupt them.

When Nick came back into the room, looking close to killing someone she knew their morning playtime was over. He already had a pair of black pants on and was pulling on a light green shirt when he saw her. It was hard to miss the large bulge in his pants or the way it jerked when he saw her. It was actually flattering, but unfortunately it turned her on even further.

"What's going on?" she asked, unable to tear her eyes away from that bulge.

"That was Holly," he said tightly. "Apparently someone in the office got the times mixed up and the convention starts in fifteen minutes, not two hours."

"Oh," she said, unable to stop from pouting.

Nick closed the distance between them and cupped her face in his hands as he pressed a gentle kiss to her lips. "We will finish this later, Jamie, but right now we have to haul ass so that we don't disappoint your fans."

\* \* \* \*

She watched as Nick headed her way, but once again Holly stepped in front of him, blocking his path and grabbing his attention. This had been going on since they arrived five hours ago. Every time that she needed to speak with Nick, Holly intervened and whenever he finished with one problem and started to walk towards her, Holly would catch his attention and point out another problem for him to handle.

Why exactly was the woman here if she needed Nick to do absolutely everything, Jamie wondered as she shot another hopeful look towards the bathroom. She'd been desperate for the bathroom for the last two hours, but she could never seem to get anyone's attention. Every time she tried to get Holly to manage the line of people waiting to speak to her so that she could use the bathroom, the woman got distracted.

By Nick.

## A Reclusive Heart: A Hollywood Heart's novel

The woman was constantly hovering around him and whenever he was alone Holly would rush over to him. She seemed desperate to be around him. Unfortunately, she didn't seem to realize that Nick looked rather annoyed with all the attention. If Jamie didn't have to pee so badly, she'd probably find the whole thing entertaining.

Okay, the whole thing did amuse her, but she really had to go and soon. Deciding that there was no way she could hold it any longer, she got to her feet and thankfully spotted Pat, the really nice event coordinator that she'd met earlier. After quickly explaining the situation, she took off like a shot towards the bathroom only to be cut off by none other than Holly.

"Where are you going?" Holly asked even though it really should be self-explanatory since she was heading straight for the women's room.

"I have to use the bathroom," Jamie explained as she tried to step around the woman.

"There's a bathroom set up for the authors," Holly explained, gesturing for Jamie to follow her. When Jamie didn't immediately move to follow the woman, who was giving off "Caitlyn vibes" as she liked to refer to bitchy vibes, Holly explained, "It's to make sure that you can use the bathroom in peace without having to worry about fans harassing you."

Oh, well that kind of made sense, Jamie decided as she followed the woman out of the large convention room and through a back door marked "Employees Only" and down a long hallway. By the time they took a right down another long hallway Jamie couldn't help but wonder how exactly this was convenient for authors, because she was finding it very inconvenient at the moment.

When Holly suddenly stopped, Jamie nearly did a happy dance only to discover that none of the doors were marked in any way indicating that they were restrooms. "I thought we should have a talk, woman to woman," Holly said as she faced her.

"Now?" Jamie asked, not bothering to hide her exasperation at the situation. "You can't wait until after I use the bathroom?" she asked, moving to step past the woman, more than willing to hunt down a bathroom on her own at this point.

"It's about Nick," Holly said with a worried expression.

Yeah, she just bet it was, Jamie thought, moving once again to step past the infuriating woman when she added, "He's going to get fired."

Now *that* had her attention.

She turned so that she could face the woman. "What are you talking about?"

Holly made a show of worrying her bottom lip as she wrung her hands together. "I really shouldn't say anything, but if I don't I know Nick will get in a lot of trouble."

"What exactly would he get in trouble for?" she asked, already having a pretty good idea where this was going.

"For his relationship with you," the woman said, confirming her suspicions.

"I see," Jamie murmured as she looked around the long hallway again for any signs of a bathroom. It was close to becoming an emergency.

"He's a really nice guy," Holly said on a broken sob. "I really don't want to see him get into any trouble, but if he continues to see you then Rick will fire him."

Jamie kind of doubted that since Nick had hauled her onto his lap in front of Rick and even kissed her a few times in front of the man. Rick looked more amused than anything, which reminded her that she wanted to ask Nick about that.

"Is that all?" she asked when she moved past the woman to take up her search for a bathroom once again.

## A Reclusive Heart: A Hollywood Heart's novel

"He'll get fired!" Holly pleaded, cutting her off once again.

Normally, Jamie would probably just mumble an apology and hear this woman's nonsense out, but she didn't have the patience and according to her bladder she really didn't have the time. Instead of doing what she'd normally do she faced the woman and decided to end this little game.

"Look, I get it. You're into Nick. You've probably been pining after him since the moment you met him and I'm guessing that he hasn't exactly been receptive to your attention," she said, knowing that she'd guessed right when the woman's sympathetic expression turned angry. "When you found out that you were joining this tour you probably thought that you finally had your chance, but unfortunately your timing was off because Nick and I are dating and now-"

"You're not dating!" the woman cut her off. "He's fucking you, that's it. That's all that Nick is good for. He fucks anything and everything with a pair of tits and the only reason he's with you is so that he can get ahead at work!"

"Um, he doesn't work for me," Jamie pointed out.

Holly spat out a cruel laugh. "No, but if you reach Dana Pierce's sales records he'll be able to pretty much do whatever he wants. He's just using you. That's the only reason he's with you," the woman said, destroying a huge piece of her newfound confidence as old insecurities rushed to the surface.

"Look, I'm trying to give you a head's up because once this tour is over he'll be dropping you," Holly said, storming past her to return to the convention.

"Because you want him for yourself," Jamie pointed out almost desperately.

Holly simply shrugged. "It will happen sooner or later. Nick's a man who likes to fuck and he'll eventually come my way." With that she walked off leaving Jamie feeling like she'd just been kicked in the gut and unfortunately still desperate for a bathroom. Instead of turning around and heading back the way she came she continued forward. She wasn't ready to face Nick or Holly's mocking sympathetic looks just yet.

She knew the woman would do and say anything to get Nick for herself, she wasn't an idiot after all. Thanks to Caitlyn, she knew exactly how vicious some women could be, but that didn't stop the words from having their desired effect.

This was only temporary. Nick had told her that. In fact, he'd been very honest about that little fact. When this tour ended then so did their relationship. Before this lovely little talk with Holly she assumed it was because the man couldn't commit, but now she had to wonder if there was possibly a little more to the situation than she'd first realized.

Was it possible that Nick tricked her, okay so he didn't have to trick her, but could this whole thing just be a way to get her to do what he wanted? As she continued her desperate search for a bathroom she had a hard time coming up with any other reason why a man like Nick would even look twice at a woman like her.

It kind of figured that she was in love with a man who had an agenda.

\* \* \* \*

"Here," Nick said as he went to hand over several bars of Swiss chocolate to Jamie.

"No, thank you," she murmured politely, not bothering to look up from her computer as she answered him.

## A Reclusive Heart: A Hollywood Heart's novel

He might be new to this whole relationship business, but he knew the bad signs very well since he used to use them to his own advantage. Since she returned from her long bathroom break she wouldn't look at him, touch him, or speak to him unless it was absolutely necessary. More importantly, she wouldn't let him touch her. Every time he moved closer to her, she found some reason to move away. He knew he hadn't done anything to screw this up and he also knew the source of the problem.

Holly.

She was already packing her bags and heading home. The moment she came back without Jamie he knew she'd done something. It wasn't until his sad little recluse came back and began greeting fans and looking close to tears that he knew that Holly had caused problems for him. When he explained how Jamie was acting and how the woman was beyond incompetent since she couldn't seem to do anything without his help, Rick had demanded that she be sent home.

He knew Rick wasn't pissed because a woman had put him in the doghouse with Jamie, but that the woman had screwed with one of their clients. Their job was to ensure their clients were well represented, handled properly, looked after and were presented in the best possible light to readers. Having an author who looked close to crying every time someone asked for her autograph was the last thing any of them needed on this tour.

When he asked her what the hell she said to upset Jamie, the woman tried to play innocent with him. She even had the audacity to suggest that they talk things over in her room. It wasn't until he sent her packing that she lost that cool facade. She'd glared at him before storming off, but she still didn't tell him what the hell she said to Jamie.

There was no doubt in his mind that whatever she said to Jamie was making Jamie think twice about being with him. An hour ago when he spotted her near the front desk he knew that she was there to get her own room, but he wasn't having that. He convinced her to come upstairs to work and then he'd been at a loss as to what to do. Thankfully he remembered the chocolate he snuck in his bag for her and used it to confirm his suspicions.

She was leaving him, which normally wouldn't be a problem except that he didn't want her to leave him. He wanted her to stay with him and he'd do whatever it took to make that happen.

"What the heck are you doing?" she demanded as he pulled her laptop away from her, yanked her to her feet and threw her over his shoulder.

"Are you going to tell me what's wrong?" he demanded, standing perfectly still. He waited for her to make this easy for him and just tell him what the hell was wrong so that he could fix it. Of course she didn't.

"Nothing's wrong," she said, wiggling in his arms.

"Then I guess I can't put you down," he said, heading for the door.

"Where are we going?"

"To check off another item on your list," he said with a shrug that unfortunately shifted her forward and scared the hell out of her. He shifted her back to where she belonged as he made his way down the dimly lit hallway, relieved that she didn't start screaming for help. Then again, he probably should have known that she wouldn't make a sound. She hated being the center of attention after all.

## A Reclusive Heart: A Hollywood Heart's novel

He took the back elevator all the way down to the first floor and then followed the signs for the pool. When he came to the locked door and peeked through the glass door, he noted that this was also dimly lit and apparently off limits until tomorrow morning. Not that it mattered to him since the manager had given him the master key for the pool area as a favor. He just hoped the manager remembered to make sure that all of his employees stayed clear of this area or he was going to have one embarrassed recluse on his hands.

"Why are we down here?" Jamie asked as he opened the door and made damn sure to lock it behind them.

"Are you going to tell me what's wrong?"

"Nothing's wrong!"

Since she was being so damn difficult he decided to do this the hard way. He walked over to the pool. "Do you by chance have your cell phone on you at the moment?" he asked, walking towards the deep end.

"No, why?" she asked, sounding confused.

"No special reason," he said even he shifted her off his shoulder and tossed her into the pool.

## Chapter 25

"What is wrong with you?" Jamie sputtered once she came to the surface.

"You wouldn't answer my question," Nick said accusingly as he gestured towards her with his leather shoe before he tossed it over his shoulder.

"So that means that you have to throw me in the pool?" she asked in disbelief as she moved to swim to the other side and climb out.

"Damn straight," Nick said, not bothering to try and stop her, she noted as she awkwardly climbed out of the pool and stormed towards the door. She just made it past the corner of the pool when Nick came after her, naked, hard and determined.

For a second she was so stunned by the sight that she couldn't move and it cost her. Before she could make a run for it she found herself thrown back over his shoulder, but this time he was pulling her shoes and socks off.

"What are you doing?" she demanded as he put her down.

In answer he practically ripped her slacks off. When she let out a surprised squeal and went to stop him, she stumbled back and fell in the water, sans pants. This time when she resurfaced, she didn't hesitate in trying to make a run for it, but unfortunately for her, Nick was quicker.

Just as she was moving to climb out of the water he yanked her back in and had her blouse off within seconds. Her bra quickly followed after that. When he went for her panties she somehow managed to shift away and swim, but not before she felt her panties rip and then she was left naked in the pool, a *public* pool where anyone could see, she realized with dismay.

"What is wrong with you?" she practically screeched as she swam to the deep end and moved into the corner to hide.

"I'm just helping you with your list, Jamie," he said calmly as he swam after her.

## A Reclusive Heart: A Hollywood Heart's novel

"You could have asked!"

He shook his head as he continued towards her. "You would have said no," he explained as he stopped in front of her and caged her in. "Now tell me what's going on."

"Nothing," she muttered, looking anywhere but at his beautiful green eyes.

"If nothing is wrong then why are you pulling away from me, Jamie," he asked softly. He gently cupped her chin between his thumb and finger and raised her face until she found herself eye to eye with him.

"I'm not-" she started to lie, but he cut her off.

"Don't lie to me, Jamie," he said, pushing a strand of wet hair out of her face. "I know you're pulling away from me. I just don't know why."

When all she could do was struggle not to cry he pulled her into his arms and held her. "Baby, what's wrong? What did I do?"

She wrapped her arms around his neck and held him tightly. "Look, I know Holly said something to upset you-"

"I don't like her," she mumbled against his damp warm skin.

He chuckled softly as he pressed a kiss against her cheek. "She's not my favorite person at the moment either, baby. Tell me what she said to you that had you so upset that you actually passed up chocolate."

"She said that you were just using me," she admitted softly.

Nick went completely still against her. "How exactly am I using you?" he demanded as he pulled away to look at her.

"To get my cooperation on this tour," she said, hating the way all the tenderness in his expression disappeared.

"And you believed her?" he asked, not bothering to hide his disgust as he moved away from her.

## R.L. Mathewson

"Why wouldn't I?" she asked, choking on a sob.

"I don't need to sleep with a woman to get her to do what I want, Jamie, especially a pushover like you," he said, making her wince. "We both know that it wouldn't take much to get you to do what I want so why the hell would I have to resort to sleeping with you to get your cooperation?"

She opened her mouth to argue, but realized that there was nothing to say. He was absolutely right. Even when she was mad at him before he promised to help her with her list she would have probably backed off complaining to Rick with just the right amount of persuasion. It never took much to make her bend to someone's will and everyone knew it.

"I'm pathetic," she muttered, not realizing just how pathetic she really was until that moment. It was one thing to believe that everyone else realized they could walk all over her, but quite another to actually have it thrown in her face. She turned away from him and moved to climb out when he wrapped an arm around her and pulled her back against his chest as he reached out and placed his other hand on edge of the pool to help keep them afloat.

"You're not pathetic, Jamie. You just have a problem with standing up for yourself," he explained, pressing a kiss against her earlobe.

"How exactly is that not pathetic?" she asked, sniffling.

"You're not pathetic, Jamie, and you sure as hell aren't the same woman I found crawling on the floor of the men's room," he said, chuckling softly.

She cringed at the memory. "I thought it was the woman's room," she explained needlessly.

"So I gathered. The point is that you've come a long way in a very short time, Jamie."

"So you don't think I'm a pushover anymore?" she asked, too eager to hide it.

## A Reclusive Heart: A Hollywood Heart's novel

"Let's just say that you're doing a lot better about standing up for yourself and for those times that you're not able to you have me," he said, pressing a kiss to her neck.

"But I don't," she said, sounding sad even to her own ears.

"What the hell are you talking about?" he asked tightly as he turned her around and gently placed her against the wall where she could hold herself up by propping her elbows up on the side of the pool.

He placed his hands near hers and he closed the distance once again. "I need you to help me out, baby, and tell me what else she said that upset you," he said when she didn't answer him.

She sighed warily as she reached out with one hand and ran her fingers through his damp hair, loving the way it felt between her fingers. "I'm not sure how she knew-,"

"Knew what?" he asked, interrupting her.

As she toyed with a strand of his hair she answered, "That this was going to end when the tour was over."

"And that's why you thought I'd whore myself out to keep you under my thumb?" he asked casually, but there was no missing the hurt in his tone.

She released the strand of hair she'd been playing with to run her fingers over the slight stubble covering his jaw. "Is that what your mother did?" she asked, already having figured it out from the comment he made about losing his virginity.

For a moment he didn't say anything as he looked away from her. She thought that maybe she'd gone too far and opened her mouth to apologize when he cut her off.

"My mother was sixteen when she had me. She was a typical teenage runaway. She got mixed up in drugs and sex and had parents who didn't look too favorably on her behavior. She decided that she didn't need them and took off for California where she thought she was going to be a movie star," he said, ramming his fingers through his hair as he looked back at her.

"She got mixed up with the wrong kind of people very early on. When she discovered that she was pregnant, she and about five friends who were also hookers rented a three bedroom apartment. They set up two of the rooms to work out of and shared the third room. When I came along the initial plan had been to give me away, but it was Christmas and most of them were young kids and thought that my birth was a sign of good times to come so they named me Nicholas," he said with a mocking smile.

Her heart broke for him as he continued. "They set my room up in the walk in closet off their room and whenever there was a John in the house they took turns locking themselves up with me until the John left. Needless to say with six hookers in one house I spent a lot of time in that closet. When I was about four they decided I was old enough to watch out for myself."

"You don't have to tell me about this if you don't want to, Nick," she whispered as she traced his strong jaw.

"It's fine, baby," he said, leaning in to press a kiss against her forehead. "I didn't think much about the women living there walking around naked or blowing some guy on the couch while I watched my cartoons. It wasn't until I started school and noticed that the other kids' mothers didn't behave like mine."

"As much as I hated living there," he said tightly as his hands clenched into fists, "and how I fucking hated it, I couldn't leave. I always thought, hoped really, that my mother would wake up one day and decide to be a mother to me like the other children had, but she never changed and when I was old enough I walked away and started my own life and never looked back."

"I'm sorry, Nick," she said, not knowing what else to say.

## A Reclusive Heart: A Hollywood Heart's novel

"Don't be," he said, forcing a smile, "I'm over it."

She didn't think that he was. In fact, she was pretty sure that the reason that he worked so hard was to put distance between himself and his past. She could relate to that. She didn't want people knowing that she was a pushover or how pathetic she used to be. All she wanted was a chance to live her life without anyone trying to keep her down.

He looked so sad at that moment and she wanted to make it better for him, to let him know without words that he was loved. She leaned forward and brushed her lips against his. At first he didn't move and she feared that perhaps Holly was right, but then with a sigh he moved his lips against hers.

"I don't want you to worry about anything, Jamie. I'm going to take care of you," he promised as he gave her the sweetest kiss of her life.

As good as it sounded she knew that he wouldn't be able to keep his word. As soon as the tour was over he was going to break her heart and she would be left with unimaginable pain, but she refused to focus on that. Right now she was in his arms and he was hers. She didn't want to waste a second of their time together since she already knew that it wouldn't last.

Soon the kiss turned hungry and they couldn't stop running their hands over each other. There was really nothing better than being in Nick's arms, she thought as she ran her hands over his wide shoulders and down his back, enjoying the feel of hard muscle tightening beneath her touch.

"Up you go, baby," Nick said huskily against her mouth as he pressed one last kiss against her lips.

When he went to raise her out of the water she stopped him with a simple shake of her head. Frowning, he put her back in the water. He opened his mouth, probably to ask her what was wrong, when she gestured for him to get his butt out of the water. With an amused smile and a quick kiss he did just that. Once he was sitting on the edge she realized something very important.

She was kind of short.

Nick must have realized the problem because he lowered himself off the edge until his large erection was at eye level with her and although that was a pretty impressive sight she couldn't seem to take her eyes off the muscles flexing in his arms and chest as he held himself up. When she caught his amused smile she forced herself to focus. She leaned in and pressed a kiss to his hip.

She'd only done this a few times, but it was easily one of her favorite things to do for him. She knew that she probably wasn't very good at this yet, but she was more than willing to keep trying. As she kissed and nibbled her way to the neatly trimmed patch of hair surrounding the root of the large erection that demanded her attention she couldn't help but wonder what it would be like to take him to completion in her mouth. Whenever she thought he was close he always pulled away, but maybe now she'd get her chance, at least she hoped she would.

When she came to his erection she continued to take her time pressing teasing kisses against the hot skin until she couldn't resist gliding her tongue over it. His low groan encouraged her to do it again. This time she took her time tracing her tongue over the thick vein that ran along the underside of his thick erection. She flicked her tongue over the tip, licking away the excitement there before she took just the very tip into her mouth and suckled on it while she slowly traced the tiny slit with her tongue.

"Aw, fuck," Nick groaned when she took him in hand and slowly stroked him. The movement pushed more of his erection into her mouth, but not enough. She looked up and met his hungry gaze as she moved forward and took more of him in her mouth. He sucked in a breath as he moved to pull away from her, but she refused to let him go, not when she had him where she wanted him.

"I need to be inside of you," he ground out between clenched teeth as he tried to pull away from her.

## A Reclusive Heart: A Hollywood Heart's novel

Never pausing in her slow strokes, she pulled her mouth away long enough to point out, "You are inside of me," before taking him back into her mouth and doubled her efforts.

He was panting hard and she couldn't help but love the sound of a strong man like Nick losing control because of her. It wasn't long before he was slowly thrusting in and out of her mouth. When he became impossibly thicker in her mouth and let out a sexy growl she knew that she had him. It was confirmed seconds later when he shouted her name and he released that salty sweet treat that she was beginning to love.

As he pulled away she pressed one last kiss to the tip of the soft velvety head and couldn't help but smile when he shivered. Her smile quickly disappeared when she found herself suddenly yanked out of the water and in his arms.

Without a word, he moved back on the tiled floor until only his legs were in the water and laid back. Just as she was about to ask him what he was doing, she found herself moved up his body and straddling his face. She wasn't exactly sure what was going on until she felt the first swipe of his tongue and then she decided that she simply didn't care as long as he did that again.

When he gripped her bottom and encouraged her to move she did, hesitantly. She wasn't really sure what to do, but when he slid his tongue inside of her, she decided that she'd figure it out later. Her hands as if they had a mind of their own slid up her damp stomach and over her breasts, pretending that they were his hands.

His grip tightened on her bottom as his tongue went wild inside of her. She pinched her nipples the way he did and she was surprised at how good it felt. She'd never really touched or explored herself, too shy to even try that, but right now it felt too good to stop. As she continued to gently squeeze and caress her left breast she slid her trembling hand down her stomach.

The few times she'd attempted to touch herself down there had never felt good. But the way he was licking inside of her was making the little nub between her legs swell up almost painfully. It was practically begging for attention and when her fingertips brushed up against it, she couldn't hold back the gasp of pleasure that slid through her.

She watched as his eyes closed to half mast as he watched her touch herself. He looked like he was in ecstasy as he continued to lick her. It felt so good. She never thought that anything could feel this wonderful. She loved when he touched her, craved it in fact, but the way he was giving her free reign to enjoy him made every little touch and sensation so much more powerful.

All too soon she was throwing her head back as she cried, screamed really, his name. She was still screaming his name when she found herself suddenly lifted off his mouth and pressed down onto his newly restored erection. He sat up and wrapped his arms around her as he took her mouth in a hungry kiss that quickly ignited her need for him again.

Her fingers tangled in his hair as she returned the hungry almost brutal kiss as they ground their lower bodies together. It wasn't long before she was panting and struggling to hold back, but he wouldn't allow it. He used his hold on her to slam her down hard on his rock hard shaft as he thrust forward. It was too much, too soon and she lost the battle. She screamed his name, barely aware that he was chanting hers almost reverently.

When the last tremor of pleasure left her body she felt him smiling against her mouth and it wasn't until that moment that she realized that she was smiling as well.

He pressed a kiss against her mouth before he lowered them back into the pool. "Now, let's see if we can do that in the pool this time so that we can check it off your list," he suggested as his hand slid between her legs.

## Chapter 26

"Is it time to get up?" Jamie mumbled as she snuggled into the covers.

"No, not yet, baby. Go back to sleep," he said, pressing a light kiss against her lips.

She followed his lips as he pulled away and he couldn't help but chuckle. It seemed that he'd created a little addict. That thought was quickly confirmed when she sleepily mumbled, "Is it time for more sex? I want sex."

"I can tell," he said, smiling as she started to drift off again. For a moment he sat there watching her sleep, perfectly content just to be near her. She is so beautiful, he thought as he reached over and swept her hair away from her face. She sighed softly in her sleep, tempting him to crawl back in bed with her and hold her, but he had work to do.

He was exhausted, he thought with a smile as he stumbled his way towards the bathroom. They'd made love twice in the pool and then once more when they made it back to their room. It was funny that with Jamie he thought of it as making love and not just fucking or sex. It didn't matter how hard or hot the sex was, it was making love in his mind. Thinking of it in any other way didn't sit well with him.

Jamie was........

Special.

She wasn't like any of the women he'd been with before. She was better, pure, sweet, kind and made him happy. He wanted to take care of her, to be there for her and it didn't matter that those thoughts should scare the hell out of him, but he couldn't stop wanting them.

He wasn't right for her and would never be good enough for her, he reminded himself and he'd never hated himself more than he did at that moment. He was the bastard son of a whore and completely incapable of being what she needed him to be. He didn't trust himself not to hurt her. How could he?

What the hell did he know about making a woman happy? He had absolutely no idea how to make a woman happy in the long term or to even make a relationship work. Growing up the way that he did, he saw the "happily married" men around town one day with their wives and kids and the next zipping up as they left the bedrooms of his mother and "aunts."

The only decent relationships that he'd seen over the years was Rick and his wife and of course Edward and Dana and there was no way in hell that he was going to kid himself and say that he could have a relationship like those two. Even after five years it was more than obvious that the two of them were more in love now than when they first got married.

He knew from the times that he went with Edward to catch a game or grab a drink that the man wasn't playing around. He wouldn't so much as look at another woman and whenever someone mentioned Dana his expression said it all. There would never be another woman for him but Dana. Dana would never have to worry about Edward coming home late or smelling like another woman, which was good because if he ever hurt her, Nick would beat the shit out of him.

Jamie deserved to have a man like Edward by her side and as much as it pained him to admit this, he wasn't that man. He couldn't trust himself not to revert to his old ways when things got tough or he got bored. It would kill him to hurt her. He'd let things die out between them and the moment it did, he would step back, wish her luck and move on.

Shoving away the rather depressing thoughts, he took a quick shower. Twenty minutes later he was stepping out of the bathroom, wrapping a towel around his waist when something on the floor in front of the door caught his eye. He didn't give the large white envelope much thought as he picked it up, figuring that it was just promotional paperwork that one of the venders had the front desk slip under his door. When he turned the envelope over he felt his heart drop to his stomach.

*YOU CAN'T HIDE*

## A Reclusive Heart: A Hollywood Heart's novel

The words were written in big bold black letters and he didn't need to open it to know who it was for. Cursing under his breath, he quickly pulled on a pair of pants, grabbed his key card and left the room, ready to kill someone. When he didn't find anyone in the hallway he ran and checked the stairwell at the end of each side of the building, hoping to find someone lurking in the shadows, but he didn't.

The son of a bitch hell-bent on tormenting his little recluse had been close, too damn close and he hadn't been able to do a damn thing to keep the sick bastard away. Realizing that he'd left his little recluse all alone when the sick fuck was nearby had him rushing back to his room.

Once inside he had to make sure that she was okay. He found her curled up on her side and fast asleep. He pulled the covers up over her shoulders and pressed a kiss to her cheek. He watched her for another minute before he grabbed his cell phone, double checked the lock on the door and shut himself in the bathroom. Praying that it was just a coincidence and some kid's sick idea of a joke, he carefully opened the envelope, trying not to fuck up any evidence just in case he needed to call the police.

What he found inside had him reaching for his phone and making that call.

\* \* \* \*

"I don't care who you are, you are not watching those DVD's without my presence!" Jamie snapped, surprising the heck out of herself and judging by the curious look Nick shot her, him as well.

For over two hours, she'd waited patiently in an interrogation room while Nick paced like a caged animal. The only thing they were told when they were shown into the room was that the detective needed to make some calls to the police department back home to verify their story. Being forced to wait after reading and re-reading that letter had been one of the worst experiences of her life.

Even though the Detective had moved them to a decent sized office, she still couldn't' shake the feeling that someone was watching her. When she'd opened the death threats the other day at the office she consoled herself with the fact that this happened to a lot of people in the spotlight and that it was no big deal. The truth was she'd been too freaked out to actually give it the proper attention it deserved. She'd hoped that if she ignored it that it would go away. She'd been wrong. Not only had it not gone away, but it had followed her to Texas.

"Miss Harris, perhaps it would be best if you allowed us to view the video first," Detective Mathers, a middle aged man with a friendly smile, said gently.

As much as she would love to leave and pretend that this never happened, she couldn't. She took a steadying breath as she shook her head. "No, I'm staying. I want to know what's on those discs," she said firmly.

Nick's hand tightened around hers as he said, "I'm staying as well."

With a resigned sigh, the detective picked up the disc marked, "Jamie Harris the whore" and placed it into the computer drive. He typed something and seconds later an image of the pool from the hotel popped up on the flat screen television mounted on the wall in front of them. Her breath caught in her throat as she watched Nick storm into the picture with her over his shoulder.

"Oh no," she mumbled weakly.

"Stop the movie," Nick demanded, getting to his feet, but thankfully keeping hold of her hand.

"Is there a problem, Mr. Quinn?" Detective Mathers asked as he paused the movie.

Nick gestured to the other three men and the woman in the office. "I really think it would be best if we cleared the room for this."

## A Reclusive Heart: A Hollywood Heart's novel

"That's fine, Mr. Quinn, but please realize that this video may have to be viewed by other officers at a later time," the detective explained as he gestured for the officers to leave the room.

"That's fine, but I don't think they need to be here this time," Nick said with a nod of thanks as he sat back down and put his arm around her.

Once the door was shut the Detective started the movie.

"*Why are we down here?*" the recorded version of her asked as Nick double checked the lock.

"*Are you going to tell me what's wrong?*" Nick asked as he moved towards the pool and she felt the air in her lungs freeze as the camera moved with the action.

Someone had been in the pool room with them last night. Thanks to the dimly lit area, changing rooms and equipment there apparently had been plenty of places to hide.

"*Nothing's wrong!*"

"*Do you by chance have your cell phone on you at the moment?*" Nick asked as he walked towards the deep end of the pool.

"*No, why?*" she asked, sounding confused.

"*No special reason,*" he said before he tossed her into the pool.

Knowing exactly what was coming, Jamie dropped her face into her hands and listened as the entire event that occurred in the pool area played out.

When it was done she almost fell out of her chair in relief. That is until Nick practically jumped to his feet and started flipping out. Wondering what had him mad, well besides the obvious, she looked up and nearly cried as she read the words on the screen.

**You'll be dead within the month, but before that happens I thought the world should know that the famous J.L. Lewis is nothing but a whore.**

**By 10:00 AM this video and the lovely audio I recorded of your bedroom activities will have already hit the internet.**

**Enjoy your fifteen minutes of fame, Bitch.**

"Play the audio tape," Nick said tightly as he reached out and pulled her into his arms.

Without a word the detective carefully switched out the DVD and within seconds an audio recording of what happened once they reached their room last night began to play.

"*You're not tired, huh?*" Nick's voice asked teasingly.

"*Not for you, Nick,*" she heard herself answer in a husky voice that surprised her.

"*What if I told you that I wanted to finish what we started this morning, hmm? Would you get back on your hands and knees for me, Jamie?*"

When Nick's deep chuckle echoed throughout the office she squeezed her eyes shut and pressed her face against Nick's chest, dreading what came next.

"*That easy, huh? Tell me, baby, are you wet for me?*"

"*Why don't you come check?*"

"Can we can skip to the end to see if whoever the hell did this left another message?" Nick suddenly asked, thankfully cutting off what came next.

A moment of silence followed before the sound of grunting and cries of pleasure echoed throughout the room. She felt her cheeks burn as it played out. Once it was done she nearly sagged with relief. It didn't take long before she realized that there was no message.

## A Reclusive Heart: A Hollywood Heart's novel

"Can we check to see if they've been released online yet?" Nick asked, giving her a comforting squeeze.

"Sure," she heard the Detective say, but refused to leave the safety of Nick's chest and face the man. That would pretty much be impossible now that he'd watched a video of her having sex.

"Son of a bitch," Nick bit out.

"It's on the internet, isn't it?" she asked, biting her bottom lip anxiously.

"Yes."

A video and audio file of her having sex with Nick was now on the internet. People all over the world could watch and listen to her having sex and there was nothing that she could do to stop it. She knew the police could try and have the files pulled off, but they'd just pop up somewhere else. Worse yet, whoever did this had followed through with the threat, which meant that they probably had every intention of following through with the second threat.

Within a month someone was going to try to kill her, she realized with something close to panic. The thought absolutely terrified her, but surprisingly she wasn't worried about herself, she realized. She was worried about Nick. If he was around, he could get caught in the crossfire and she didn't want to see him hurt. It would destroy her if anything happened to him because of her.

She wanted him safe and the only way to guarantee that was to keep as far away from him as possible. There was only one way she knew how to do that and it would have the added benefit of taking her out of the limelight and giving her a chance to figure out who she'd upset so much that they were willing to kill her over it.

"Nick?" she said, pulling back just far enough to look up at him.

"Yes?" he said, looking down at her with so much tenderness that she almost cried.

"I'm done with the tour," she announced, knowing that it meant they were over, but not caring one bit. Well, she did, but she was more concerned about getting him to safety and that meant taking away every reason he had for being near her.

"That goes without saying, Jamie," he said on a sigh as he leaned down and pressed a kiss to forehead as she tried to hold back her hurt feelings.

That was it? Seriously? After all they went through he was going to let her walk away that easily? Then again there did appear to be a psycho on her tail so maybe it was for the best that he was giving her up so easily.

Knowing that it was for the best she didn't argue with him. She decided to hold back the tears until she got to her new place and could drown her sorrows in chocolate. As long as Nick was safe she could handle anything, even having her heart broken by the big jerk.

## Chapter 27

"Are you still ignoring me?" he asked, throwing Jamie a sideways glance as he pulled to a stop at a four-way intersection.

"I'm not ignoring you, Nick. I'm just trying to get this file edited before tomorrow," she said, not bothering to look up from the computer balanced on her knees. Her words and tone were polite, but they felt all wrong. He might be new to relationships, but it didn't exactly take a genius to figure out what was wrong with his little recluse.

She was pissed and for good reason. He'd screwed up and hadn't protected her. Now thanks to him, someone managed to invade a very private moment and made it public. As he pulled onto his street he idly wondered how Edward handled it after it happened to him and Dana. If anyone knew how to handle a bullshit situation like this it would be Edward and Dana.

"Okay, do you want to grab some food?" he asked, slowing down before he reached his house.

"If it's okay with you, I'd rather just call it a night and get settled in," she said, not bothering to look up from her computer.

"That's fine," he said, deciding that they'd just order in tonight. Tomorrow he'd have plenty of time to go food shopping since he most likely just lost his job today.

It was one thing to have a discrete relationship with one of his clients, but quite another to get caught having sex with her and have the video plastered all over the internet. There was also the fact that he had about thirty conventions and interviews to cancel tomorrow, which wouldn't make Rerum Publishing House very popular. It was a tossup which one they'd take issue with, but he was willing to bet his, thankfully large, bank account on being canned for the video.

"Is this it?" Jamie asked, looking up from her computer for the first time in hours.

"Yes," he said, throwing the car into park and shutting off the engine.

Jamie sighed as she shut down her computer. "Thank you for the ride, Nick. I really appreciate it, but you don't have to stick around. If you could just give me the key I think I'll be all set," she said, sliding her computer into her bag as she shifted nervously next to him.

"You don't want me to stick around?" he asked slowly, starting to have a good idea where this was going.

"I, um," she cleared her throat uncomfortably as she shifted again, "think that might be for the best."

Holy shit, she was breaking up with him, he thought with a humorless chuckle. "So now that the tour is over, you want to end this, is that right?" he asked, cocking his head to the side to study her as she struggled to answer. If he hadn't been looking at her, he probably would have missed the way her little chin quivered or the way her eyes filled with tears.

She looked away from him as she nodded. "The tour's over and we said this would end along with the tour," she said softly, giving him a helpless shrug.

"I see," he said evenly as he climbed out of his car and slammed the door shut, violently rocking the car. He couldn't fucking believe this. He was giving up his job and his way of life for this woman and she was giving him the brush off? Not fucking happening.

He grabbed most of their things from the trunk before slamming it shut and stalking towards the bottom level of his three story house. He unlocked the door and quickly disarmed the alarm. His little recluse reluctantly followed and when she looked around the garage filled with his black Mustang and his motorcycles her brows creased in confusion.

"This way," he said, shutting the door and resetting the alarm once again before walking past his bikes to the door that led to the second level of his home.

## A Reclusive Heart: A Hollywood Heart's novel

He dumped their things on one of the leather couches as he walked through the living room and headed towards the kitchen section of the large open area. He grabbed an ice cold beer out of the fridge, popped the top and leaned back as he watched his little recluse stop in the middle of the living room and slowly look around.

"Am I renting someone's house while they're away?" she asked, sounding so damn hopeful.

"Nope," he said, letting the word pop as he watched her.

"This is your house?" she asked, looking anywhere but at him.

"Mmmhmm," he said, taking a sip of his beer.

"Is there perhaps a chance that we're merely stopping here on the way to my new place?"

"Not a chance in hell," he said, watching her reaction.

"Oh," she said, her shoulders drooping a bit as she opened her mouth to say something but nothing came out.

"Awkward, huh?"

"You could say that," she mumbled.

"We had to get your stuff out of there quickly. We stored your stuff here and planned to have a place set up for you by the time you returned, but we had to cut the tour short. We don't have a place set up for you yet," he explained before taking another sip of his beer, his eyes never leaving her.

"Oh," she said weakly.

"I just happen to live alone and have plenty of room so I thought I'd let my girlfriend stay with me, but it seems that she just dumped my ass not even ten minutes ago so now we're stuck in a very awkward situation," he said, placing his beer on the counter before he crossed his arms over his chest and glared at her.

"Is there any chance that you can give me a ride to my car wherever it is so that I can find a hotel for the night?" she asked.

He shook his head as he said, "No way in hell. You're staying here until this asshole is caught."

"I-I c-can take care of myself!" she sputtered, but he wasn't buying it.

"No," he simply said, pushing away from the counter and walked into the living room.

"What the heck do you mean 'no'?" she demanded, following after him as he scooped up her bags and headed down the hall and up the second flight of stairs. He didn't have to look back to know that she was following him. He paused by the first guest room, but it wouldn't do. He walked down the hall and shoved open the door to the master bedroom and set her things down. As he stood up, he spotted her boxed belongings piled in the corner and nearly groaned. Leave it to Rick to take the initiative and screw him over.

"You didn't answer me," she pointed out as she joined him in the room.

"And I'm not going to. You're staying here and that's final."

"That's not your decision," she snapped, coming up behind him.

"Yes, it is," he said more calmly than he felt as he headed for the door. "This is your room while you stay. Make yourself comfortable."

"I'm not staying," she said, picking up her bags and nearly toppling over under the weight.

"Yes, you are, Jamie. If you try to leave I'll just drag your cute little ass right back here."

"That's kidnapping!"

## A Reclusive Heart: A Hollywood Heart's novel

"Call it whatever you want, Jamie, but you're not going anywhere right now," he said, heading for the door only to have his little recluse drop everything and rush to cut him off.

When he moved to step past her, she held up her hands in a staying motion. "Look, I appreciate your concern. I really do, but I can't stay here. I just can't. So if you could just tell me where my car is, I can call a taxi and make some arrangements to have my things removed and then I'll never bother you again."

"No," he said firmly, moving again to walk past her, but the damn woman wasn't having it. It actually surprised him that she wasn't backing down.

"I really need to leave, Nick. Please just-"

Something in him snapped. While he couldn't get enough of her, she wanted nothing to do with him. Worse, she couldn't get away from him fast enough. He moved forward, crowding her until she had no choice but to back up. When her back hit the wall he caged her in by slapping his palms against the wall as he leaned into her.

"Why?"

"Why what?" she asked, licking her lips nervously as she glanced towards her right and probably what she deemed as freedom.

"Why the hell are you so eager to get away from me, Jamie? Hmm? Tell me exactly what I did to set this off," he demanded, leaning in to run his nose over her neck, inhaling her sweet scent.

"You didn't do anything, Nick. It was just time. Please just let me go," she said, putting her hands on his shoulders, moving to push him away, but instead she clutched almost desperately to him.

"Why the hell are you doing this to me?" he whispered hoarsely as his hands clenched tightly into fists.

"I'm not doing anything to you. I-"

"Bullshit!" he snapped, pulling back slightly and slamming his fists against the wall, damaging the drywall and scaring the hell out of his little recluse.

"I'm not doing anything to you!"

"Yes, you are!" he snapped, glaring down at her.

"What exactly am I doing to you? You're the one who decided that this wasn't going to continue past the tour. It ended early and so did we. I accepted it so why can't you?"

"Because I fucking love you!" he shouted.

As soon as the words were out he wanted to take them back. He opened his mouth to do just that, but he realized that he couldn't. He loved her. He was head over heels in love with this woman and he knew it was pointless to deny it. Where other women had failed, his little recluse had not only succeeded in bringing him to his knees, but once he was down she dropped kicked him in the balls for good measure.

This hurt so fucking bad, he thought as he struggled for control. She didn't love him, didn't want him. She wasn't the pathetic one, he was. He'd only loved two women in his life and both of them could have cared less, first his mother and now Jamie.

He didn't want to love her. A long time ago he closed his heart off and it should have damn well stayed closed. She had no fucking business making him fall in love with her, he thought bitterly as he reached for her and how fucked up was that? He knew that she didn't love him, but he couldn't help but hope, pray that she cared at least a little bit for him to take the edge off the tightness in his chest.

"No, you don't!" she cried, shoving him away.

"Yes, I do!" he snapped back, reaching for her again only to have her weakly slap his hands away.

## A Reclusive Heart: A Hollywood Heart's novel

"You can't!"

"Why the hell not?" he demanded.

"Because you'll get yourself killed, you jackass!" she snapped back and not even a second later she slapped both of her hands against her mouth as her eyes widened in surprise at what she probably thought was profanity since he noticed that she didn't swear or the fact that she'd just said a little too much.

"What did you just say?" he asked, stepping in front of her as she tried to head back down the hall and the hell away from him.

"Nothing," she mumbled, trying to get past him, but he refused to move.

"It didn't sound like nothing to me, Jamie. What did you say?" he asked, not allowing himself to hope that maybe, just maybe she cared about him too.

"Just let me go, Nick. *Please!*"

Let her go? There was no way in hell that he was going to let that happen. Not now. Not when there was a possibility that for once, someone loved him back. She folded her arms over her chest defensively and turned away from him, he stepped up behind her, careful not to touch her in any way.

"Tell me that you don't care about me, Jamie, and you can go," he said softly.

"I don't!" she cried, but he didn't believe her.

"You're lying," he said tightly, keeping his voice low and even as he resisted the urge to take her into his arms and shake some sense into her.

"No, I'm not, Nick. We're over. I don't care about you and I never want to see you again," she said, her voice breaking as she struggled not to cry.

"Look me in the eye and say that," he said, praying like hell that he wasn't wrong. He couldn't be wrong, not about her. She was his little recluse, his sweet, loving Jamie and he knew that she cared about him.

Slowly, so damn slowly that he thought his heart was going to burst in two, she turned around. When she looked up at him and didn't quite meet his eyes he had his answer.

"I don't love you, Nick. Please just let me go," she said, keeping her eyes averted to the right, her chin trembling and her body shaking as she struggled to hold back the sobs that he knew were threatening to escape.

"You're a liar," he said softly as he reached over and gently cupped her face in his hands.

"No, I'm not!" she cried out as tears began to stream down her face. She tried to step away from him, but he wouldn't allow it. He was done playing this game and wanted to know why she was so damn willing to break his heart.

"Look me in the eye, Jamie, and tell me that you don't love me," he demanded softly. He carefully wiped her tears away with the pads of his thumbs.

"I did," she mumbled, sounding miserable.

"No, you didn't, baby. Look me right in the eye and tell me that you don't love me and I will let you go, Jamie," he promised, knowing he would, but that it would probably kill him.

Beautiful, glimmering, caramel eyes looked up and locked on his. He watched as she worked her mouth soundlessly for several minutes before finally closing her mouth and looking away from him in defeat.

"If you can't tell me that you don't love me, then why don't you tell me why you're willing to lie to me, Jamie?" he suggested, pressing a kiss to her forehead. "Tell me why you're willing to break my heart," he whispered against her forehead.

## A Reclusive Heart: A Hollywood Heart's novel

Instead of answering him, she shook her head, but thankfully didn't try to step away from him. He dropped his hands from her face and without a word swept her up into his arms and carried her down the hallway. When she still didn't speak he started to become a little nervous. He sat down on the leather loveseat and adjusted her in his arms until she was straddling his lap. Once he was done he took both of her cool hands into his and pressed a kiss to each palm.

"Are you upset about the video?" he asked, feeling like an idiot. Of course she was up about the video, but he didn't know if that was the reason that she was pulling away. "If I had known, I-"

"It's not the video," she whispered.

"Then what is it?"

"I shouldn't be around you."

"Why? Because I'm a bad influence?" he asked teasingly, hoping to get her to smile. When her lips twitched he damn near sighed in relief.

"Because of the threat. If you're around me you might get hurt."

"And you don't want me to get hurt?" he guessed.

She shook her head.

"Because you love me?"

"Maybe," she mumbled, pulling her hands away so that she could play with one of the buttons on his shirt.

"Maybe?" he repeated, trying not to glare at the stubborn woman as he continued. "You thought by pushing me away that you were protecting me."

"If you're not around me then you won't be hurt," she said firmly as she looked up and met his eyes.

"Uh huh," he said, wondering if he should just spank her ass now or cut off her chocolate supply. It was his job to protect her and he really didn't appreciate her interference. It was touching that she cared about him enough to protect him, but really the woman needed to let him do his damn job, he decided with a shrug as he rearranged her on his lap until she was lying across his knees.

## Chapter 28

"Oh, no you don't," Nick said, swiping the large coffee roll with extra icing out of her hand.

"But I need that!" She made a mad grab for it, but Nick simply ignored her as he put it back in the white bakery box and dropped the box in the top drawer of the tall black filing cabinet near his desk. When he closed the drawer and locked it she considered kicking him in the shin and stealing the key out of his hand.

"No, you don't," he murmured as he pulled her into his arms and pressed a soft kiss against her lips. "You've already met your sugar quota this morning," he explained before taking her hand and pulling her towards the door.

"Hey! You don't get to set my sugar quota," she muttered pathetically as she threw a look of longing over her shoulder at the filing cabinet.

"I do when I wake up at three in the morning to discover a mound of empty candy bar wrappers-"

"It wasn't a mound," she muttered, ducking her head in embarrassment the second he pulled her into the busy hallway.

He of course ignored her denial and kept going. "-the bedroom light on and you were tearing through your boxes and bags in search of your next fix," he said, sounding amused, but she really couldn't tell since he was looking ahead and of course she was still staring at the ground.

"I was hungry," she pointed out only partially lying. She had been hungry since they didn't get a chance to eat last night. After he spanked her, and she still couldn't believe the big jerk did that or more importantly her reaction to it, he'd taken her in what seemed like every room and every position he could think of as if he were trying to prove something. The only thing he managed to prove was that the man was a god in bed, or rather on the couch, stairs, against the wall, shower, etc.

When he'd finally had enough around one this morning and passed out she'd been left exhausted, but too worried to fall asleep. She was worried about his job and she knew that it was in jeopardy even though he tried to play it off like it was nothing to worry about. She was also worried that the stubborn man was going to get himself killed by staying around her.

The few times that she got an opportunity to try and explain that he needed to put some space between them had ended with a murderous glare and her screaming his name until she thought her head would explode. The man was too stubborn to think clearly. She knew that he thought he was in love with her, but she also noticed that he hadn't spoken a word about the future. There was no point in asking if there was a future when she knew that there wouldn't be. He'd told her that he couldn't give her a future and she knew that his telling her that he loved her hadn't changed that.

As much as it hurt, it was also a bit of a relief, because that meant that she still had a chance to explain things and help him see that he really shouldn't be taking any chances by being around her. She knew that he felt protective of her and that was sweet, but she really could take care of herself and besides, the police were looking into it. Plus, she was planning on being careful, really careful so there really was nothing to worry about.

After a moment, she realized that the usually busy office that made her nervous with its constant "Go, go, go" mentality was eerily quiet. Had everyone left? she wondered as she chanced a peek and immediately wished that she hadn't. The normally busy office was still overflowing with people, but instead of rushing off here and there like they normally did, they were all standing around, staring at her and Nick.

## A Reclusive Heart: A Hollywood Heart's novel

Her cheeks burned as she registered looks of disgust from most of the women and a few leering looks from some of the men. Of course they'd seen the video, she realized, feeling like an idiot. Everyone on earth probably saw that video by now and thanks to that little performance they probably thought that she was a slut. That thought was confirmed by a few gestures and soft chuckles directed her way. What she wouldn't give to be able to make a run for it at that moment.

Nick suddenly stopped, causing her to slam into his back, but he barely noticed as he leveled a scowl on the onlookers. "Is there a problem?" he asked calmly, but there was no hiding the fury in his tone or his challenging stance as he silently dared anyone to say something. If she hadn't been so stressed or worried about Nick at the moment, the way they jumped back into whatever it was that they had been doing before they spotted her and Nick would have made her smile. As it was it barely took the edge off of her humiliation.

He gave her hand a gentle squeeze as he once again headed down the now thankfully busy hall towards the boardrooms. When he pulled her through the open doorway of the room she recognized as the one they held their morning meeting in, she became very nervous. If two minutes of being stared at by her co-workers, the same co-workers she had a legal contract forcing her to face when she was required to come to the office, was unsettling she doubted that an hour or more under the same scrutiny would do anything to ease her nerves.

"Dana? What the hell are you doing here?" Nick asked, drawing her attention to the beautiful woman sitting at the large table. She wasn't too surprised when she spotted Edward Pierce sitting to her right, holding her hand.

Jamie watched as the beautiful woman shrugged. "I decided to attend this meeting since it affects my next book," Dana explained, sending her a discrete wink that had her chewing her bottom lip nervously as she looked around the room to find a very somber Rick sitting at the table along with several men and women she was pretty sure that she didn't know, but was pretty sure judging by the looks they were sending Dana and Edward that they were not happy with the power couple's presence.

"Please have a seat," Rick said, giving them a forced smile as he gestured for them to sit across from Dana and Edward.

As much as she would love to run away she forced herself to walk the ten feet and sit down. She needed to do this for Nick. She needed to help save his job and do whatever she could to keep him safe. The scent of cheap perfume hit her nose a few seconds before she heard the sounds of heels clipping against the floor. When she looked up she wasn't too surprised to see Holly, whom she kind of thought had been fired, walk into the room, looking smug.

Jamie watched as the woman walked around the table and took a seat near an older gentleman, who didn't look pleased with her sitting next to him. Not that she could blame the man. Even from here the perfume was starting to sting her nose and eyes.

"Why don't we begin?" Nick asked pleasantly as he entwined their fingers and faced off against the men and women that were probably seconds away from firing him.

If, no there weren't really any *ifs*, when they fired him she fully planned on walking out with him. The only problem she had would be finding a lawyer good enough to get her out of the iron clad contract that she'd signed. She didn't like the idea of staying here without Nick. It didn't feel right that she got to stay while he had to-

"Miss Harris, I'm sorry to say this, but you're fired," the man in the coal gray suit who was sitting next to Rick said, kind of shocking her.

### A Reclusive Heart: A Hollywood Heart's novel

"You're letting me out of my contract?" she asked, trying not to sound too eager. If they did, that meant that she could go with Nick. She wasn't allowed to start up another publishing company, but he would be able to do that. She didn't think that they'd really have any kind of future, but she could show her thanks by signing on with him and maybe J.L. Lewis could help him build a lucrative business.

The man shook his head. "No, you're still contracted through us for J.L. Lewis, but we've decided that as Jamie Harris you will no longer be associated with Rerum Publishing House," he explained before shifting his eyes to Nick.

"I'm sorry, Mr. Quinn, but I'm afraid you're fired as well," he said, surprisingly not sounding very happy about it at all.

Then again from what she saw, Nick was a hard worker. His personal life might have drawn concerns, but his work ethic was irreproachable. He worked hard, put in long hours and wasn't afraid of doubling his workload to get the job done. Personally, she thought they were foolish to let the man go.

"I understand," was all Nick said.

What the heck? He was just going to sit back and let this happen? This was her fault, not his. None of this would have happened if it weren't for her and she sure as heck wasn't about to sit around while they destroyed Nick's career. She opened her mouth to say, well, she really wasn't sure what the heck she was going to say, when Dana spoke.

"I guess this is where I tell you that I will not be signing my contract to continue with Rerum Publishing," she said quietly. Rick for some strange reason looked slightly relieved while the rest of them, even Holly, looked panicked.

"Let's talk about this, Mrs. Pierce," the man who'd fired them said almost desperately.

Dana simply shook her head. "I'm sorry, but I don't feel comfortable signing with Rerum Publishing when you're releasing one of the main reasons that I enjoy working with this company in the first place. Mr. Quinn has always double checked my work for me, helped plan my tours when I decided to take them and if I can't reach Rick for some reason Nick's the person I go to. If I can no longer count on having someone like Mr. Quinn for support then I don't believe I will continue with Rerum Publishing."

"Mrs. Pierce, any of our agents can do that for you. They'd be more than happy to help you with any problems that you have," a middle aged woman with graying chestnut hair that was pulled back into a painful looking bun explained imploringly.

"Although I have the utmost respect for your employees, none of them are as dedicated as Mr. Quinn."

"Our hands are tied on this matter, Mrs. Pierce. Not only did Mr. Quinn have an inappropriate relationship with his client and employee, but he also put Rerum into a very unpleasant situation by canceling dozens of interviews and personal appearances. That's not something that we can simply-"

Edward Pierce cut the man off. "I've known Mr. Quinn for several years now and I've never known him to act inappropriately with clients or employees for that matter, which is pretty impressive given his personal reputation. I can understand that you're not thrilled with the situation, but from what I saw on the video this is not a simple fling nor did either one intend on making their situation public. It appears to me that two people very much in love had a very personal moment stolen from them and exploited," he said before throwing her a wink that had the blush that she was pretty sure was going to reduce her to ashes intensifying.

She felt her eyes widen and a whimper work its way up her throat at the realization that Edward Pierce and no doubt Dana Pierce, judging by the soft blush painting the woman's cheeks, had watched her have sex. Oh god......

## A Reclusive Heart: A Hollywood Heart's novel

Everyone in this room had watched the video but her, she realized with horror. When the detective played the video she'd been too mortified with him in the room to look up. Of course, she could have watched it from any number of sites on the internet, but she hadn't exactly been in a rush to see any negative comments like, "Fat ass" or "How could he sleep with her?" which she was sure were all over the web by now. Maybe she should watch the video so that she at least knew how horrible it was.

"With all due respect, Mr. Pierce, but this doesn't concern you or your wife," a man said with a crisp voice that was as hard as ice, but instead of finding out who'd spoken she kept her eyes on the table, too humiliated to do anything else. "If you would like to arrange a meeting to discuss your contract we'd be happy to accommodate you, but for right now I'm afraid that I'm going to have to ask you to-"

"I'm afraid it does concern us if you ever expect my wife to do any promotions for the books that you currently have her contracted for. If memory serves me correctly, she has the right to refuse any promotional event that makes her uncomfortable and I have to be honest," Edward said, drawing her attention against her will. She looked up to find the man leaning back in his chair, looking comfortable as he addressed the men and women who were visibly panicking. "Having my wife work with a company who would place profit before her safety is not making me very comfortable," he said firmly, leaving no doubt in her mind at least that the man didn't play games when it came to his wife.

"I support Mr. Quinn's decision to cancel the promotional dates considering the situation," Rick said. "Between the video and the threats I think he made the right choice."

"It wasn't his call to make," the woman with the severe bun explained tightly.

That was the main problem? Jamie thought with an inward snort. Well, she could clear that up right now. "Mr. Quinn didn't cancel the rest of the tour. I-"

"I canceled the tour," Nick explained, cutting her off as he gave her hand a warning squeeze, "because I could not guarantee her safety as long as there was a threat out there. After speaking with the police, it was agreed that until they caught whoever sent the threats was identified or caught that it would be better to get the attention away from her."

"You should have spoken with us before you made that decision," the man with the crisp voice said. Jamie looked to her right to find the man sitting next to the still smug Holly was the one who had spoken.

"I apologize for that. However, I felt an obligation to cancel the most immediate dates out of respect for our contracts. I explained the situation and told them that the contracts would be honored as soon as the matter was cleared up," Nick smoothly explained. The men and women didn't look happy about it, but they did seem less tense at the moment.

"Right now my only concern is Miss Harris. There's obviously a very disturbed person out there with a fixation on her. I don't think it would be appropriate or fair to ask her to put herself in danger to promote her books. Until the matter is settled I believe there are other methods better used to promote her books at the moment that I think should be utilized," Nick suggested calmly.

"Thank you, Mr. Quinn. We'll look into it," crisp voice man said in clear dismissal.

"Fine," Dana said with a sigh as she got to her feet. "Just let me know where you end up or if you decide to start your own company and I'll be more than happy to sign with you."

"Wait!" crisp voice man said, sounding desperate. "Please reconsider, Mrs. Pierce!"

Jamie tightened her hold on Nick's hand as she took a deep breath and stood up, hating all the attention as every set of eyes settled on her expectantly, but she had to do this.

### A Reclusive Heart: A Hollywood Heart's novel

"This is probably where I should tell you that the last two books that I contracted with Rerum Publishing are done and that I won't be renewing my contract as well."

With that announcement that seemed to have stunned everyone, including Nick, into silence she walked out of the room, forcing herself to walk slowly until she reached the hallway and closed the door behind her. The second it was closed, she turned and rushed off towards Nick's office in desperate need of that coffee roll now more than ever.

## Chapter 29

"Good luck, Nick," Dana said softly as she gave his hand a comforting squeeze, but his attention was on the double doors. He wanted to go after his little recluse and make sure that she was alright and didn't consume a shit load of sugar, but he had to fix the damn problem she'd just created for herself.

She'd worked too damn hard to throw it away now and as much as he appreciated her trying to help him out he could take care of himself. He knew that every publishing company in the world would probably kill to sign her, but he wanted her here where Rick could watch over her. Once Dana and Edward walked out of the room all hell broke loose.

"Can somebody please explain to me how in the hell we just lost our two top clients in one day?" Jonathan demanded in that crisp voice that always annoyed Nick.

"Because instead of allowing me to explain the situation you listened to Miss Johnson," Rick explained tightly as he stood up and walked over to the mini bar to poor himself a drink. "And now we not only lost one of our best editors," he said, gesturing towards Nick with his drink, "But two of the top authors in the world."

Who in the hell was Miss Johnson, he wondered as he joined Rick at the bar for a drink. Since no one had called security on him yet, he thought he'd stick around and try to fix this mess before his little recluse got in over her head.

"I'm not too concerned with my job, but I think you should reconsider your position on Miss Harris' job. She's a damn good editor and our clients trust her. They rely on her in fact and taking her away will be like taking away their support system," Nick said before taking a sip of his drink.

"He's right. The second they hear that she's no longer working for us they'll pull back and the ones that were considering signing with us will go elsewhere," Rick said, backing him up.

## A Reclusive Heart: A Hollywood Heart's novel

"I didn't want to fire either of them in the first place, but after what Miss Johnson said, I didn't feel as though we had a choice and now look at the mess that we're in," Margaret said, running a hand over her tight bun as she walked over to the bar and gestured for him to get her a drink.

With a shrug, he made hers a double as he asked, "Who is Miss Johnson and what exactly did she say that cost me my job?" he asked, forcing himself to remain relaxed as he wondered who had just fucked them over.

"Holly," Rick drawled.

Nick looked around the room for the woman so that he could strangle her, but at some point she'd snuck off. He should have known the woman would do something when he sent her packing, but admittedly his focus had been elsewhere.

"Oh? What exactly did she say?" Nick asked in a bored tone as he took a sip of his drink, welcoming the burn as it coated his throat.

"Apparently she decided to go behind my back after I refused to allow her to return to help with the tour," Rick said, surprising him. The woman actually tried to come back? That was a little odd.

"She claimed that under your direction Miss Harris wasn't getting much work done and you were ignoring your duties to be with her. At first we didn't think much of it," Jonathan said as he joined them for a drink. "But after that video, the tour cancelation and of course the complaints we received in the past couple of days-"

"What's this about complaints?" Nick asked, interrupting the man.

Anthony, who'd been pretty quiet up to this point, joined them for a drink. "We started to receive calls that you and Miss Harris were caught in several indecent situations over the past couple of days. There were also complaints that the two of you were constantly ducking out of conventions. When we asked Miss Johnson about it she reluctantly admitted that it was difficult to find you, you refused to help her and that Miss Harris disappeared for a good hour, leaving the convention coordinators high and dry."

"Why didn't you ask me what happened?" Nick asked, pouring the man a drink and handing it to him. "I could have cleared this whole thing up. I don't know about the complaints, but we never left a convention early. In fact, Jamie worked her ass off and stayed as long as it took to meet every single fan because she felt bad about them waiting to meet her. In case you haven't noticed she's painfully shy and that was a hell of a lot of stress for the woman, but she did it," Nick said, noting the look his bosses, well, technically ex-bosses now, shared.

His little recluse had worked her ass off and shouldn't be facing this bullshit. She had enough to deal with. Her family screwed her over and lied to her and thanks to a few well placed calls he now knew they'd fucked her over once again. She just lost her home. She had a psycho on her ass and he'd be damned if he let them take away something she truly enjoyed doing.

"As far as Miss Johnson is concerned," he said tightly, "I'm afraid you've been mislead. During the brief time Miss Johnson accompanied us on this tour she proved to not only be incompetent, but resentful as I explained to Rick. She caused problems that I was forced to deal with and she left Miss Harris near tears. Before the convention was over, I decided that she was not capable of doing her job and asked Rick to remove her."

"He did," Rick agreed, finishing off his drink. "But, before I got a chance to speak with Holly, she went over my head and filed complaints with your offices. If you had explained what was happening, I would have been more than happy to go over this with you."

## A Reclusive Heart: A Hollywood Heart's novel

They let out a collective sigh as they shared another one of those looks that gave him hope that they'd let his little recluse back. "I apologize for the misunderstanding, Mr. Quinn. Would you please consider forgetting this incident and continuing with us?" Jonathan asked, looking suddenly exhausted. Not that he could blame the man since this little episode left his head reeling.

"As long as you allow Miss Harris to do the same," Nick clarified.

Jonathan didn't bother looking at his partners as he nodded. "Consider it done."

"Thank you," Nick said, more than willing to let this go as long as his little recluse was safe and happy. He was just about to head after her when one of the secretaries burst through the doors. "The police are here and they're looking for Miss Johnson," she said anxiously.

For some reason he really wasn't at all surprised, he thought as he put his drink down and went to hunt down his little recluse.

\* \* \* \*

"Stupid lock," Jamie muttered as she gave up her attempts to break into the filing cabinet and rescue her poor, lonely, little coffee roll that desperately needed her attention.

She was a little stressed out and honestly, she didn't do well with stress. She needed a sugar fix and she needed it quick. Then, when she was done, she fully planned on trying to figure out what to do with the rest of her life since she'd just lost her job and pretty much her contract within the last hour. Her game plan had been to follow Nick wherever he went, but now that she was out of the situation and thinking a little clearer she realized that he just might not appreciate that one bit.

After all, he'd just lost his job and probably his reputation, because of her. Why would he want her to go with him? He probably wanted to get the heck away from her as fast as he could and she really couldn't blame him.

She needed chocolate, sugar, caffeine, just something sweet to calm her down, she thought as she left his office. For a moment she stood there contemplating her options. There weren't many. For one thing she couldn't leave the building. Well, she could, but then she'd have to face the paparazzi that were stationed outside. She did have her car, but she doubted they'd let her get to it without harassing the heck out of her.

Granted, she had to leave sometime. Why not now? She needed to get some sugar, clear her head, and think and there was no way that she could do that with an office full of people who'd seen her have sex. Yeah, it was definitely time for her to leave, she decided as she lowered her gaze to the floor and made her way to her office.

Less than five feet from her office the scent of cheap perfume hit her hard. She wrinkled her nose in distaste at the offending odor as she headed for her door, hoping the scent hadn't seeped into her office. When she opened her office door she was hit full blast by the offensive fragrance. It took her a moment before she managed to get her focus off the horrible scent and onto the woman standing frozen at her desk in front of Jamie's laptop computer, her laptop computer that should still be in her bag and beneath her desk, but wasn't.

"What are you doing in here?" she asked, walking to her desk just as the woman ejected a disc from her laptop and placed the disc in the front pocket of her brown blazer.

"I was just leaving you a note," Holly said, smiling as she stepped away from the desk and headed for the door.

"On my computer?" Jamie asked, frowning down at her computer. It was open to her desktop and she wondered how the woman got past her password.

"It was open," the woman lied.

"No, it wasn't," Jamie said, clicking open the recent documents folder and what she saw there had her seeing red. "You went through my books and private files?" she asked in disbelief.

## A Reclusive Heart: A Hollywood Heart's novel

"Someone must have gone through it before I walked in, Miss Harris. I only came in here to leave you a note," she explained as she headed for the door.

"Then where's the note?" Jamie demanded, fighting back tears of frustration. Even though everything in her screamed for her to shut up and leave it be, she just couldn't. The woman had gone through the books she'd just written, her e-mails, and the two lists she made.

Out of everything the lists were the things that upset her the most. She'd accepted that people took one look at her and realized that they could walk all over her without a problem, but they couldn't have known about the things that she'd inadvertently admitted to in the list. No one knew that she was a virgin, they could guess, but they would have never known for sure. Worse, Holly now knew that she'd never been kissed before Nick.

It didn't bother her that Nick was the only man she ever kissed. Actually, it made it feel even more special. She liked the idea of Nick giving her, her first kiss. He was so sweet with her, kind and funny and took such good care of her. The way he treated her and looked at her made her want to hope for the impossible, that he was truly in love with her, but Jamie wasn't an idiot.

There was nothing even remotely special about her. She might look better than she did a year ago, but there were still prettier and sexier women out there and Nick could probably have any woman that he wanted. Unfortunately for her, she was also still Jamie. Just because she'd expanded her outlook on life and tried new things didn't change the fact that deep down she was and probably always would be the painfully shy woman that hated to be the center of any sort of attention.

Nick didn't need a woman like her by his side. He was handsome, charming and didn't mind having all eyes on him. He needed a woman that was outgoing and matched him in personality and looks and she was not that person. As much as she would love to be, she could never be that woman. She didn't know what hurt worse, the knowledge that she would always be "Jamie" or that she didn't have what it took to keep a man like Nick.

"I figured out what I needed, so I guess I didn't need to leave a note after all," Holly said, dragging her attention to more important matters like the woman who'd just gone through her personal files.

Maybe she wasn't the old Jamie after all, she thought as she picked up the phone. The old Jamie would have simply shut her mouth and wallowed in self-pity, but she was done with that. She might not turn into the life of the party, but she was done with allowing people to push her around.

"Fine. Then we'll just let Rick handle this," she said, starting to press the extension for Rick's office only to find the phone suddenly pulled away.

"You can't do that!" Holly snapped, looking nervous.

"Watch me," Jamie said, reaching out to take the phone back only to find the woman jumping back and out of reach. "Holly, give me-*What the heck did you do to my computer?*" she practically screeched as she watched the icons on the desktop begin to flicker before disappearing all together.

She ignored the woman in front of her as she tried to figure out how to stop whatever was happening to her computer. Every time she tried to click on an icon that icon would disappear instantly. She watched in horror as everything on her desktop disappeared until the screen turned a stomach clenching black and she knew that all of her work was gone.

Two books that she'd slaved over whenever she had a moment of free time no matter what time of day it was were now gone. Not only were they the two books she owed to Rerum Publishing and were due next month, but they were her favorite books so far. There was no way that she was going to be able to write two new books in time. Even if she worked day and night there was no way that she could do it.

"Why?" she demanded, fighting back tears as she looked up at the woman who looked on the verge of panicking.

## A Reclusive Heart: A Hollywood Heart's novel

"I-I.....," the woman stammered as she put the phone down and moved to flee, but Jamie cut off the taller woman by stepping in her path.

"Why did you destroy my work?" Jamie demanded.

Holly noticeably swallowed as she shifted to the side to dart past Jamie, but she wasn't having that. She was done with letting people push her around. All her life, people took advantage of her, walked all over her and openly dismissed her, not caring that it left her feeling hollow inside or so alone that sometimes it was a struggle just to breathe. She was done playing the victim.

"If you don't tell me what you did right now then I'm going to call the police," Jamie bit out through clenched teeth.

Holly's eyes widened in panic as she reached for Jamie. Unfortunately for Jamie, the other woman was faster and bigger. Holly managed to grab Jamie by her arms and was squeezing painfully before she could stop her or get out of the way.

"You can't do that!" Holly snapped, giving Jamie a good shake. "I'll be ruined if you do, Jamie. Just let me make this up to you!" she pleaded, looking slightly crazed as she gave Jamie another shake.

"Let go of me!" Jamie ground out as she struggled to get away from the woman, but Holly refused to let her go, desperate to convince Jamie to give her a chance.

"I can fix this. I'll get Rick to push back the date on your contract. I already planned to do that. Now that Nick's gone and everyone else has their hands full I know that Rick would pick me to work with you," she shot a nervous glance over her shoulder at Jamie's computer as her hands tightened further around Jamie's arms. The woman's long manicured fingernails bit into her skin and Jamie barely bit back a wince at the stinging sensation.

"If Nick had just backed off like he was supposed to I would have never had to resort to destroying your books, Jamie. You have to believe me. I just needed him to back off so that I could take over. He didn't need you, not like I needed you," Holly said with a crazed look in her eye that actually frightened her.

"What are you talking about?" Jamie asked, trying to pull free again, but the woman refused to let her go.

"Nick's already a senior editor. He didn't need you, but that bastard was too selfish to give anyone else a shot. Don't you understand?" she shook Jamie roughly to get her point across. "I had the best chance of getting J.L. Lewis. I'd been here the longest and was next up for consideration, but *Nick*," the woman bit out with such distaste that Jamie momentarily forgot about the pain in her arms as she watched Holly struggle to stay in control.

"I thought you wanted Nick," Jamie said quietly, only to have Holly give her a violent shake, slamming her head into the wall that she'd apparently backed her into.

"Want him?" she asked with a humorless laugh. "Why would I want him? He's a whore just like his mother, only he does it for free," she said acidly. "But before you came along he was the key to everything."

## Chapter 30

"Say that again," Nick said, pinching the bridge of his nose as he fought back the headache that he knew was coming.

"They wanted her out of the apartment," the detective explained again with a weary sigh.

"So they sent her death threats?" Nick asked in disgust as he dropped his hands to his sides.

Detective Michaels nodded. "It seemed that they didn't realize that Miss Harris had been evicted yet and decided that she needed another threat to scare her away. We caught Mrs. Briggs stuffing an envelope in Miss Harris' mail slot at three this morning and Mr. Ames stuffing a letter in her mail slot around four this morning and then one beneath her door just in case she missed the first one," he drawled.

"And why were they doing this again?" Rick asked as he leaned a hip against the corner of his desk.

When the police arrived a half hour ago, he'd been eager, more like desperate, to go hunt down his little recluse. Detective Michaels explained that he had a few things that he needed cleared up while his men searched the building for Holly, who more than likely, already split since the police weren't here for even a minute before word spread about the reason behind their visit.

Detective Michaels' lips twitched as he said, "According to Mrs. Briggs, Miss Harris blasted her television day and night, was loud, and had drunken parties every weekend."

Nick couldn't help but frown as he shared a surprised look with Rick. His little recluse was loud? That was bullshit. She didn't like the volume when she was watching television or listening to the radio up loud. In fact, most of the time while they were driving he had to raise the volume so that he could hear the damn thing. He couldn't even begin to describe what was wrong with the drunken party accusation.

"Apparently these last two months have been particularly bad. Mrs. Briggs complained to the manager, but nothing was done, so the woman decided to take matters into her own hands," the Detective explained.

"She hasn't been in the state in the last two months," Rick said, sounding just as confused as he felt.

The Detective cleared his throat. "Well, it appears that Mrs. Briggs hearing aid was not only set too high, but she also has difficulty pinpointing the direction in which sounds come from. As it turns out, it was the neighbors on her other side that were causing the problems, five twenty year old college kids."

"And Mr. Ames?" Nick found himself asking when all he wanted to do was hunt down his little recluse and pull her into his arms.

"He was convinced that she'd been stealing his mail."

"Why would he think that?" Rick asked, pouring himself another drink, Nick noted. If this conversation wasn't enough to drive a man to drink he didn't know what was, he decided as he snatched Rick's drink and downed half of it in one swallow before shoving it back into Rick's hand. With a grumble and a glare Rick finished it off and placed the glass on his desk.

### A Reclusive Heart: A Hollywood Heart's novel

"According to Mr. Ames, he doesn't trust quiet people because they're always up to something. So he felt it was his obligation to see what she was up to. After he broke into her mail slot and discovered letters addressed to J.L. Lewis he determined that she was a criminal and that Jamie Harris was the alias. When he didn't win the *Publisher's Clearance House* after sending them ten entries every day for the past year he concluded that it was because of Miss Harris. He believed that Miss Harris didn't have a job because she was living off his prize money."

"Were they working together?" Rick asked, sounding somewhat amused and pissing him right the hell off.

This wasn't funny. These two nut jobs had gone out of their way to scare the hell out of his little recluse and almost cost him any type of a future with her. That thought made everything in him still.

A future?

Did he want a future with her? He loved her, absolutely adored her, but he hadn't given any real thought to anything long term mostly because he was scared out of his mind that he would hurt her. It made him wonder if a future with her was even possible. Did he trust himself not to hurt her?

Surprisingly, yes.

He'd rather die than hurt her and he knew that feeling would only intensify over the years. But just to make sure, he tried imagining touching another woman. The thought left a sour taste in his mouth and he knew he would never want to stray. Jamie turned him on like no other woman and she was fucking fantastic in bed. She was still pretty new to sex and would only get better in time, he thought, fighting back a huge shit eating grin.

He was a lucky bastard and damn well knew it.

"No. As far as we can tell neither one of them was aware of what the other was doing," the detective explained, thankfully pulling him out of his thoughts before his body gave away his thoughts. The last thing he needed was a hard on with two guys in the room, he thought dryly.

"What does Miss Johnson have to do with this?" Rick asked and Nick was thankful that the man was focused because he sure as hell wasn't. All he could think of was grabbing his little recluse, hunting down a jar of hot fudge and letting her go to town licking it off his body.

With a silent curse he forced himself to focus again.

"We're not exactly sure yet, but we do know that she was behind the videos in Texas. We were actually hoping that you could help shed some light on the subject before we spoke with her."

He felt every muscle in his body go rigid at that announcement. "She was the one that threatened Jamie?" he demanded in a cold even tone as he contemplated killing someone for the first time in his life.

"It would appear so. When the IT department in Texas went through the hotel's surveillance videos again they spotted her in the corner of the lobby watching you as you spoke with the manager, we're presuming it was when you asked for the pool keycard. Then they looked at an earlier on the employee hall surveillance camera and found her sneaking in the back door of the pool area and slipping into one of the dressing rooms. We weren't sure until we zoomed in on that spot because the fitting room area was nearly pitch black while you were using the pool, but we spotted slight movement when you entered the pool area and spotted her running into the employee hall minutes after you and Miss Harris left. Unfortunately there are no cameras in the guest elevator or the halls so we can't prove that she was the one who recorded the audio CD, but we did manage to lift a partial print from the CD. I just need you to confirm that you didn't speak with her the next morning and that as far as you know she didn't handle the CD."

### A Reclusive Heart: A Hollywood Heart's novel

Nick shook his head. "She was supposed to leave that day. I don't think she was around the next morning."

Detective Michaels pulled a small notebook out of his pocket and flipped through several pages before he found what he was looking for. "She caught the ten a.m. flight to Los Angeles, California the next morning."

"Of course she did," he said, rubbing his hands down his face and feeling like an idiot. "She had to be there the next morning to drop the envelope off at our room."

"Do you know where Miss Harris is at the moment? I need to speak to her while my men look for Miss Johnson."

"She's probably looking for a fix," Nick said.

"She has an addiction problem?" the detective asked, looking less than pleased with the announcement.

"Yeah, she's a sugar addict and if we don't find her soon she'll probably be too wired to answer your questions," he said, sighing as he gestured for the man to follow him.

\* \* \* \*

"The key to what?" Jamie found herself asking as she desperately tried to ignore the sharp pain in the back of her head and the hot liquid seeping over her scalp.

Holly slammed her against the wall, again. This time Jamie gave up her useless struggles to push the woman off. It was clear that the woman was stronger than Jamie, so she focused all of her attention on kicking Holly. She got in one good kick and was instantly rewarded with another shove into the hard wall behind her before Holly moved her legs out of kicking distance, leaving Jamie with no way to protect herself. How in the heck did the woman get so freakishly strong?

"To get to the top. What else?" Holly asked with a mocking smile. "It shouldn't have been too hard. The man seemed to fuck anything and everything. When I first came here, I waited for him to make his move and when he didn't I had to initiate it, but apparently the male whore has a rule about not fucking co-workers. My initial plan was to let him fuck me and then manipulate him into putting a good word in for me and if that didn't work I was going to threaten to sue for sexual harassment, but I couldn't get the bastard to ignore his rules and fuck me."

"Well, he's not desperate," Jamie found herself saying and was of course rewarded with another slam against the wall, but it had been worth it.

"When you signed on I knew you were going to be my big break. All the senior editors were busy and I'd been kissing ass for months. I should have been placed as your editor. Never in a million years would I have suspected that Nick wanted you. He didn't need you, not the way I needed you. I tried to talk Rick into placing me with you, but the bastard wouldn't listen."

"So, you sent me death threats?" Jamie guessed.

The woman looked insulted. "No! I didn't send you death threats, but I will admit that when I found out about them I thought they would be enough to send Nick running. He doesn't like drama or complications and having some psycho after you should have scared him off, but it didn't."

"Let me go," Jamie bit out as she tried to shove the woman's arms away, but it was like pushing against steel. The woman would not budge so much as an inch.

"I decided to push the whole stalker angle when Rick told me that I was going to be tagging along as an assistant." Her expression turned cruel as she spat out, "I am too good to be anybody's assistant. Rick should have handed you over to me, but instead he insisted that I tag along and play gofer to the bastard.

# A Reclusive Heart: A Hollywood Heart's novel

Holly gave Jamie another shove against the wall that caused black spots to dance around her vision. She sucked in a breath as she fought against the urge to vomit. Her head was throbbing and she was pretty sure that a few more well placed slams would knock her out. Jamie was truly afraid of what this crazy woman would do to her then.

"As you can imagine I was not happy at all about the situation, but then I walked in on the two of you kissing in the break room and I was sure that I found my key to getting Nick to step aside and let me take over. When we got to the hotel I planned on blackmailing the bastard, but he gave me the brush off and decided to openly spend the night with you, taking away my hope to blackmail him. If he didn't care enough to hide it I knew he wouldn't care if Rick found out. I tried to convince you that he was only using you, but instead that bastard called Rick and had me sent home."

Her hands tightened around Jamie's shoulders, moving slightly closer to Jamie's neck when she gave her another forceful shake. "I knew Rick was going to fire me or worse, demote me to handle nobodies that wouldn't get me anywhere so when I heard Nick make his little pool plans, I took a chance and it worked," she said smugly. "Granted, I thought he'd quit to save his own ass, but him getting fired worked in my favor." Her expression turned murderous once again as her eyes zeroed in on her. "That is until I discovered that you fulfilled your contract and weren't going to sign again. I couldn't have that. Not after all my hard work."

Jamie tried to shove the woman away, but Holly's hands came around her neck and gave a warning squeeze. "Now listen to me, you bitch. I haven't worked my ass off all these years for you to wreck me. You're going to sign the contract if you know what's good for you and you're going to *beg* Rick to assign me to you."

"And if I don't?" Jamie asked as she desperately tried to remove Holly's hands from around her neck.

"There are no ifs about this, bitch," Holly said, tightening her hands around Jamie's neck until it became a struggle just to breathe. "Do you understand? From now on you will do exactly what I tell you to do."

Jamie shook her head as she struggled desperately for air and freedom. "No, I won't!" she said on a choked whisper.

Not only did she not want to be within a hundred miles of this psychotic woman or her nauseating perfume, but her pushover days were long gone. She would never let anyone boss her around again or belittle her in anyway. Thanks to Nick she knew she deserved better than that.

Holly released a screech as her hands tightened impossibly further, cutting off the rest of Jamie's air. As her vision flickered in and out she slapped, pushed, yanked, and even dug her nails into the woman's arm to get away, but her efforts only seemed to infuriate the woman. She had just resigned herself to this being the end when she realized that Holly had moved closer to her in order to keep her hold on Jamie. It gave her an idea that she wasn't sure would work, but she needed to try anyway.

Gathering her last reserve of energy as her lungs burned and her world began to fade around her, Jamie brought her knee up hard between the much taller woman's legs and nearly jumped for joy when the woman let out a surprised gasp and a groan of pain. Her hands loosened somewhat around her neck. It wasn't much, but it was enough to allow her to suck in a lungful of air.

Jamie didn't waste any time in shoving the surprised woman away. She stumbled to the side, giving Jamie a chance to run for it. Unfortunately the crazed woman was blocking the only exit in the room so Jamie settled for running to the other side of the small office and putting the desk between them.

"You've ruined everything!" Holly screeched as she slammed her fists against the desk. "Everything!" When Jamie saw the woman's glare drop down to the sharp letter opener lying in its case near the computer she decided that it was past time to make a run for it. She took off running, taking the woman by surprise and managed to run past her.

### A Reclusive Heart: A Hollywood Heart's novel

Her hand fumbled with the door as adrenaline surged through her body. She couldn't stop shaking as she tried desperately not to think about the insane woman coming after her. After a few failed attempts she managed to grip the doorknob and open the door with a loud bang. She ran into the hallway, not sure where to go or what to do when she heard him.

"Jamie!"

She turned around and spotted Nick running her way with Rick hot on his heels and what appeared to be several officers. A sob broke loose as she ran towards him, happy to have this nightmare finally over. She couldn't wait to hold him, to kiss him and tell him how much she loved him. She realized with dismay that she'd never told him that. It was silly and stupid and she should have told him the second that she realized what he meant to her, but she'd been too-

Something slammed into her, knocking her into the wall. She barely had time to register the thought when she found the heavy weight yanked away and Nick was pulling her into his arms.

"Baby, are you okay?" he asked, cupping her face with shaky hands.

"Fine," she lied in a hoarse whisper with a wobbly smile. Her head really hurt. Her neck ached and her throat burned with every breath she took. As Nick pulled her to her feet she idly wondered if she could use this as an excuse to drown her sorrows in ice cream.

"Jamie, you're bleeding," Nick said with an edge of panic laced in his voice.

She reached up and carefully touched the back of her head and winced at the slight sting. "It's fine. Just a little cut." She hoped at least. He'd probably think that she was a big baby, but she didn't want any stitches. The idea of a needle sliding through her skin was enough to make her stomach hurt. Not that she was surprised considering the one and only time she had stitches she'd passed out on the doctor when he pulled the needle out of the sanitized package.

"Oh shit," Nick muttered, drawing her attention.

Frowning, she followed his glance down to her stomach. It took a moment for all the blood to register in her mind. When it did the pain decided to make its presence known. She looked up in time to see the officers wrestle the bloodied letter opener from the still screeching Holly as she was slammed to the ground.

"Oh, that can't be good," she heard herself say hollowly as her legs gave out and everything went black.

## Chapter 31

"Chocolate," Jamie whispered and Nick couldn't remember ever hearing a more beautiful word in his life. He chuckled in relief as he left his chair, ignoring the aches and pains that came along with sitting in the chair for three days straight and went to his little recluse's side.

He cupped her face in one hand, careful of her oxygen tube, as he leaned in and pressed a kiss to her dry lips. "Welcome back, sweetheart," he said softly.

"Did I go somewhere?" she asked sleepily, giving him a soft smile.

"It's not important right now," he said, unable to stop smiling. The last couple of days had been the worst days of his life. A few times it had been touch and go, but she pulled through. His little recluse was a fighter.

"I'm tired," Jamie muttered around a yawn as her eyes closed.

"That's fine, baby. Go to sleep and I'll be right here waiting when you wake up," he whispered, pressing another kiss to her lips.

"Okay," she mumbled. "With chocolate," she added barely coherant thanks to the pain killers in her system, he assumed.

Chuckling, he pressed a kiss to her forehead. "A huge basket of chocolate, Jamie."

\* \* \* \*

"You lied," Jamie said accusingly as the nurse fussed with her tubes and wires, but that adorable little glare never wavered.

"The doctor hasn't cleared you for solids yet, but the second she does I'll have a truck full of chocolate delivered," he said, hoping to appease his grumpy little recluse.

Five days without sugar and she looked close to killing someone. Maybe he should sneak her in a chocolate milkshake, a Coke, or something, before she tried to escape from her bed, again. Her doctor thought he was kidding when he suggested she pump pure sugar into Jamie's body. He hadn't been. In fact, he was pretty sure that she'd be a very pleasant patient once she got sugar into her system.

She looked up at him, pouting as she allowed her little chin to quiver as she said, "But I love you, doesn't that mean anything?"

Grinning like a fool, he leaned over and kissed the tip of her nose. "It means everything, but until your doctor clears it you're not getting any chocolate." When she opened her mouth, probably to argue, he added, "Or sugar."

"Big jerk," she mumbled under her breath as she dropped back against the pillows.

"Yeah, but you love me," he said, sitting next to her on the bed so that he was facing her. He carefully took her hand in his, nervous that he'd hurt her if he accidentally touched the IV's in her hand.

She sighed heavily. "I suppose I do."

"Does your stomach hurt, sweetheart?" he asked, raising her hand to his lips to press a soft kiss to her thankfully now warm skin. For a little while, it had been ice cold and he'd been scared to death that he was going to lose her. Thanks to surgery and donated blood she was going to pull through. Several times he had to fight back the urge to go hunt down the blood donors and get on his hands and knees and thank them. They'd never know what a precious gift they'd given him.

"Just sore," she said, shifting her hand in his until she could entwine their fingers together.

He watched her look around the room curiously. "Are these all for me?" she asked, sounding unsure, shy and absolutely perfect.

## A Reclusive Heart: A Hollywood Heart's novel

"Yes," he said, smiling when her glance turned predatory as she looked over the flowers, bowls of fruit, teddy bears, and hundreds of cards that were taped all over the walls. "I had the nurses lock up the chocolate," he said, chuckling when her bottom lip jutted out.

For a moment she didn't speak and he was content to just sit there and enjoy being with her. He still couldn't believe how close he'd come to losing her. If it hadn't been for the fast thinking of the police officers she probably wouldn't be here now. While he'd been too busy begging her to wake up, an officer applied pressure against her stomach and bought her a little more time.

When they loaded her into that ambulance, he felt as though his heart was being ripped out of his chest. He wanted to ride with her, to hold her in his arms, but they wouldn't let him. Rick and a few officers had to hold him back when they drove off with her. He would have killed the bastard, but he needed the man to take him to the hospital.

Once he made it to the hospital no one would tell him a damn thing because he wasn't family. They ended up throwing him out a few times when he flipped out, but he came back each and every time demanding to see her. She was *his* and he'd be damned if he let anyone tell him otherwise.

When they called her ungrateful family in he'd had a hell of a time keeping it together. Thankfully Edward and Rick had the presence of mind to grab a hold of him before he could beat the shit out of her lying heartless father. The only one who seemed shaken was Jamie's brother-in-law, which appeased him somewhat until he realized that the man had feelings for his little recluse. That was confirmed when he shook his head in disgust when her sister made a cruel comment that set Dana off.

Dana was one of the best women he knew. She was kind, considerate, liked everyone and everyone loved her. It took a lot for someone to upset her, never mind piss her off, but Jamie's sister had his best friend seeing red and going for her throat. Edward barely managed to grab his wife around the waist and yank her back, but that didn't stop Dana from telling the woman in minute detail what she thought of her.

The only decent thing her father did as far as he was concerned was sign over Jamie's medical proxy to him. Nick calmly thanked the man before he walked him outside. Once they were in the parking lot he decked the son of a bitch, breaking his nose in the process. He did it for all the years the bastard happily ignored his little recluse. While the man's wife had treated Jamie like nothing because Jamie was the reminder of her husband's infidelity her father had ignored her because she was the reminder of what he'd done to a seventeen year old girl who sure as hell didn't know better. He also did it for keeping Jamie's mother out of her life.

"Did my family visit while I was sleeping?"

She asked the same question every day and every day it nearly broke his heart. They only came once and that was to see how bad she was and to sign over her care to him, while she was unable to do it for herself. Other than that they didn't visit or call. They were done with her and it was all because of him.

He'd given the bastard the choice of telling her the truth or getting the hell out of her life. He'd chosen to get out of her life and save his own ass. It was his loss. Jamie was a beautiful person inside and out and brought nothing but joy into his life. If the son of a bitch had looked at her, really looked at her for even one moment he would have realized what a precious gift he'd been given.

"No, baby, I'm sorry," he said, wishing like hell that things were different for her. She deserved a family to love and take care of her, but that didn't seem to be in the cards for her.

At least not yet.

### A Reclusive Heart: A Hollywood Heart's novel

"It's okay," she said with a forced smile as she peered around the room. "Do you know if my doctor's here yet?"

"I haven't seen her yet."

"She's very pretty," she pointed out conversationally.

"I guess," he said slowly, wondering where she was going with this.

"I, um, think she might be interested in you," she said quietly while she looked down at their entwined hands.

*Shit.*

His little recluse was jealous. Was she worried that he was interested in her doctor? He wasn't and he hated the idea of her being hurt because some woman was showing him interest. Not that he was bragging, but it happened a lot and if they were going to give this a chance she was going to have to realize that he wanted her and no one-

"Do you think you could maybe flirt with her a little bit? Maybe take her out for a coffee?" his little recluse asked, sounding hopeful as she shot him a quick glance.

What. The. Hell?

"You want me to sleep with another woman?" he asked, shocked beyond words. Why in the hell would she want him to sleep with another woman? Was she crazy or was she doped out of her fucking mind?

Jamie rolled her eyes, giving his hand a playful slap. "No, I don't want you to sleep with another woman," she said in an exasperated tone. "I just want you to butter her up a bit and then maybe when she's putty in your hands you could maybe ask her about the chocolate?"

"You're willing to whore me out for chocolate?" he demanded as he came to his feet and pulled his hand away from hers.

She rolled her eyes as she settled her hands in her lap. "No, I was just kind of hoping that you'd use that pretty smile of yours to get me some sugar."

"Pretty?" he spat out in disgust.

"Well, yeah," she said, shrugging. "You have a very pretty smile."

"*Pretty?*" he couldn't help repeat in disbelief. His smile wasn't *pretty*. It was charming and boyish, but pretty? Hell no. By all rights he should have stormed out of the room, but he was still too shaken up to leave her side for more than five minutes at a time so he decided to sit in the chair and settle on glaring at her.

When she sent him a cute little wave and a hopeful smile he had to struggle not to smile back. It was difficult but he managed to do it. Her willingness to whore him out for chocolate pleased him immensely, not because he was fine with her using him, which he was, but because she wasn't jealous. His shy little recluse knew that he loved her and would never have to worry that he would hurt her.

He sure as hell hoped at least.

"I'm not asking, Jamie," he said firmly.

"But-"

"No."

"Maybe-"

"No."

"You won't even hear me out. I-"

"You're not having any chocolate until your doctor says so, so let it go, baby," he said, smiling when she let out the cutest little frustrated growl he'd ever heard.

## A Reclusive Heart: A Hollywood Heart's novel

"Fine. Then let's talk about something else," she grumbled, settling back against her pillows as she glared up at the ceiling.

"What would you like to talk about?" he asked, deciding that he'd punished her for traitorous ways long enough. He moved back onto the bed and took her hand into his. With a sigh, she stopped glaring at the ceiling to smile softly at him.

"Any luck on the job front?" she asked, nibbling her lip nervously.

He inwardly winced when he realized that there were a few things that he'd failed to tell her, but in his defense when she wasn't passed out she was drugged out of her mind. Today was the first day that she'd been coherent enough that he could actually talk to her.

"I'm staying with Rerum Publishing, sweetheart. After you left we sorted it out and realized that Holly was behind the firing. We're actually pretty sure she was the one behind the complaints as well," he said, giving her hand a comforting squeeze.

"Oh," she said, frowning. "Do I still have a job?"

"If you want it, it's yours," he said casually as he silently prayed that she stayed. He loved working with her, but more importantly he loved being with her.

"Will they still let you handle my books?" she asked, worrying her bottom lip.

"Yes," he said, knowing that if they tried to assign anyone else to her that he'd quit for real. J.L. Lewis was *his* and the key to his happiness. As long as he handled J.L. Lewis he would be the lucky son of a bitch that spent time with Jamie. He'd do anything to be with her. She was his heart, his soul and the only woman he would ever love.

"Then I'll sign the contract, but there's something you should know," she said, looking close to tears.

"Are you okay?" he asked, concerned that the painkillers were wearing off and leaving his little recluse in pain. He'd rather die than see her suffer.

"I'm fine, but the two books I wrote were destroyed. Holly did something to my computer and I think it's dead," she mumbled with a little sniffle that damn near broke his heart.

He leaned in and pressed a kiss to her lips. "It's okay, sweetheart."

"No, it's not, Nick. I really liked those books. They were due next month and I'm afraid I won't be able to replace them."

"Shhh, baby, you don't have to," he said soothingly as he gently cupped her face in his hand.

"Yes, I do. I signed a contract and now I don't have the books, so they're going to-"

"You have the books, baby. I installed software onto your computer that automatically backed up your files online. It's all there, sweetheart. Everything's fine," he said, pressing a kiss against her mouth. "Everything is fine."

"Oh," she said against his lips.

When he pulled back just enough to look at her, he couldn't help but smile as she pursed her lips in thought. "Is there something else, Jamie?"

"I was just wondering if we were going to get a chance to finish the tour. We never got to go to Vegas, Hawaii or do the rest of the things on the list."

He bit back a smile as he asked. "Is there something in particular that you wanted to do, sweetheart?"

She shrugged in indifference, but he wasn't buying it. "What do you want to do, sweetheart? You know that we don't have to wait for the tour to do it."

"I just don't want to go back to being the old boring Jamie that's all," she muttered shyly.

## A Reclusive Heart: A Hollywood Heart's novel

He chuckled as he leaned forward and pressed a kiss to the tip of her nose. "You were never boring, sweetheart, but you should know that we can do whatever you want, sweetheart. Anything you want to try we'll try and I will be right there by your side."

"Promise?"

"I promise, Jamie. Anything you want," he promised, moving his lips back to hers.

"Then can I have chocolate?" she asked, sounding so damn hopeful that he couldn't help but laugh.

"No yet."

"I hate you."

"You love me."

"No, I love chocolate. I hate you," she clarified even as she smiled so damn sweetly up at him.

"Really?"

"Mmmmhmm, really," she said, nodding solemnly.

"What if I sneak you in a double chocolate milkshake, hmm? Will you love me then?"

"Will it have a shot of hot fudge?" she asked, appearing to think it over.

"It will have anything you want in it, sweetheart."

She reached up and cupped his face. "What if I want you? Can I have you?"

"You already have me, Jamie," he swore, turning his head to press a kiss against her palm.

"In that case I'll take a double shot of hot fudge in it," she said, grinning impishly up at him.

He chuckled as he leaned down and kissed her. "I guess it's too bad that I lied then, huh?"

"I really do hate you," she said, sighing against his lips as she kissed him back.

"Too late, Jamie. I already know that you love me."

"Do you love me?" she asked, shyly.

He moved back just enough to look into her beautiful caramel eyes. "So much that it hurts, Jamie. You're my world."

"I think you should prove it with chocolate."

"I just bet that you do," he said, chuckling as he leaned in to cut off her protests with a kiss that probably wasn't appropriate for a hospital room, but he couldn't help himself. The little recluse set him on fire and holy hell did he burn for her.

## Chapter 32

Three months later.........

Ten miles outside of Hershey, Pennsylvania

"Is my surprise a visit to heaven on earth?" Jamie asked, trying not to sound too eager and failed. All she knew was that he better not have brought her this close to the Hershey factory without any intention of bringing her there.

Nick's deep chuckle relaxed her somewhat as he picked up their entwined hands and pressed a kiss against her knuckles. She noticed that he did that a lot, kissing her that is. He couldn't seem to be around her without touching her or kissing her. It made her happy and helped ease the anxious part of her that waited everyday for him to break her heart when he decided that he couldn't handle being with her any longer.

After four months they were still going strong. It surprised her how well they were doing. Even more surprising was the fact that they seemed to be living together. It wasn't something that they discussed. It just kind of sort of happened. When they finally released her from the hospital she'd been too weak to go through the hassle of searching for a new home and moving. Thankfully Nick told her that there wasn't a rush and that she could wait until she was fully recovered.

When her doctor announced that she was able to return to work, well, go to the office instead of just working from Nick's bed, he didn't say anything and neither did she. They just kind of fell into a routine of making love in the morning, having breakfast together, driving to work separately because of the different schedule demands they each had. Some nights they managed to have dinner together and other nights she ignored the cute little post-it notes he taped to the cabinets and refrigerator imploring her to have a normal meal and usually indulged in her love for sweets. No matter what they did or where they traveled they always ended the day making love.

Life, right now, was perfect and she wasn't going to wreck it by wondering about tomorrow. She was going to live each day to its fullest and enjoy her time with Nick. If it ended tomorrow, she would be devastated, but she was thankful for the memories they'd created together.

"Do you really think I'd bring you this close to the motherland and not take you? You'd try to smother me in my sleep if I did that," he said, smiling in that way that drove her crazy and made her consider asking him to pull over so that she could check a certain item off her list, again.

"Then what are we doing here? I heard you telling Rick that you had to schedule a stopover during this tour so I'm guessing this is the stopover. What is it?" she asked, turning in her seat to look at him.

He let out an exasperated sigh that she wasn't buying for a minute before answering her. "It's a surprise, my little eavesdropper."

She shrugged off his teasing. "Is it a good surprise or a bad surprise?"

"I'm hoping that it's a good surprise, Jamie," he said, turning all serious on her.

"Should I be worried?" she asked, wondering what kind of surprise would require them to take a few days off during their tour to come to Pennsylvania. Maybe he was bringing her to a Hershey's outlet store and was going to let her fill the trunk and backseat with chocolate. She could hope at least.

"There's nothing to worry about," he said, pressing another kiss to her hand as he pulled into the parking lot of a 50's era diner with a sign that boasted the largest dessert menu on the east coast, something the sugar addict in her was more than willing to look into.

"Why don't we grab lunch?" Nick suggested as he parked their rental car.

## A Reclusive Heart: A Hollywood Heart's novel

"That sounds like a good idea," she said, wondering if he was going to count that donut she snuck earlier against her. The man was so damn stubborn when it came to her sugar intake, but in a sweet cranky sort of way that actually made her smile.

That is when he wasn't coming between her and sugar.

She watched him loosen his tie as he walked around the front of the car and nearly sighed. The man was a sight to behold. He was handsome, hot, masculine and so damn sexy that sometimes it was a struggle, like now, not to tackle him to the ground and have her dirty little way with him. By the time he made it around the car to open her door she was focused on what was important, a huge dessert menu calling her name.

He leaned down and brushed his lips teasingly over hers as he took her hand in his before they headed towards the front doors. The scent of home cooking hit her before they made it to the doors, making her stomach growl viciously. Perhaps she'd eat lunch before hitting the dessert menu, she decided as they walked into the diner and nearly tripped over her own feet when she got her first look of the interior.

The diner was large, homey, and crowded. Instead of the 50's memorabilia that she expected it had old fashioned dessert and candy pictures everywhere, but that's not what took her by surprise. Not even close. It was framed pictures, magazine covers and newspapers articles of J.L. Lewis books placed among the yummy looking photos. At the front counter where a smiling woman stood near the cashier there were even J.L. Lewis books on sale among the homemade candies and treats being sold.

"What is this?" she asked distractedly as she ran her eyes over everything once again, sure that she was seeing things.

"How many?" the smiling woman behind the counter asked, her smile slipping a little as she looked Jamie over. "You look very familiar, Miss, have you been here before?"

"No," Jamie said weakly, feeling a little overwhelmed. She didn't like attention, but she normally was able to deal with it. She wasn't so sure she'd be able to do that in a place that was set up as a living shrine to her. It was a little unnerving.

"It's our first time here. Who's the big J.L. Lewis fan?" Nick asked, gesturing lazily to the large stack of books on sale behind the cashier.

The woman's smile returned full force. "That would be Aubrey. She's the owner and the nicest woman you could ever meet," the woman said warmly.

"Is she here?" Nick asked and Jamie just barely fought back the urge to give his shin a good solid kick. What in the heck was he thinking? He knew how nervous overexcited fans made her. If the promise of a large dessert menu didn't intrigue her, she would so be out of here, but it did so she was staying. She was also having more than one dessert because of this, and if he didn't like it then that was too bad for him.

"She'll be here soon," the woman said, picking up two menus as she stepped around the counter to show them to their seats.

"When she comes here could you give her my card," Nick asked, pulling a business card out of his pocket and handing it to the woman, "and tell her that I would love to meet her."

She took the card as she gestured them towards an oversized booth near the jukebox. "I sure will."

"What was all that about?" Jamie asked once the woman walked away.

Nick shrugged as he looked down at his menu. "Just curious to meet her that's all," he said, but she wasn't buying it. If her eyes hadn't landed on the most enticing appetizer menu that she'd ever seen she would have questioned him further.

## A Reclusive Heart: A Hollywood Heart's novel

"You do realize that I'm going to have to get several desserts here, right?" she asked as she ran her eyes over the largest dessert menu she'd ever seen. Did she just whimper? She just might have.

"I packed the aspirin, heating pad and ice packs so you can have whatever you want," Nick said, surprising her, not that he was prepared for one of her sugar binges, but that he was accepting it so easily.

Something was wrong. Something was very wrong. The one and only time he'd encouraged her to indulge in too much sugar had been right after she was released from the hospital and he had to break the news to her that her family had yet again screwed her over. Finding out that her family had made money by selling the journal she'd kept when she was fifteen had not been her favorite day. It was difficult knowing that people all over the world could read about her private thoughts from one of the most difficult times in her life.

Of course, that little action helped her get over missing them real quick. They didn't love her. She knew that. It was fine. She didn't need them. She had Nick and some really good friends now. Although it would have been nice to have someone to call her own. she didn't need them.

"Do you want to start off with a shake?" Nick asked.

Oh god.......

He was now pushing sugar on her. This was going to be very bad. She just knew it.

"What's wrong, Nick?" she asked, dreading his next words.

"Nothing's wrong," he said, smiling as he reached over and took her hand into his.

"Then why are you pushing sugar on me?" she demanded.

"I just thought you'd like a milkshake," he said, linking their fingers together. "But if you don't want one then you don't have to get one."

"Oh, I'm getting one, buddy, and you should know that I know that you're up to something."

When he sent her a wink she decided that she was going to make that milkshake a double and watch how he reacted. Nick Quinn was a sneaky man and as long as she remembered that she-

"Hello," a warm feminine voice said, "Catherine told me that you would like to speak with me. My name is Aubrey and I.....I......*oh my god*," the woman ended in a harsh whisper that somehow managed to draw Jamie's attention from the impressive list of milkshakes.

She really hoped the woman didn't start crying and screaming for joy. That happened to her a few times and she'd die happy if it never happened to her again. She looked up to find a middle aged woman with kind eyes and beautiful blonde hair staring at her. Her skin was pale and she looked seconds away from passing out.

"Are you okay?" Jamie asked, actually preferring the women's screaming and crying to this. This frightened her. She quickly scrambled out of the booth and took the woman's shaky hand into hers and helped her sit down in her freshly vacated seat.

Once the woman sat down she refused to release Jamie's hand as she stared up at her. It was really starting to freak her out. She threw Nick a pleading look only to find him watching them intently. Really helpful, she thought dryly as she turned her attention back to the trembling woman.

"Are you okay?" she asked, forcing a smile as she looked into the woman's pretty face.

"No, I mean yes," Aubrey said weakly, still holding Jamie's hand tightly.

"Aubrey, are you okay?" a man at the next booth asked, looking as concerned as Jamie felt.

## A Reclusive Heart: A Hollywood Heart's novel

"I-I'm fine, John," Aubrey said, giving him a watery smile even though her eyes never left Jamie's. "I'm perfect in fact."

"Are you the man I spoke to last week?" Aubrey asked and it took a few seconds for her to realize that she was speaking to Nick.

"Yes," Nick said, surprising her.

This was planned? Why? She didn't know what was going on or why Nick would plan something like this. It certainly wasn't easing her anxiety.

"Jamie, I would like you to meet Aubrey O'Shea," he said before adding, "Your mother."

"What?" Jamie asked, well, nearly shouted, startling the people dinning around them. "What are you talking about?"

Her mother was dead. Her father said so. Plus this woman didn't look old enough to have a child nearing thirty. She didn't. There was no way, she thought even as she noted the woman had her eyes, nose and smile.

"You have no idea how long I've waited to hold you again," Aubrey said, choking back a sob as she dropped Jamie's hands and pulled her into a hug that Jamie was too stunned to refuse, but once she found herself in the woman's arms she was helpless to fight it. It felt.....

Right. Perfect. God help her but it felt like she belonged. For the second time in her life she felt like she belonged to someone.

"I am so proud of you," her mother whispered fiercely against the top of her head as she pressed a kiss against her hair. "So proud, Jamie."

She didn't realize that she was crying somewhat hysterically until she felt Nick kneel behind her and run a soothing hand down her back. "Shhhh, Jamie, it's okay."

It really wasn't okay, she thought as a loud sob rocked her body. She was so happy, but at the same time she was scared out of her mind. She was afraid that this was a dream or a sick joke and any second now she was going to wake up or the woman in her arms that was holding her tightly was going to pull back and tell her that it was a mistake.

Please don't let this be a mistake, she prayed as she tightened her hold around the woman she prayed was her mother. Until that moment, she didn't realize just how badly she needed this woman, a mother. For years she'd accepted the fact that her mother, father and sister didn't want her and pretended that it didn't hurt, but it did. She never realized how badly she needed a reassuring smile, a pat on the head or a kind word from her family until that moment.

"I never wanted to let you go, Jamie," her mother said, sniffling. "I was so young, Jamie. I quit school to have you and worked two jobs, but it wasn't enough, sweetheart. It wasn't enough. When I had to choose between putting food in your stomach or a roof over your head I made the biggest mistake of my life and gave you to your father. I shouldn't have done that, Jamie. I should have worked harder and found a way to make it work, but you were so small and I just couldn't watch you suffer another minute. I'm so sorry, Jamie, so sorry," she said, squeezing Jamie tightly against her.

"She tried to come back for you, sweetheart," Nick said softly near her ear as he continued to rub her back. "She saved every penny she could and when the time came she went back for you, but your father wouldn't give you up. I don't think he wanted to deal with people asking too many questions. Your father convinced her that you were being taken care of and that she would only confuse you and hurt you by getting involved in your life, sweetheart, but she's been keeping an eye on you. She loves you just as much as I love you, Jamie," Nick said, pressing a kiss against the back of her head.

## A Reclusive Heart: A Hollywood Heart's novel

Sniffling, she pulled back and looked into the caramel eyes that matched her own. "Is that true?" she asked, hoping like crazy that it was. It would mean that her mother hadn't given her up because she was unlovable or a nuisance, but because she really did love her and wanted her happy.

Her mother smiled warmly as she cupped her face. "I've always been your biggest fan, Jamie."

## Epilogue

One year later..........

"Is this the line for the bathroom?" the cute guy who'd been eying her since she stepped onto the airplane an hour ago asked as he stepped up behind her.

She smiled up at him as she nodded.

"My name's Vince. What's yours?" he asked in a charming tone as he continued to smile down at her.

"Jamie," she said, shaking his hand.

"Are you going to Pennsylvania for business or pleasure?" he asked, releasing her hand as he leaned a shoulder against the gray wall.

"A little of both," she said before reconsidering it. "Well, I guess I'm not really going there to work since I'm just tagging along. Mostly I'm going so that I can spend a few days with my mother," she said, smiling hugely at the thought.

She didn't mention that she made this trip once a month or that her mother stayed with her for a week every month as well. Even after a year she still found herself excited and giddy at the prospect of spending time with her mother. Most people would probably think she was being silly, but she had a lot of lost time to make up for.

"I guess that means I can't offer to show you around," he said, giving her a boyish smile that was rather cute.

"Her husband might have a problem with that," Nick said as he stepped up behind the poor guy.

Vince noticeably started as he looked over his shoulder and up at Nick, who was glaring down at him. She watched as Vince swallowed hard. "I-I thought you were with the other woman," he said, referring to Patti, the blonde knockout who was one of Nick's clients and the reason that they were traveling to Pennsylvania. She was attending a sci-fi writer's convention while Jamie visited with her mother and hit Hershey Park, again.

It didn't bother her that he thought that Nick was with the gorgeous woman. A lot of people actually made the same mistake. She didn't care because she knew that the man looking close to killing the poor guy absolutely adored her so it didn't matter what anyone thought.

"Asshole," Nick grumbled as Vince made a hasty retreat.

"He was just being nice," Jamie said, secretly pleased by the attention. Not that she enjoyed making her husband jealous, well, she kind of did, but she would never do it on purpose. It was just nice to get noticed instead of being treated like wallpaper and she didn't think she'd ever get used to it.

Nick snorted his disbelief as he stepped up behind her and put his arm around her. "Yeah, real nice," he said tightly as he pointedly raised her left hand and looked at the wedding band and engagement ring on her finger.

With a soft chuckle and an eye roll she pulled her hand away. He was just so damn cute when he got all jealous. She stood up on her toes and pressed a quick kiss to his cheek that only made him grumble more. She ignored him as she turned around. Not even a minute later the bathroom was freed up and she was closing the door on Nick, but not before she caught the murderous glare he was sending Vince's way.

The whole thing was rather ridiculous, she thought as she washed her hands. Like she'd ever want another man. He really should know better. She was his whether he wanted her or not. He'd married her and she was never going to let him go. She loved and adored the grumpy man, she thought with a smile as she opened the door only to find herself suddenly backed up into the room and the small space suddenly smaller as Nick closed and locked the door behind him.

"What are you doing?" she asked even though she had a pretty good idea what the sexy grin he was giving her meant.

"What do you think I want?" he asked, backing her up impossibly farther into the small space until her back hit the plastic wall.

"I'm not that kind of girl," she said as she spread her legs and made a show of raising the skirt of her floral summer dress.

"Are you sure? Because I have this list that I could a use a hand with," he said in a husky voice that sent a shiver through her body.

"What kind of list?" she asked, licking her lips hungrily as he hooked a finger in each side of her panties and pulled them down until she was able to step out of them.

"It's a very naughty list," Nick said, reaching for his zipper. He never took his eyes off her as he pulled the zipper down.

"What exactly is on this naughty list that you need my help with?" she asked, watching in anticipation as he reached into his pants and pulled out the large erection that still managed to make her body tremble and tighten in need.

"I was sort of hoping you'd let me have my naughty way with you in this bathroom," he said, slowly running his hand over his shaft as he slid his hand between her legs and traced her already wet slit.

"What's in it for me?" she asked, panting as she fought against the urge to roll her hips against his hand.

"A life altering orgasm?" he suggested as he slid his finger inside of her.

"My husband gives me at least five of those every day," she explained as she gave in and rolled her hips against his finger.

His lips twitched up into a cocky grin as he watched his glistening finger slide in and out of her. "He sounds like a very generous guy."

"He is," she agreed on a moan.

"How about a body massage later tonight?" he asked, stepping forward as he removed his finger. She spread her legs further until her right foot hit the side of the bench that held the toilet and decided to place her foot on the edge since it worked so well last month when they flew to Florida and did this.

Nick growled approvingly as the new position opened her up more and gave him a clear view of her sex. He pressed the tip of his erection against her open slit as he continued to stroke himself. She loved it when he teased her and he darn well knew it.

"My husband gives me those every night as well. What else do you have?" she asked, running her hands over her stomach and breasts as he continued to tease her.

"How about a bar of Belgian chocolate, hmmm?" he asked, cupping the back of her neck as he moved in to kiss her. "I happen to have a bar of my wife's chocolate in my carryon bag. It's all yours if you let me slide inside of you right now," he said, brushing his lips against hers as he continued to tease her.

"Won't your wife be mad that you're giving away her chocolate?" she asked against his lips as she moved her hips against him, desperately trying to get him where she needed him, but the stubborn man pulled back just enough to deny her what they both wanted, needed.

"I have another one in my suitcase that she doesn't know about. I'll give her that and she'll never have to know about this," he said, emphasizing "this" by rubbing the hot velvety tip of his erection around her sensitive nub, coating it in her juices.

"I want both," she said against his lips.

"Greedy," he said approvingly against her mouth seconds before he stopped playing around and deepened the kiss.

She fisted his hair in her hands as she held him right where she wanted him. He suckled on her tongue as he slid inside of her, knowing how wet and crazy the move would make her. When she started to moan loudly he stopped kissing her to cover her mouth with his hand as he continued to thrust inside of her.

He kept his eyes locked with hers as he took her slowly, deeply and so darn perfectly that it wasn't long before she was screaming her release against his hand. He licked his lips as he watched her find her moment and when she was done he removed his hand and took her mouth in a hungry, wild kiss that had her wrapping her arms around his neck and clinging tightly against him.

"Love you, Jamie," he groaned against her mouth as he found his release.

She was still clinging to him when the banging on the door started. Nick simply chuckled as she struggled not to die of mortification. That mortification only intensified when Nick picked up her panties and pocketed them.

When she arched a brow in demand and held out her hand he chuckled. "Sorry, sweetheart, but I need these for another item on my list."

"Planning on wearing them?" she asked teasingly.

He shook his head good naturedly as he fixed his pants. "No, I'm planning on having my wife wrap it around my cock later and stroke me off," he said with a wink as she struggled not to jump him again as the image of doing just that set her body on fire. That was definitely going on the list, she decided as she followed him out of the bathroom and past the short line or irritated passengers.

She stepped past Patti to get to her seat and ignored the woman's pout. It wasn't too hard to guess the reason behind the pout. She wanted Nick, but then again most women that met him did. As long as the woman respected the ring that Nick wore proudly on his finger then she was fine with the woman's obvious crush.

Nick was hers and she never had to worry, because he never gave her a reason to worry. He loved her and she never had to question that. She also knew that he hated to be apart from her which was why whenever he had to go on the road he always brought her along. Rick didn't seem to mind since she stayed out of Nick's way and whatever author he was promoting. It also didn't hurt that her book sales were still off the charts and of course she was working on a second book with Dana Pierce since the first one had broken sales records.

Life really couldn't get any better, she thought as Nick put her tray down and placed his laptop in front of her, already on a Scrabble game. He placed his hand on her knee, gently caressing her skin as he spoke with Patti. They went over the next week's schedule while she kicked some serious butt at Scrabble.

A little while later when he slipped her the chocolate bar he'd promised her she couldn't help but smile. She had her dream job, a great mother, an incredible guy who spoiled her with chocolate. What more could a girl want? she thought as she leaned over and kissed Nick's cheek. He immediately stopped talking to Patti to turn his head and brush a quick kiss against her lips before returning his attention back to Patti, picking up right where he left off.

It really didn't get any better than this, she decided as she slipped another bite of chocolate in her mouth and took Nick's hand into hers. She changed her opinion a moment later when Nick turned to whisper something in her ear.

"I love you, Jamie."

Maybe being plain old Jamie wasn't so bad after all, she thought with a smile.

Made in the USA
San Bernardino, CA
28 December 2014